Ben Grant stood about six feet tall, with a moderately strong build and above-average good looks. His rumpled dark hair was attractively cut to just brush his collar. He was probably in his mid-thirties.

With his salt-stained Topsiders and blue chambray shirt worn with a loosely knotted black knit tie, he presented a safe, identifiable look, one that engendered trust in the casual observer.

All surface. Looking into his eyes, Julia felt she was gazing down the barrel of a .44 Magnum. They were the most penetrating eyes she'd ever seen. Dark blue and fringed with black lashes, they seemed capable of burning through stone.

He wasn't from the island. Not only would she have remembered him, but beneath that casual facade he was too sharp, too tough, too city-wise.

And she thought, *What is someone like you doing in Harmony?*

Charlie exhaled a long-suffering sigh and explained, "Ben is the new editor of the *Island Record.*"

Julia frowned. "Oh. Did I interrupt an interview or something?"

Charlie took her arm. "No, you didn't interrupt a thing. Ben was ready to leave, anyway. Weren't you, Ben?"

"Sure...Chief Slocum," Ben answered with a low chuckle. "Nice meeting you, Julia." She heard at least ten shades of meaning sliding around in that one remark.

She didn't return the sentiment.

Dear Reader,

Julia marks the beginning of an exciting new venture for me, a series entitled CIRCLE OF FRIENDS about a group of people who share the unusual experience of having grown up together on a small island off the southeast coast of New England.

Although Harmony Island is a fictional place, it is based on my fascination with the islands that really do exist in this area, a fascination that began thirty years ago when my husband and I visited Nantucket on our honeymoon. Since then we've vacationed on other islands—Martha's Vineyard, Block Island and tiny Cuttyhunk, part of the Elizabeth chain, which is usually visible from the shores of the town where we live.

Gazing at those islands, especially in stormy weather, always sparks my imagination. I wonder what it would be like to be living out there, to have grown up there, coping with the isolation in winter and the tourists in summer. I imagine the people as being resourceful, independent and individualistic, yet singularly close-knit—just the sort who make wonderful characters in a romance novel.

I hope you enjoy reading *Julia* as much as I enjoyed writing it, and you'll look for *Lauren* in December 1999 and *Cathryn* a year later. (Each is a self-contained story.)

My best to you,

Shannon Waverly

JULIA
Shannon Waverly

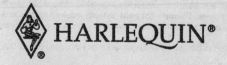

HARLEQUIN®

TORONTO • NEW YORK • LONDON
AMSTERDAM • PARIS • SYDNEY • HAMBURG
STOCKHOLM • ATHENS • TOKYO • MILAN • MADRID
PRAGUE • WARSAW • BUDAPEST • AUCKLAND

ISBN 0-373-70813-0

JULIA

Copyright © 1998 by Kathleen Shannon.

Printed in U.S.A.

JULIA

PROLOGUE

CHANGE WAS IN THE AIR.

Julia Lewis saw it in the clarity of the night sky, its stars swept clean of August's milky haze. She smelled it in the ripeness of wild rose hips, heard it in the heightened song of the insects in the marsh behind the dunes.

But mostly Julia saw it when she gazed around the campfire at her friends, gathered one last time for Cathryn Hill's annual end-of-summer clambake.

The entire graduating class was present, all ten of them, plus several spillover friends from other classes, a generation of teenagers who'd grown up together on these fifteen square miles of isolation and innocence called Harmony Island, their home and their universe—until now.

Only a few would stay on. For the rest it was time to leave. College and trade school and better job prospects were taking them away, and Julia doubted many would be back.

Although Harmony's population swelled to ten thousand during the summer, augmented by a hundred thousand day-trippers, the year-round population numbered barely six hundred. Most professions couldn't subsist on a population of six hundred. You couldn't be a lawyer or an accountant, for instance; couldn't be an ad executive or an athlete, a model or a medical specialist. And you certainly couldn't pursue a career in radio broadcasting, she thought, reminded of her own personal dilemma.

All Harmony had was its natural beauty and convenient location off the southeast coast of Massachusetts, and unless you were involved in the tourist trade somehow or were independently wealthy, you were better off moving on.

Julia's gaze drifted around the firelit circle, seeking out the girls who'd gone through school with her—Lauren DeStefano, Amber Loring, Cathryn. Her lifelong friends. Of the four of them, only Cathryn knew unequivocally that she would be staying. She was perfectly content here, engaged to another die-hard islander and already planning her wedding.

Lauren certainly wouldn't be back. Her family had just lost their house and moved off-island. From here she would be heading to the state university and then, she maintained, a career in whatever would make her the most money. Amber would be going off to school, as well, to a two-year course at a business college, after which she hoped to work as an executive secretary.

Until recently Julia had thought higher education was beyond her means, but thanks to a couple of scholarships, a hefty financial-aid package and the generosity of Charlie and Pauline Slocum, who'd taken her in after her mother's death, she, too, would soon be shipping out. Her destination—Emerson College in Boston, where she planned to study communications.

She knew with certainty that broadcasting was where she wanted to take her life, because she'd spent the past couple of years working at WHAR, a quirky little radio station on Harmony, run by a quirky little man named Preston Finch. The experience had been transformational.

Quiet and introspective by nature, Julia had gone into a

tailspin of withdrawal after her mother's death. But broadcasting had pulled her out of it, and once she'd discovered the joy of reaching out over the airwaves, she'd positively blossomed.

That didn't mean she wasn't still terrified of going away to school. Growing up on an island, people tended to be, well, insular, and she was no exception. But she was determined to make the most of the experience. She knew she could make a good living in broadcasting, and that fact, maybe even more than her love of the field, would get her through.

She remembered too well the hand-to-mouth existence she and her mother had lived at the mercy of Harmony's limited economy, and she refused to ever live that way again. She wouldn't depend on a husband to support her, either. As her father had so ably proved, you couldn't trust a man as far as you could throw him. Instead, she'd be self-reliant and find contentment in herself, in her work, her hobbies and wherever she happened to end up living.

Oh, but would she ever again know friends as dear as these? She missed them already, especially Amber, for although the four girls were close, Amber was Julia's best friend.

As if sensing Julia's attention, Amber turned from the conversation she was engaged in and started her way.

"What are you doing over here, sitting all by your lonesome? Are you okay?"

"Sure. Just feeling a little sad, thinking this is probably the last time we'll all be together like this."

Amber folded her legs under her and scanned the group. "Don't be silly. We'll be together again in four short months. Cathryn's already planning her usual Christmas party."

Julia shook her head. "Lauren won't come back. She's

too angry at the world. And Barry's going into the service. Who knows where he'll be stationed?''

"I hadn't thought of that.'' Amber's expression became as meditative as Julia's.

"And even those who do come back…we'll be different. We'll have met new people, done new things, faced problems and made decisions, and we'll have done all those things on our own.''

Amber sighed softly. "Until now we've done everything together, haven't we?''

Julia nodded. "We've grown in step.''

Amber was quiet awhile, her big blue eyes fixed on the fire, its light dancing in her pale blond hair. She and Julia had always been such opposites, not just in looks but also in temperament. Julia often wondered what made them best friends.

Eventually Amber turned from the fire and gave Julia one of her perennially buoyant smiles. "But *we'll* always be the same, Julia—you and me. Even though we're heading in different directions, we'll stay close. We'll call each other all the time and we'll visit. Heck, our schools are only forty miles apart.''

Julia returned Amber's smile and said, "Of course,'' hoping she sounded as if she believed it.

"We'll do lunch and go shopping,'' Amber continued. "Even beyond school we'll do those things. After all, you're going to be my maid of honor when I get married, remember?''

"You'd be mine, too, except that I'm planning to be an old maid. You can come help me feed my cats, though.''

The two girls laughed and went back to watching the fire and listening to Seth Connor playing his guitar while the others sang. But a few minutes later Amber pulled a tissue from her jeans pocket and surreptitiously blotted her eyes.

"What's the matter?" Julia asked quietly.

Some people thought of Amber as a dumb blonde, maybe because whenever they saw her she was giggling or gabbing a mile a minute. She was far from dumb. "Thanks for being in my life, friend," she said.

"Thanks..." Julia had to stop to clear her throat. "Thanks for being in mine."

On the other side of the fire, Mike Fearing got to his feet. "Well, I gotta split. It's way past my bedtime." Mike was lobstering with his father full-time now, and their boat left the dock before dawn.

"I've got to go, too," Lauren said. "I have to be on the ferry first thing tomorrow."

"But it's so early," Cathryn wailed, trying to hold them together. Her protest went unheeded, however, as here and there teenagers got to their feet and started folding blankets. Cathryn sighed in resignation. "Oh, well, see you in December."

Several people nodded and there were murmurs of "Sure" and "We'll be here," but Julia also heard an undercurrent of uncertainty. The party was breaking up, the circle of friendship unraveling. They'd reached the fullness of their time together, and though they might get together upon occasion in the future, things would never be quite the same.

Julia's gaze drifted one more time over her friends, intent on storing memories of them in a place in her heart safe from the ravages of time and distance, a place that kept childhood golden. And then she, too, got to her feet and gathered up her blanket. It was time.

Change was in the air.

CHAPTER ONE

Eleven years later

"I HAVE A CALL from a *what?*" Julia swiveled from the digital cartridge player and frowned at her young producer, ensconced in his high-tech, glass-enclosed control room.

"A cop," he answered, his voice coming to her tinnily through her headset. "Switchboard has him on hold for you. He said he'd wait, since you're so close to quitting time and all." A grin creased his bearded face. "Oh, Jules, what've you been up to now?"

That was what she was wondering, too. Swallowing her apprehension, she snapped her fingers. "Must be that bank heist I botched last weekend." With her producer's laughter still ringing in her ears, she scooted her chair back to the control board and pressed the button that activated her microphone. "That was the out*rage*ous new group, Slow Drip, capping off another ten-in-a-row here on Hot FM with their number-four hit single this week 'Nowhere to Run.' The temperature outside our KHOT studios this twenty-sixth day of September is eighty-one degrees..."

As she spoke, her gaze moved ceaselessly over the board, from the clock to the timer to the gauges that registered sound modulation. Equally busy were her hands, adjusting one vertical slide, then another.

"And the time is five-fifty-eight. That's two minutes to the top of the hour and the traffic update with Beverly

Kane, which means it's time for yours truly to shuffle on outta here and join the rest of you lucky folks sitting out there in freeway gridlock.''

With the flip of a switch Julia got her last selection started. "As always, it's been a pleasure spending the afternoon with you. Till tomorrow, 1:00 p.m.—" ever so slowly she shifted a slide as the timer ticked down the seconds "—this is Julia Lewis for KHOT-FM. Take care, Los Angeles.''

With perfect timing the vocals swelled to the foreground. She switched off her microphone, removed her headset and carefully placed it on the console.

"Good show, Jules," her producer said out of habit, his voice coming through the intercom now.

"Thanks." She smiled but didn't meet his eyes. Lord knew she tried to do a good job, but since the station had been sold and the format changed from light jazz to Top 40, she was finding it increasingly difficult to sustain her enthusiasm.

She filed her program log, fished her shoes out from under the table, then relinquished her seat to the next deejay.

"Julia?" the producer called again. "Don't forget your cop call." As if she could! "You can take it in Studio D," he added with a grin, "if you'd like some privacy."

Julia obliged his teasing with an exaggerated smirk, picked up her purse and with a wave slipped out the door.

Studio D was a small, seldom-used cubicle with an outdated board and a stainless-steel rack half-full of dust-covered tapes. Julia turned on the overhead light, settled into the chair at the console and reached for the phone.

"Hi. This is Julia Lewis," she said as soon as the switchboard had connected her. "I'm sorry to keep you waiting."

"Well, you ought to be, Julia Ann," came a gruff voice.

"Do you know how much this call is costing the good citizens of Harmony Island?"

Recognition hit like a storm of confetti. Julia sat up, board straight and astounded. "Charlie?" Her usually well-modulated voice squeaked. "Charlie Slocum?"

Her caller laughed. It was a warm gravelly sound. "Hi, Funny Face."

Julia opened her mouth, but nothing came out. Her mind whirled, and for one crazy moment her grip on reality became totally unhinged. Although she knew perfectly well where she was, she felt the clearest sensation of simultaneously being back East, on the small quiet island where she'd grown up.

"Charlie, oh, my God! My producer told me I had a call from a cop. He didn't say anything about a chief of police."

"I wanted to surprise you."

"You certainly did that!" Smiling, Julia sank more deeply into the chair. She'd always been fond of Charlie Slocum, even as a child when he was just a family friend, coming to visit her and her mother with his wife. He was tall and solid, a great block of a man, with dark springy hair, an open friendly face and eyes the color of milk chocolate. Julia had especially liked the way he talked. He meted out his words with a reassuring calmness that said, Slow down. There's an answer to this problem, and there's time enough to find it.

Actually, never having known her own father, Julia had been more than just fond of Charlie Slocum. He was every fantasy of paternal strength she'd ever dreamed, every vision of dependability, chivalry and honor. That vision hadn't diminished with time, either. Rather, it had moved from the realm of fantasy to one of fact when she was sixteen and her mother died, and Charlie and Pauline took her in.

"It's so good to hear your voice, Charlie."

"Good to hear yours. It's been a while."

"It sure has." Two years, in fact, since she'd called to express her sadness at Pauline's death.

Julia still felt terrible about not returning for the funeral. Pauline had been a warm nurturing woman who'd always been there for her, and although she hadn't played as influential a role in Julia's life as Charlie had, mostly because Julia had already had a mother, Julia still loved her and certainly would've attended her funeral. But she'd been on the road when Charlie tried to reach her, behind the wheel of a U-Haul, moving from Mobile to Omaha. She hadn't gotten the news until it was too late.

"How've you been?" he asked, slipping right past the painful subject.

"Good. Living clean. Staying out of trouble." Over the phone line she thought she heard him sip a drink, ice cubes clinking.

Swallowing, he said, "I couldn't believe it when I got your Christmas card last December and read you were in Los Angeles. *Los Angeles,* I said to myself. What's my little girl doing in Los Angeles? Last time I looked you were in Nebraska."

Julia sighed in chagrin. "That job didn't quite work out." In the silence that followed she wondered if Charlie was tallying up all the jobs she'd had, all the places she'd lived, that hadn't "quite worked out."

"So how do you like it there in Los Angeles?"

"It's incredible, Charlie," she said with forced enthusiasm. "It's so big flying in, you can't even see the ends of it. It just sprawls forever."

"Hm." He didn't sound impressed. "Are you living in a safe neighborhood?"

"Yes, it's quite safe." She smiled. "I have an apartment

in a nice complex. It has a pool and tennis courts and a
gym. You'll have to come visit me sometime."

Charlie ignored the invitation. "Are you seeing anybody
I should know about?"

She growled with affectionate impatience. "No."

"No! What's the matter with the men out there in California? Are they all blind or something?"

"I go out, Charlie. I date all the time. I'm just not serious
about anyone." It was the answer she'd been giving him
all her adult life, and most of the time it was true. She'd
only had two long-term relationships, two close calls, the
first with a dentist in Buffalo named Brian, the second with
a radio executive in Mobile named David. Both had been
pleasant good-looking men, sociable, mature and financially stable. Both had wanted to marry her. Neither had
understood why she didn't want to marry them. And so
she'd moved on.

"Ever hear from that fella in Buffalo?" Charlie asked.

"Good Lord, Charlie, of course not. That was six years
ago."

"Oh, well. Can't fault an old man for asking. I worry
about you, out there all by yourself."

"All by myself is exactly how I like it."

Charlie grunted. "You always were too independent for
your own good."

"No such thing."

There was a sigh. "How's the job?" The man knew
when to change a subject. "Are you happy with it?"

"It's terrific, Charlie. It's…everything I left Harmony
for." She plucked at a loose thread on her trousers, her
mood drifting in a direction she preferred not to go.

That was the only serious argument she'd ever had with
Charlie, the one about her leaving. But how could she have
stayed? There was nothing for her on Harmony. Eventually

he'd come to see her point and then, as usual, he'd gone overboard trying to help her with her career. However, she was sure he hadn't bargained on her moving *this* far away.

"So, to what do I owe the pleasure of this call?" She, too, knew when to change a subject.

Charlie took a swallow of whatever he was drinking, then sighed again. "I'm sorry to be calling you at work like this. But it's nine o'clock here and I'm bushed. It's been a long day. I'm going to bed soon and didn't want to just leave a message on your machine."

"No problem, Charlie. So, what's up?"

"I, uh…I'm afraid I have some bad news."

Her body stilled and tightened in a protective clench. "Bad news?"

"Mm. There's been a death here on the island."

A death. She squinched her eyes tight as the most likely candidate came to mind. "It isn't Preston Finch, is it?" Preston, her old mentor at WHAR, had to be in his late seventies by now.

"Preston?" Charlie seemed surprised. "No, Preston's fine. Actually he's more than fine. The old coot got himself married last spring."

"Married!" Julia's eyes widened. She'd always thought of Preston as unchanging as the cliffs that rimmed his part of the island.

"Yep. To a cottager. A pretty lady from New Jersey."

"I can't imagine it." Julia's relief was shortlived, though. "If it wasn't Preston…" Her dread returned, cutting off the rest of her sentence.

Ice cubes clinked over the phone line. "It was one of your old classmates."

Julia started. That was the last thing she'd expected Charlie to say. "One of my classmates?" That couldn't be. Her classmates were *her* age, only twenty-nine. Then, "Oh,

God.'' When an entire school contained only a hundred students, and when your own class consisted of a mere ten... ''Which one?''

''I'm sorry, Julia. It was—'' Another sigh. Suddenly he sounded very tired. ''It was Amber.''

Julia didn't move an eyelash. She just stared, her gaze fixed, while the walls and equipment and tape racks around her faded to nothing.

After a moment of silence Charlie asked quietly, ''Honey, are you okay?''

No, she wasn't okay. She was confused. Charlie's message didn't make any sense. ''Amber *Loring?*'' she demanded, surprised by an unexpected flash of anger.

''Yes. She was married, though. Her last name was Davoll.''

''Don't you think I know that? I was her maid of honor, for heaven's sake!''

Charlie remained unruffled through her outburst. ''I'm sorry, sweetheart. I hate to have to be the one giving you this news, but the family isn't up to making a lot of calls. They asked if I'd get in touch with you.''

Julia wasn't listening. ''Amber?'' she asked again, still incredulous, still angry, but this time, for some reason, her voice had grown toneless and insubstantial. ''Amber...died?''

''Yes, honey.''

All at once color and definition came flooding back into the room. All at once Julia understood. Shock streaked through her, stealing her breath and electrifying her nerves. ''Oh, no,'' she said, shaking her head. ''That can't be.''

''I wish I could say different, sweetheart, but she was found this morning about seven-fifteen, our time.''

Julia's heart pounded. Was found? *Was found* could

mean only one thing—a sudden death, an accident of some sort. An auto accident? she wondered.

She shrank from the image of Amber, twice a beauty queen, damaged in a car crash. Maybe it was something health-related, like…like meningitis…or food poisoning.

Julia gathered her courage. "What happened?"

"From all indications, it seems she—" Charlie hesitated again.

"It's okay, Charlie. I haven't seen Amber in years. We may have been best friends when we were kids, but that was a long time ago. We've drifted apart. So go on, just tell me. I'll be all right."

He sighed heavily. "From all indications, it appears she took her own life."

Despite her avowal of emotional distance, Julia was stunned.

"I know," Charlie commiserated without her having to utter a word. "It's the worst thing possible. So young."

Julia began to tremble. She wrapped an arm around her middle and hunched forward over the console. "How…how did she do it?"

Just when she thought she was done being shocked, Charlie said, "Shot herself. One bullet to the head."

"Amber?" Julia straightened, her voice spiking up an octave.

"Yes."

"Are we talking about the same Amber who used to spend forty minutes before school putting on her makeup and another forty fixing her hair?"

"I know. It's hard to—"

"It isn't just hard, Charlie. Try impossible." Abruptly Julia covered her eyes with her hand. "Oh, God, what am I saying? I didn't mean to imply she was vain or anything. She wasn't. She only wanted to look nice."

"That's all right. I understand."

Julia pulled in a long shaky breath and let it out on an even shakier groan. "Killed herself. Wow. That's gonna take some getting used to."

"Yep. Everybody here is just, well, flabbergasted."

Julia's chest tightened with momentary anger. "I can't believe it. Of all the stupid things to pull! She had so much going for her. She was pretty and popular, never had any trouble getting the guys. And her folks...I mean, they weren't the richest people on earth, but she never knew a day of want."

"That was a long time ago, honey," Charlie said softly.

Julia frowned, pained by the truth of his words. "You're right," she said, her anger done in. "You're right." She traced an idle pattern over the console, between the slides, around the buttons.

"Charlie?" she said after a thoughtful pause. Her voice was smaller and weaker than intended.

He coughed uneasily. "Yes?"

"Why did Amber kill herself?"

"Why?"

"Yes." A stretch of silence divided them. *Help me understand this, Charlie,* she pleaded. *Help me the way you used to when I was a child.*

Charlie's sigh was voluble. "Aw, hell, Funny Face, I don't know. *Why* is a question that never has a satisfactory answer when suicide is involved."

"Did she leave a note?"

"No."

"Say anything to anybody?"

"Not that I've heard."

Julia pushed her hand through her hair. "There has to be something."

"Well, if you absolutely need a reason," Charlie said

slowly, his words slurring slightly, "we found some prescription antidepressants in her medicine cabinet."

Julia felt the room cant. "She was being treated for depression? Amber?"

"Apparently."

Julia frowned. "I can't picture it. She was always so upbeat, always laughing."

"She wasn't doing too much of that lately, I'm afraid."

"I'm not sure I understand what you mean."

"Well, you know, her divorce and all."

If the room had tipped before, now it was spinning. "Amber was divorced?"

"Almost. She and Bruce were in the process. It would've been final in another month or so." Charlie seemed a bit confused. "You didn't know?"

"Uh, no."

"When was the last time you spoke to her?"

"It's...been a while." Her voice sank with guilt.

"Yep, she and Bruce split up last winter sometime. It hasn't been easy on her, trying to swing the house by herself, fighting over who gets what..."

Julia sat speechless, trying to grasp this new vision of a friend who'd always been so happy-go-lucky. Unable to make the two visions mesh, she gave up trying and asked, "Do you know when the funeral will be?"

"Monday, I think. Yep, three days from now." Charlie paused abruptly. "Why? Are you coming home?"

"I'm not sure. It might be hard to get time off work at such short notice."

Charlie said nothing.

"Flying cross-country won't be cheap, either."

Still he said nothing. His silence weighed on her. She groaned. "What am I saying? Of course I'm coming home."

She heard the smile in Charlie's voice when he said, "It'll be great seeing you again, Funny Face. You haven't been home in ages."

"Yeah, seven years," she admitted with a sad smile. "Not since Amber's wedding. It'll be nice seeing you, too."

"When will you be arriving?"

"I don't know yet. I'll have to call the airline."

"Well, you be sure and ring me as soon as you do. I'll meet you at the airport."

"That's not nec—"

"And another thing—where do you intend to stay?"

"Oh, I don't—"

"I'd offer you your old room. I still keep it as a spare. But to be honest, since Pauline died, the house has gone to hell. I just don't keep it up the way she used to."

"That's okay. I assumed I'd be staying at a hotel anyway."

"Hold your horses. I'm still thinking this through. How about... I know! Preston's house!"

"What?"

"Sure. Preston's isn't being used. He and his bride've been gone since early June. They're traveling around in a camper seeing the country. Montana. That's where they were the last time he called me. I keep an eye on his place for him. It's been rented out all summer, but the renters are gone now, and Press won't be back until November."

"I can't stay at Preston's place!"

"Sure you can. In fact, if I know Press, he'd be mad if you didn't stay there."

Julia gave up. When Charlie was determined to take care of you, there was nothing you could do but be taken care of. "Fine. I'd love to stay at Preston's," she said, rolling her eyes.

She paused in midroll. Actually she would. It was a nice old house with beautiful views over the island. Besides, WHAR was there. It would be fun revisiting the old station where she'd made her first broadcast.

Charlie was pleased. "Great. I'll give him a ring right away."

"Thanks, Charlie."

"My pleasure."

"And thank you for calling."

"Wish it could've been under better circumstances."

Julia's smile faded. "Yeah, me too," she murmured. Slowly she hung up the phone. "Me, too."

She looked at the clock on the console. With any luck she'd catch the station manager still in his office. As long as she was asking for time off, maybe she'd try for the entire two weeks she still had coming to her. It was silly to fly three thousand miles just to turn around a couple of days later and fly back.

Still, Julia didn't move. Her heart was too heavy with the news she'd just gotten, her need to make sense of it too great.

But sense eluded her. Instead, her mind raced, tumbling over fragments of memories and images: Amber's stunning blue eyes and pale blond hair, her ditsy giggle; the times they'd trudged to school together through autumn leaves, through winter snows...

From out of nowhere Julia's throat tightened and tears stung her eyes. It was true that their lives had taken different paths, but before the divergence, they'd shared so much. There had been school pageants and church suppers, beach walks and endless talks, borrowing sweaters and cutting each other's hair—a million experiences that bound their lives in an invisible fabric that neither time nor distance could rend.

Amber had been her best friend growing up, her companion and confidante and strongest support. But she was gone now, and although Julia hadn't seen her in several years, she realized she was going to miss her terribly.

Julia's memories gave way to grief then, grief that deepened immeasurably when she remembered the particular way Amber had died. How unnecessary it was. How wasteful.

What problems could've been so weighty that she'd been unable to endure them? Why hadn't someone close to her seen the danger signs and helped?

Julia's heart pounded. What if *she* had helped? She could've called more often, could've made Amber talk out what was bothering her. She'd always had that knack.

Guilt-ridden and heart-heavy, she pulled a tissue out of her handbag and blew her nose. She couldn't imagine attending the funeral. Didn't have a clue how to say goodbye. Amber was too young to be gone. She should still be alive, now and for decades to come.

Julia surged out of her seat and began to pace. Why *wasn't* Amber still alive? Suicide was about depression, about running out of options and giving up hope. Hard as she tried, she still couldn't fit that picture with the Amber she'd grown up with.

Julia gave the stainless-steel music rack an angry twirl.

Maybe she just didn't know her friend anymore. Maybe Amber had changed. That was possible. They'd lost touch over the years, and as Charlie said, Amber had problems. It was unfair to think she'd remained the same, frozen in some sort of never-never land.

Suddenly going home seemed like a very good idea to Julia. It would give her the chance to talk to people, old friends, maybe even the Lorings, tactfully of course, to find out who Amber was and what had been troubling her. She needed to hear reasons, needed to hear others say there was nothing anybody could have done.

Not even her.

The music rack stopped spinning. With a wry smile Julia noticed the title of the tape just above her fingertips. Remembering the songs it contained, she pried it out, wiped off the dust and returned to the console.

Yes, she'd go home, she thought, putting on a set of earphones and cuing up a selection. She'd attend the funeral and pay homage to her friend, but along the way she'd also find out why she died. Somehow she'd make sense of this most dark and senseless occurrence. She would. But in the meantime...

The song began. Julia closed her eyes, shutting out her surroundings and immersing herself in the music, her element, the thing that had accompanied her through every vicissitude in her life.

She'd always enjoyed James Taylor's voice, and now its sweet clarity cut right to the heart of her. Her lips moved silently, mouthing the lyrics along with the singer as the years scrolled by, all the places she'd drifted, all the people she'd come to know and enjoy and say goodbye to since leaving Harmony. She, too, had seen fire and rain; she, too, had known days she thought would never end.

Unaware of the tears sliding down her cheeks, she whispered, "But I always thought I'd see you one more time, my friend."

CHAPTER TWO

KELLY CARTER was looking for trouble—of the sexual kind. Ben Grant had been down that road often enough in his misspent youth to know the signs.

"So, what are you gonna do this weekend, Benjamin?" she asked, lounging across the worktable, one hand propping her blond head, the middle finger of her other hand seductively tracing the rim of her plastic champagne glass.

Ben removed his reading glasses, crossed his arms and wondered how he was going to get out of this one. As editor of the *Island Record,* he certainly wasn't opposed to socializing with his staff. In fact, that was exactly what they'd been doing until about ten minutes ago. The aroma of pizza still hung in the air, as it usually did on Friday evenings after the paper was put to bed.

But the rest of the staff was gone now, and he didn't think it would help the *Record*'s creative health if the paper wasn't the only thing to be put to bed tonight.

"I'm hoping to do some kayaking out on Cook Pond if the weather holds," he said neutrally.

Kelly lifted her gaze to his mouth, her lashes sweeping up, coming at him for round two. "Any plans for tonight?"

Think, he told himself. Kelly was an exceptionally attractive young woman, but she was a little on the young side, just a couple of years out of college, and he was pushing thirty-six. Even more importantly she was his best reporter. Becoming involved with someone so essential to the paper would only lead to trouble.

He delayed too long.

"I have an idea." She reached across the table so that her fingertips fell just inches short of his arm. "Come over to my place. We can rent a movie, pop some popcorn. How's that?"

"Thanks, it sounds great..." Actually it did. It sounded like it would be a lot of fun, but only for one night, maybe two or three. After that someone was bound to get bored, the other one hurt, and then there'd be hell to pay at work. It wasn't worth it. He was pleased with the way the paper was evolving. He didn't want to jeopardize any of those gains now.

As owner and editor of his own newspaper, Ben was finally living out a boyhood dream, one he thought he'd outgrown and forgotten along with his old Olivetti and the "Neighborhood News" he used to generate on it. Moreover, he was living his dream in a place he loved.

He'd fallen for the island on his very first visit. That had been two years ago. He'd taken the ferry over with a couple of friends, just a weekend of R and R away from Boston and the hectic pace of the *Globe*. Less than a year later he'd moved here permanently, no little shock to the family and friends of this born-and-bred city boy.

Living here these past thirteen months had only deepened his love affair with the island. Geographically Harmony was every bit as beautiful as Martha's Vineyard or Nantucket, but it was far quieter than the former and less expensive than the latter. Its pace was calm, its community tight-knit, and its weekly police log read like a page out of "Mayberry RFD." In a time of increasing craziness, Harmony was a corner of the world that still made sense.

What had really brought him here, though, was the paper.

It had been up for sale. Colleagues had thought he was crazy leaving the *Globe* to sink his hard-earned savings into a small weekly. At times he'd believed they were right.

But since then every one of his doubts had vanished. He loved working on the *Record*. He enjoyed being a vital cog in a small wheel—this community. He didn't feel he was working below his talents, either. He had only to remind himself of the nationally acclaimed *Gazette* over on the Vineyard to know how much could be done with a small paper. If he could have a career like the *Gazette*'s legendary editor and essayist, Henry Beetle Hough, he'd die a happy man.

"Well?" Kelly urged, bringing him back to the moment.

Ben looked the young woman over a second time, reconsidering, but then gave his head the tiniest shake. The paper was too important to him. It didn't need the tension of an office romance. Besides, Kelly had "short-term" written all over her, and Ben wasn't much interested in short-term stuff anymore. He was sick to death of it, in fact.

Maybe it was his age. Maybe it was just genetic—he came from excessively family-oriented folks. But whatever the reason, since moving here, he'd been giving the idea of settling down more and more thought.

Unfortunately no one he'd dated so far on Harmony lit the least spark of interest. That worried him, since they'd all been interesting attractive women. Had he gone past falling for someone? Having dated so many, had he become desensitized? Irrevocably jaded?

This, however, was the wrong time to be worrying about such matters. His young reporter was waiting.

"I'm sorry, Kell. I really can't make it."

"Why not?"

He didn't prevaricate. "Mixing business and pleasure isn't wise, you know that."

Her face dropped, and the sensuality she'd been oozing melted away, leaving her looking bruised and embarrassed. "Oh, well, it was just a thought."

"A nice thought. Thanks." Ben moved around to her side of the table and put a hand under her elbow. "Come on, we'd better call it a night."

Ben had just seen Kelly off and was closing the blinds in the front window when he noticed someone emerge from a shadowed doorway across the street and head toward the office. Ben didn't know the young man's name, but he recognized him as one of the eight or nine auxiliary policemen hired for the summer to augment Harmony's regular three-man force.

He opened the door without waiting for a knock. The night was cool and starless and, as always, redolent of the sea.

"Hi. What can I do for you?"

The kid was dressed in a heavy sweatshirt and jeans. His hair was sweat-damp and his eyes looked tired. "I didn't think anyone was here," he said in a hushed tone, "but then I saw your light. Do you have a few minutes?" His gaze flicked past Ben into the office.

Although Ben had no reason to feel suspicious, his reporter's intuition woke up—but sluggishly, like a bear who'd been hibernating too long.

"Sure. Come on in."

The young man stepped over the threshold, his gaze scanning the office and its clutter of desks, computers, typewriters, in-bins, out-bins, file cabinets and paper. Paper everywhere.

The office occupied the ground floor of a century-old wood-frame building in the center of town that had originally been a dry-goods store. Above the office was the one-and-a-half-story apartment where Ben lived.

Ben shut the door. "I don't think I know your name," he said, extending his hand to the young policeman.

"Scott Bowen."

"Ben Grant," Ben said as they shook hands.

Scott followed Ben to his desk at the back of the wide-open office, where Ben removed a half-empty bottle of champagne from a chair before motioning for the young officer to sit. He grinned apologetically. "We had a small celebration earlier. It was a year ago today that I took over as editor here. My staff thinks that's a reason to celebrate."

The young man nodded vacantly, too preoccupied, it seemed, to care about what had been, to Ben, a touching tribute.

"I'm surprised you're still working on the island." As he talked, Ben picked up some of the papers littering his desk and filed them in the wooden bins on the back wall. "I thought all the summer recruits left after Labor Day."

"Most do. But a couple of us were hired to stay on through September."

"The swing month," Ben said with a nod. Although the island quieted down considerably in September, there were still enough visitors to warrant extra help. He closed his file drawer, stacked some books—he was guilty of reading on the job, Dilbert cartoons mostly—and aligned his Rolodex with the pictures of his five nieces and nephews.

Finally he dropped into his leather chair just as Scott was saying, "This is my last weekend, though."

"Where do you go from here?" Ben knew that most of the auxiliaries were college kids enrolled in criminal-justice programs, or they'd already completed their police training and were in the process of applying for permanent jobs.

Working here gave them valuable training in the field, as well as a summer at the beach.

"I've got a couple weeks off, then I join the Wellington Police Force. That's up near Boston."

Ben knew where Wellington was. "Congratulations," he said.

"Thanks." The kid offered up a brief smile before his thoughts sobered him again. Ben waited.

"You heard about the suicide today, right?"

Ben's mood took a dive. "Yeah, I heard. The funeral home called with the information for the obituary." Ordinarily he got news of that nature immediately through his police scanner. But this morning when the call went out, he'd still been asleep. "A damn shame, isn't it? She was so young, so pretty."

"It was horrible."

Ben glanced up at the hollowness of the young man's voice. A vacant look still glazed his eyes, but now Ben noticed it wasn't so much preoccupied as it was haunted.

"I, uh, really didn't know her," Ben said, backing off from the uneasiness he suddenly felt. "I might've talked to her a couple of times—"

"I was the first officer on the scene," the young man interrupted.

"Oh."

"I work the midnight-to-eight shift, so I was still on duty. I was the one the dispatcher called."

"Ever been called to a suicide before?"

"Hell, no. This was my first death, period."

And he's come to dump it on me, Ben thought, feeling distinctly like the character in *Rime of the Ancient Mariner,* accosted on his way to a wedding by a crazed old man in need of unloading his horrific tale.

"The reason I'm here, Mr. Grant—I like what you've

done with the *Record.* I've worked on the island for a few summers now, so I know the paper. I like how it's changed. How *you've* changed it.''

"I've made it longer," Ben said wryly.

"You've done more than that. The columns are better. And your editorials are really…'' He searched for a word, searched and finally, reluctantly, said, "They're really good.''

"Thanks.'' Ben couldn't help but be pleased.

"You care about things on Harmony, the politics, the ecology, health care, and you're not afraid to speak up when you think something's wrong.''

"Maybe I should be. Some weeks the letters-to-the-editor section threatens to take over the paper.''

"Oh, that's the best part.''

Ben took the praise with a grain of salt. He knew the kid hadn't dropped by just to clap him on the back. "So, what does this have to do with the suicide this morning?''

Scott bowed his head. "This isn't easy for me to say. Chief Slocum's been good to me. He wrote the best recommendation…''

Ben sat forward. "This is about Charlie Slocum?''

Scott nodded.

"How so?''

"Let's just say he could've done a better job this morning.''

"How so?'' Ben asked again.

Scott swallowed. "Well, for one thing, there isn't going to be an autopsy. Did you know that?''

Ben frowned. "Aren't suicides always autopsied?''

"I guess not.'' Scott pressed his lips together. "Especially if they happen on Harmony.''

Ben's neck prickled. "Okay. Tell me what happened, the whole story, so I get a good picture.''

Ben settled into his chair as the young man told his tale: about the neighbor out jogging early in the morning; about the barking dog, chained in the yard, drawing his attention; about that neighbor's checking the house, seeing the body through the bedroom window and running to the victim's parents' house up the road to call 911.

"And you drew the short straw," Ben said when the kid paused, looking lost in anguished thought.

"Yeah." Scott sighed. "I sure did."

"So what happened when you got there?"

"The parents were at the house already. They didn't wait for me."

Ben winced.

"Yeah, it was pretty bad. Took me a while to calm them down. But once I had them sitting still, I called the station just to make sure Chief Slocum was on his way."

"Was he?" Ben prompted softly.

"The dispatcher had called him, yes."

That didn't answer Ben's question. "How long before he showed up?"

"Twenty minutes."

Ben drummed his fingers on his desk, unable to hide his displeasure. "What did you do in the meantime?"

"I wrote my report. You know, the time, the weather conditions, all that stuff we're taught to do."

"Did you check out the body?"

"Yes, I tried." Scott swallowed. "I looked around the bedroom, too. A little. And the bathroom."

Ben sat quietly, waiting, while Scott got up and paced.

"Anyway, Chief Slocum finally showed up. He talked with the Lorings first, but mostly he just acted like any neighbor would, grieving with them—which isn't bad, I guess..."

"But it sure doesn't get a report written."

"No. No, it doesn't." The kid dropped into his chair again. "After a while he got around to asking them about their daughter, her recent behavior, the last time they saw her, that sort of thing. They didn't have much to say. They'd seen her the evening before, but nothing had seemed unusual. They did say she'd been treated for nerves a while back—nerves, that was their term—but I'd already figured that out. I saw some antidepressants and Valium in the bathroom."

Scott went on to relate how he and the chief had checked out the bedroom. Scott had taken pictures while Slocum "poked around" and bagged evidence. From Scott's tone, Ben could tell he didn't think much of Slocum's evidence-gathering capabilities.

"After that he called the state." The troubled look in the young man's eyes deepened significantly. "Y'know, he didn't even bother to cover the phone when he picked it up. Just put his clammy hands all over it—and whatever fingerprints might've been there. That's what's bothering me, no proper procedure. It was the shabbiest investigation I've ever seen."

Ben weighed the statement carefully, in light of how much experience the kid could've had in his twenty-odd years.

"So he called the medical examiner..."

"Yes. And reported the death. I tried to listen in, but I missed some of it. He had me taking the evidence out to his car. When I returned he was off the phone. I asked him when the M.E. would be flying in. That's when he told me nobody was coming. That in fact, there wasn't going to be an autopsy."

"Did you ask him why?"

"Sure. He said he and the M.E. decided it wasn't necessary. Can you believe it? Wasn't necessary. Just like that.''

Ben tried not to react. "No other reason?''

"Yeah. We're in hard times, he said, lots of cutbacks in state budgets. Unless foul play is suspected, the M.E. just isn't going to grant an autopsy. No time, no money.''

Ben picked up a pen and turned it end to end. "Sad to say, that doesn't surprise me, Scott. It may seem unfair...''

The kid was shaking his head. "I know about the cutbacks. I also know you can get anything you want if you push. That's what I said to the chief, too. But he said the suicide was as routine as they get, so why bother putting the family through all that grief for nothing?''

"He may have a point there.''

"No.'' The young man shook his head again, firmly. "That's no excuse. Even if something *is* routine, it still deserves a complete investigation. A police officer has no right to just assume things and write up a report on appearances.''

Ben agreed but kept his opinion to himself. "Who filled out the death certificate?''

"Dr. Winters from the Medical Center. The chief called him right after talking to the M.E. Winters came over and examined the body—did an okay job, too, but let's face it, he's not an M.E. He wrote the certificate, put in death by gunshot, manner suicide, and that was that, case closed. Off the body went to the funeral parlor.''

Ben dragged a hand down his face. "I'm not sure what you expect me to do with this, Scott,'' he said, deciding to be forthright. He didn't have enough verifiable information to turn it into an article, and even if he did, suicide was too delicate a matter to center a public debate on. There were relatives and friends of the victim out there in the community, people who would be unnecessarily hurt by the exposure.

The kid sagged. "I'm not sure, either, Mr. Grant. You weren't there. I don't know how you're supposed to write about an investigation you didn't see."

"And you'd rather not be dragged into it, right?"

"I will if I have to be, but it sure wouldn't look good to my next commanding officer." He balled his fist and gave his thigh a series of controlled thumps. His mouth worked. "I really hate laying this problem on your desk. It's just, I'm leaving tomorrow and, well, you've taken on the chief before."

"You really think he should be 'taken on' over this issue?"

Scott nodded. "If you want to know the truth, off the record of course, I think the guy ought to get canned. I've worked for him for three summers now and watched him slacking off more and more." He paused. "He's been drinking more, too. Not on the job, but he drinks, comes in with red eyes and lots of mouthwash on his breath but not enough to cover the liquor." Scott shook his head. "I don't know. Maybe he just needs a rest." He looked up, directly into Ben's eyes. "All I know is, on this island, with Charlie Slocum as police chief, you could probably get away with murder."

The hair on Ben's arms stood up, and for a moment he couldn't speak. He came back to life with a rush of adrenaline. "Whoa. What are you saying? What are you *not* saying?"

Scott muttered a curse under his breath, probably regretting the can of worms he'd opened. "Look, I'm not saying anything. I'm just upset about Chief Slocum's procedures and think people ought to find out about 'em, that's all."

Ben's eyes narrowed. "You're bothered by more than that."

Scott gave his thigh a few more thumps, his eyes downcast.

"Come on, Scott. What're you chewing on?" Ben got up and came around his desk.

"Damn. I'm not saying this case was anything but a suicide. Really. I mean, Ms. Davoll *did* have a history of depression, and she *was* going through a messy divorce..."

"But?"

"I don't know. Call it instinct." The kid pressed his fingers to his eyes. "Women don't usually kill themselves that way, with a gun to the head. With a gun, period." He dropped his hands and looked at Ben. "Especially when they have a medicine cabinet full of pills."

"Pills. What sort of pills? Barbiturates? Painkillers?"

"No. Nothing like that. Just, like I said, her antidepressants and some Valium. All legally prescribed."

"They still could've taken her out, though, right?"

"Of course they could've."

And with a lot more grace, Ben thought.

"You do know that the stats on women committing suicide by gun have changed," Ben said. "*Women* have changed."

Scott shook his head. "Not here on Harmony. Here, everything's about thirty years behind the times. Besides, there was something else. I saw a couple of tickets on the bureau to an upcoming Sting concert. The chief didn't think much of it, but I've got a sister about that woman's age, and I know she sure as hell wouldn't kill herself if she had tickets to see Sting."

Ben tried to smile but realized his face had frozen. He pushed off the desk and paced a tight line, his sense of unreality deepening with each step. He came to a stop in front of the young auxiliary again. "You think somebody killed her?" Even as the words hung in the air, Ben couldn't believe he'd said them. This was Harmony. Quiet, lost-in-time Harmony. A place where nothing ever happened.

"Probably not. But I'm not sure. And now, without an autopsy or decent investigation, *nobody* will ever be sure." Scott rose, coming level with Ben's gaze. "Will they?"

Ben had to remind himself to breathe.

"I'll keep my eyes open, Scott. I'll try talking it up. But to be honest I still don't know what else I can do. Why don't you appeal for an autopsy?"

"You mean, go over Chief Slocum's head?"

"Yes." Ben suspected the kid was hoping he'd get people here stirred up enough to do it for him.

Scott avoided his eyes. "I'm not sure of the procedure."

"I'm not, either, but I can give you a couple of names, phone numbers, people who can tell you what to do and how to do it."

Scott shifted his weight, one foot to the other. Finally he nodded. "Okay."

Ben flipped through his Rolodex, then wrote the pertinent information on one of his business cards. Scott slipped the card into his back pocket and said thanks, but Ben wondered if that card would end up anywhere but a wastebasket.

Ben led Scott back through the maze of desks and opened the front door. Fog had rolled in, muting the security lights in the bike-rental lot across the street and the sounds of jazz drifting from the Brass Anchor on the corner.

"Jeez, where'd this come from?" Scott lifted his gaze to the sky.

"Amazing how fast things change on this island."

Ben felt the irony right down to his bones.

"Maybe your last night'll be a quiet one," he said, accompanying the young cop farther out onto the sidewalk.

"Let's hope." Scott extended his hand. "Well, thanks for listening."

Ben shook his hand. "No problem. Listening's what I do best."

The kid waved goodbye and walked down the hill toward the harbor. Ben remained on the sidewalk, pensive, watching him disappear like a phantom through the swirling mists.

Again he thought of the wedding guest in *Rime of the Ancient Mariner*. Sadder but wiser—was that where the phrase came from? Ben definitely felt sadder. But wiser? No. His brain was as fog-soaked as the night.

He wasn't eager to make an issue of Chief Slocum's ineptitude. Charlie was part of the old guard, folks who had an us-versus-them attitude toward the outside world, and that included anyone who hadn't been on-island for at least a couple of generations. In their minds outsiders didn't understand their ways or their best interests. "We take care of our own," Ben had heard on more than one occasion.

Maybe Charlie Slocum really believed he was taking care of his own—in this instance, the Lorings and those close to them—by skipping the autopsy and minimizing their grief. Ben could appreciate that.

But who was taking care of Amber Loring Davoll? Who was delving into the whys and wherefores of her death? And who—just on the very slim chance she'd died at the hand of another—who, dear God, was taking care of the rest of the citizens of Harmony?

Slowly Ben tipped back his head and scowled at the fog. "Thanks," he muttered. "Thanks for nothing."

CHAPTER THREE

JULIA FLEW HOME on Sunday, the day before the funeral.

Other than a two-hour wait at Logan for the Harmony shuttle, the journey was smooth and uneventful. By five in the afternoon the small commuter plane was in the air, heading south from Boston. Julia would be on the island by dinnertime.

Anxiety buzzed through her like a swarm of gnats. Because of the funeral, she told herself. She didn't like funerals, and this one was bound to be one of the most painful she'd ever attended.

The worst part was, she kept thinking Amber would be waiting to meet her, that they'd go to the funeral together, lend each other moral support and afterward maybe go out to lunch.

But then she'd remember it was Amber's funeral, and the shock would hit her all over again, fresh as the first time.

Julia rested her forehead against the window by her seat, determined to get her mind on more pleasant matters, at least for a while. The two upcoming weeks she'd managed to get off work, for instance. Preston's comfortable old house that Charlie had succeeded in procuring for her. And then there was Charlie himself, waiting at the airport to meet her.

That last image brought a smile to her face. It would be great seeing Charlie again. He'd played such an important role in her life she hated to think what would've become of her if he hadn't been around.

He'd kept tabs on her schoolwork, lectured her when she got into trouble, praised her when she did well, and if she needed a shoulder to cry on, his shoulder was always there.

Of course Officer Slocum had made himself available to all the island kids, but Julia knew she was special. She'd gotten Christmas presents from him and his wife, and they'd taken her places. They'd gone to the movies or played miniature golf and afterward stopped for malts at the diner. He'd taught her how to surf cast, taken her out on his speedboat, and he and Pauline had even invited her along on a vacation to Disney World once. That had been a dream come true.

Not all of Charlie's involvement had been pleasant, though. During her midteen years, he'd watched her like a hawk, mostly for signs of drinking or drugs. He'd also butted into her love life, discouraging her from seeing certain boys and setting her up with others, usually dorks who'd held zero appeal for her.

Difficult times, those years, but they were also some of the best, because it was then that he'd introduced her to WHAR.

In a very real sense Charlie Slocum had been more of a parent than her own mother—and certainly her father, who'd taken off when she was two. Her mother had loved her of course, but she'd also been somewhat neglectful. Not of her own choosing, Julia was sure. She'd just been too tired to do anything more than turn on the TV when she came in the door at night.

In contrast Charlie had nurtured her, inspired her, guided and rooted for her. And she loved him for it. She also respected him profoundly. As a policeman, he was unarguably fair, just, brave and dedicated to protecting the community. As a private citizen, well, there just wasn't any better husband or friend. He was without a doubt one of the few truly good men who walked the earth, and Julia felt privileged to know him.

Far more at ease than she'd been in days, Julia finally let herself enjoy the view out her window. The small commuter plane was just leaving landfall behind and shooting out over Buzzard's Bay. From her vantage point she was able to see nearly all of the islands that made up the Elizabeth chain, uninhabited except for tiny Cuttyhunk. She could see Martha's Vineyard beyond, the largest and most popular of the region's islands, and farther out still, a hint of Nantucket.

And there—Julia's pulse hammered—she could also see Harmony.

She bit her thumbnail as she watched the island come into view, landmarks becoming more distinct. There was graceful West Light on one end, East Light on the other, the deep indentation of the harbor and, above the harbor, rising like the sides of a shallow bowl, the town with its myriad shops, restaurants and large Victorian hotels.

The view enthralled her. With the plane nearly over the island now, she could see the entire thing, spread out below like a huge board game.

She could see the long pale sweep of the outer beaches, their dunes and cottages and the thin white line that was the pounding surf. She could see the wild windswept bluffs to the east, rising from Petticoat Shoals; the hills, the narrow roads, patches of woods, dozens of small ponds shining like mirrors, the undulating green fields and ubiquitous stone walls that gave so much of Harmony the look of an Irish landscape. She could also see the WHAR transmitter behind the Finch house. It rose like a beacon—a personal lighthouse—drawing her back across time to her home port.

It was all so familiar, she thought, like the reflection of her own face or the back of her hand. Without warning, her heart swelled with the bittersweet pangs homecoming brought.

She hadn't expected that. After all, she didn't have a home to return to here. Neither did she have any family waiting to embrace her, for as dear as Charlie was, he wasn't a blood relative. She couldn't even say she still had friends on Harmony. Granted, Cathryn was there, and Mike Fearing, but communication with them had dwindled to Christmas cards.

Yet, here she was now, gazing down on her birthplace with an ache in her throat and mist in her eyes and suddenly realizing you could spend eleven long years putting distance between yourself and your roots, and in an eye blink find yourself right back where you'd started. A full 360-degree turn. The geometry of the heart.

The plane shot past the island and then banked, tilting Julia's view up to blue sky and blinding sun. When it leveled off, she could see it was zeroing in on the airfield. Momentarily the landing gear was rumbling over the tarmac. Julia's heart pounded. Ready or not, she was home.

BEN PARKED his Bronco in the lot across the road from the airport terminal and turned off the engine. It was late Sunday afternoon, and the air was full of the buzz of small planes—the wealthier cottagers on their way home. He envied them their leisurely weekend. Somehow his kayak had never made it out of the shed.

After Scott Bowen's visit on Friday night, Ben hadn't been able to think of anything but Charlie Slocum's inept handling of the Davoll case. Harmony deserved better than that.

Ben had wanted to start writing an article right then and

there, but caution had prevailed. He'd known better than to go out on a limb just on the word of a young inexperienced auxiliary, and so he'd spent Saturday morning checking Scott out. The kid had come up clean, smart and reliable.

Ben had felt better about his source, but he still couldn't see himself writing an article. The touchy issue of the victim's family remained.

Saturday afternoon Ben had channeled his frustrated energy into finding out more about the budget cuts that had allegedly led to the state's policy of waiving certain autopsies. He'd phoned a friend at the *Globe* who covered state government and then an old source who worked in the coroner's office.

After hearing what they had to say, Ben had picked up the phone and started dialing Charlie Slocum's number. But caution had again stepped in and he'd hung up before the call went through. Instead, he'd spent the night cruising the three bars that remained open year-round on Harmony. One of those bars was Davy's Locker, owned by Bruce Davoll, Amber's husband. Bruce never made an appearance, but Ben got an earful, anyway.

When he'd awakened this morning, he'd been determined to talk to Charlie Slocum face-to-face. Getting the chief's side of the story was the only responsible thing to do. In a corner of his mind Ben also harbored the hope that his questions would scare Charlie out of his indolence and make him procure an autopsy. Then everyone's concerns, especially his, would be put to rest.

As soon as he'd dressed and had breakfast, he'd phoned Charlie's house, twice, but each time only got the answering machine. So he'd called the station and been told it was the chief's day off. Pushing his luck, Ben had asked where he might run into the chief today. The unsuspecting woman who manned the phone on Sunday had explained that Charlie was spending the day grocery shopping and getting his hair cut and such. He had a friend coming in on the five-thirty plane.

It was now almost five-thirty. With long purposeful strides, Ben crossed the road and pushed open the glass door of the small terminal. The chief was sitting at the lunch counter, arms planted on either side of a thick white coffee mug.

"Chief Slocum?" he said.

Charlie Slocum glanced up and, recognizing Ben, lost his smile.

"Mind if I sit here?" Ben nodded at the adjacent stool.

"Nobody's name's on it, far as I can see."

Ben ignored Charlie's sarcasm and sat. He asked the waitress for a coffee, too. "Great weather we're having."

Charlie grunted. "What do you want, Grant?"

"I was wondering if we could talk."

"I'm here to meet someone. Plane's due in five minutes."

"I probably won't need that long, and anyway, the shuttle always runs late."

Charlie tapped his spoon against the countertop. "Okay, but make it fast."

The waitress placed Ben's coffee in front of him. He waited until she left. "It's about Amber Davoll's suicide."

Charlie dropped the spoon. His already florid complexion deepened. "You better not be thinking of running a story about *that*. Those poor people are suffering enough."

"Of course I'm not." Ben tipped the glass sugar-dispenser over his cup, stirred, set the dispenser down again. "But certain things about the incident have been bothering me, and I can foresee those things maybe leading to a story eventually."

"It's nobody's business, a family tragedy like that. It doesn't belong in the paper."

"I agree. But certain decisions you make do belong there. They affect everybody. People have a right to know what to expect from the department they're paying to protect them."

Charlie turned slowly to face Ben, the swivel stool complaining under him. "What the hell are you talking about?"

"I heard there isn't going to be an autopsy. That right?"

Charlie only stared at him, a study in caution.

"And the reason is state budget cuts."

Charlie turned back to his coffee. "Where'd you hear that?"

To protect his source, Ben answered, "The Water Street Diner," otherwise known as "the wind tunnel" because of its customers' propensity for gossip. Ben had learned he could ascribe almost anything to the diner, since almost everything blew through there some time or other. Since Charlie didn't take him up on it now, he figured he was safe again.

"So?" Charlie said.

"To be honest, Chief, I was pretty surprised. I thought suicides were always autopsied. So I decided to look into these cutbacks, see who'd voted them in, the repercussions on the grassroots level, that sort of thing. But then I ran into something interesting. Somebody told me that the financial straps are loosening and the M.E.'s being a lot more generous these days."

The chief glanced at his watch, then toward the door where arriving passengers entered the terminal. "So?" he said again.

"So, it isn't impossible to get an autopsy for a suicide. It isn't even all that hard. All you have to do is push a little, present reasonable suspicion..."

"Well, there you go. I didn't have any suspicion."

"But women don't usually commit suicide using a gun, especially when pills are available. Couldn't you have used that?"

A vein throbbed in the older man's temple. He said nothing.

"Then there's the testimony of family and friends. I've run into at least five people myself who swear the victim was no more depressed than they were." Ben paused. Did he actually think Charlie would volunteer that he hadn't spoken to Amber's friends?

Charlie tossed a dollar bill on the counter. "I'm having trouble seeing where this conversation's going, Grant."

"I'll be honest with you, Chief. I think you should've insisted on an autopsy. It's one of those things a community just...deserves. It answers questions once and for all."

"It also puts the family through a lot of unnecessary pain."

Ben picked up his cup, stared into it, then plunked it down again. "Charlie, please. I need to know what measures you took to assure yourself this was an open-and-shut case of suicide."

The chief swore under his breath and, without answering, pushed himself to his feet.

Ben rose, too. "Did you fingerprint the house? Gather foreign material? Make sure Dr. Winters did a thorough exam? Did you send samples of everything to the lab?" Charlie started to pull away. "Dammit, Chief, did you even talk to that scum, Bruce Davoll, to see what he was doing the night his wife died?"

Ben heard the answer to his questions in Charlie's defensive anger. "Goddammit, what are you after?"

"I only want to hear your side of the story."

"No, you don't. What you want is to write some slanderous trash that'll stir people up, sell papers and have you coming out like a holy crusader.''

"I'm sorry you feel that way, because nothing could be further from the truth.''

"Like hell it couldn't.''

Ben suddenly got the feeling they weren't alone, that another presence was looming over their argument. He glanced to his left and, sure enough, someone was there, not four feet away. Her eyes were riveted on him and blazing with hostility. Her lips were parted and turned down in distaste.

Charlie Slocum swiveled toward the young woman, too. "Oh, hell,'' he ground out, his anger mixing with embarrassment.

His attitude changed almost immediately, however. Ignoring Ben, he struggled into a smile. "Hey, Funny Face!'' he called. He held out his arms and the young woman stepped into them, but stiffly, her eyes still fixed on Ben.

His curiosity soared. The dispatcher had said Charlie was expecting a friend, but this person seemed too young to be a friend. She was about the right age to be a daughter, though, but as far as Ben knew, Charlie didn't have any kids.

She wouldn't have been his offspring, anyway. She was too thin, too pretty, too fashionably dressed. There was also a book of Pablo Neruda poems tucked in the outside pocket of her carry-on.

Whoever she was, she gave the impression of someone who was thoroughly pulled together. Instead of wearing comfortable jeans, as many travelers did these days, she had on a jacket of oatmeal linen with matching trousers and a cocoa-colored blouse. An office outfit. City duds.

As attractive as the outfit was, Ben's gaze was drawn irresistibly to this woman's hair. It was dark and long and smooth, a spill of chestnut satin that gave her the cool aloof aura of a forties movie queen. Her eyes, remarkably, were the very same shade of red-brown.

Ben realized quite suddenly that he was staring. But then, so was she, those big red-brown eyes of hers narrowed and fixed on him over Charlie's shoulder as they embraced. Ben had never felt such animosity from a woman he hadn't even met.

For some crazy reason he could only smile back.

HE HAD A NERVE! Julia thought. How dared he smile so unrepentantly when he knew perfectly well she'd just overheard him haranguing Charlie? She wasn't sure what she'd walked in on exactly, but it had certainly smacked of media harassment. And the questions! Where did this guy think he was? *Who* did he think he was?

Charlie loosened his embrace and they stepped apart. "Will you look at you!" he said proudly, lifting her hands out to the sides.

Julia was still lost in her anger, but she realized Charlie came first. If he wanted to ignore whatever had been going on here, she'd comply—for the moment. She dragged her attention away from the stranger and focused it on Charlie.

What she saw made her heart sink. *He's changed,* she thought. Seven years ago only a few threads of silver had graced his dark hair. Now his entire head was salt-and-pepper gray. And his face, what deep creases lined it. How tired and puffy his eyes were.

Only to be expected, she reminded herself. *The man is fifty-eight.*

What she couldn't dismiss so easily, though, was the weight he'd put on, thirty or forty pounds. The buttons of his shirt were strained.

Not that the extra weight looked bad on him, she told

herself. Charlie Slocum was still the handsomest man this side of the moon in her estimation. He simply didn't look exactly as she remembered him.

"Hi, Charlie," she said, assuming a bright smile. "I hope you haven't been waiting long."

"Nope. I just got here. How was your flight?"

"Long, but otherwise okay."

"You must be tired."

"Actually, no. The three-hour time difference is in my favor. Unfortunately I'll feel it in the morning."

He looked past her. "Do you have any other bags?"

Julia followed his gaze to her carry-on, resting behind her on the floor. "Afraid I do. Two more." Against her will her eyes were drawn to the stranger again. He was still standing there, watching them, eavesdropping on their conversation, violating their reunion.

He didn't just irritate her, he made her uneasy, although the reason for that eluded her.

Charlie glanced at the stranger, too. He hesitated a moment before lifting her bag, probably debating whether or not to introduce them.

"Hi. Ben Grant," the stranger said, stepping forward, hand outstretched, to do the job himself.

Julia ignored his hand but allowed herself a murmured "Julia Lewis." Being rude, even to someone who deserved it, usually left her with more guilt than satisfaction.

Ben Grant shoved his hand into his pocket and nodded. "Julia," he repeated quietly, as if he was mentally doing something with the name. Analyzing it. Taking possession.

Who *was* this guy?

He stood about six feet, with a moderately strong build and above-average good looks. His rumpled dark hair was attractively cut to just brush his collar. He seemed to be in his midthirties, sort of a yuppie type in salt-stained Top-

Siders, tan pants, and a shirt of blue chambray worn with a loosely knotted black knit tie.

All in all he presented a safe identifiable look, a boyish, bookish look, one that engendered trust in the casual observer.

All surface. Looking into his eyes, Julia felt she was gazing down the barrel of a .44 Magnum. They were the most penetrating eyes she'd ever seen. Dark blue and fringed with black lashes, they seemed capable of burning through stone and sucking out its very essence.

He wasn't from the island. Not only would she have remembered him, but beneath that casual facade, he was too sharp, too tough, too city-wise.

And she thought, *What is someone like you doing on Harmony?*

Charlie exhaled a long-suffering sigh and explained, "Ben is the new editor of the *Island Record*."

Julia frowned. "The newspaper?"

"Yes," the man named Ben Grant replied.

"Oh." Things began to fall into place. Julia gave him a second look. "Did I interrupt an interview or something?"

Charlie took her arm. "No. You didn't interrupt a thing, sweetheart. Ben was ready to leave, anyway. Weren't you, Ben?"

The editor answered with a low chuckle. Charlie ignored him and nudged Julia toward the luggage cart that was just being wheeled in.

"Nice meeting you, Julia," Ben said as she walked away. She heard at least ten different shades of meaning sliding around in that one remark.

She didn't return the sentiment.

"WHAT WAS THAT all about?" she asked Charlie once they were alone, watching the luggage porter unload the cart.

Charlie made a disgusted sound, accompanied by a dismissive toss of his hand.

"Tell me," she persisted. "When I arrived you two were really going at it." Her heart ached with protectiveness, which was odd. In their relationship Charlie had always been the protector. "What was he asking you? Something about a murder investigation?"

Charlie started. "Oh, no, no. Just..." He lowered his eyes. "Just your friend's death."

"What!"

"Listen, honey—" Charlie squeezed her shoulder "—while you're home, I'd like you to do me a favor. Ignore the *Record.* Ignore Ben Grant. Every once in a while he gets a notion to stir things up, give someone flack, and more often than not that someone is me."

"You? What sort of flack can he possibly give *you?*"

"It really isn't worth explaining."

"Yes, it is. You can't leave me hanging, Charlie. What was he griping about just now?" She picked up one of her suitcases, Charlie took the other, and they started for the exit.

"He thinks I should've done a more detailed report on Amber. He thinks there should've been an autopsy." Charlie shook his head. "Hell, he wasn't there. He didn't see how bad Hank and Viv Loring were hurting. He doesn't even know them."

Charlie opened the glass door and Julia stepped through into the late-September afternoon.

"I did the best job I could as fast as I could, so they could get out of there and get on with their grieving," he said, crossing the road. "And after thirty-five years on the force, I don't need some smart-ass outsider second-guessing my judgment."

His cruiser was parked in the first row of the airport lot.

Julia noticed with some concern that he was breathing heavily as he lifted her bags into the back seat.

She waited until they were in the car before continuing. "You don't think he's going to make an issue of this, do you? Good Lord, he wouldn't write about it in the paper?"

Charlie only shrugged, leaving the possibility open.

"Why is he doing this?" Julia asked, buckling her seat belt.

Charlie backed out of the parking slot. "You know how pushy reporters can be these days. They all think they're working for the *Washington Post* or '20/20.' But what can you expect? The movies glorify the image, so we get all these Bernstein and Woodward wanna-bes, these...damn obnoxious pests."

"I'm familiar with the type." A few of the radio stations she'd worked for had affiliate TV stations. Unfailingly their news departments included at least one person whose insensitivity appalled her.

"I just think it's ludicrous, here on Harmony. I mean, we are still talking about the *Record,* right?"

"It is ludicrous, and that's why I don't want you worrying yourself over it." Charlie drove on in silence for a minute, probably hoping to drop the subject.

"What happened to the old editor?"

"Agnes? Oh, she finally retired." Charlie shook his head. "Why she handed the paper over to an outsider, I'll never understand."

Julia rolled down the window and let the fresh ocean breeze blow through her hair. "Where's he from, anyway?"

"The Boston area. I don't know what the hell he's doing here—except being a pain in the butt."

"Did he marry somebody from Harmony?"

"Nope. He isn't married at all."

Somehow Julia already knew that. "Has he been here long?"

Charlie sighed, badly hiding his irritation with the subject. "Hey, I haven't seen you in seven years. Why are we wasting our time still talking about Ben Grant?"

Feeling heat creep up her neck, Julia turned her face to the open window. "Charlie, I haven't the foggiest."

PRESTON FINCH'S HOUSE stood high on Peggoty Hill in the sparsely populated southeast quadrant of the island. Peggoty Hill wasn't the most desirable acreage on the island—that was the shoreline—but Julia had always liked it well enough. Being one of Harmony's higher knolls, it was also a perfect spot for a radio transmitter.

Now, as Charlie pulled into the long driveway, Julia gazed at that transmitter on its rise behind the house, and her pulse quickened. Memories assailed her, memories of being sixteen and Charlie bringing her here for the first time to work with Preston. How frightened she'd been. How resistant.

Preston Finch was something of an island character, which wasn't a bad thing to be. The island was rather fond of its characters. He'd garnered this distinction back in the sixties when he'd single-handedly built his own radio station. Located in a wing of his house, WHAR was properly licensed and fully operational, although Preston was its sole operator. It was, in truth, his indulgence, since he certainly made no money from it.

The station's frequency covered just the island, but that was enough for its owner. Equally quirky was its program. Preston only went on the air in the evening after dinner, and he only played music that pleased him. By no stretch of anyone's imagination was WHAR your usual radio station, and at sixteen Julia had wanted no part of it.

If only she'd known how much working here was going to do for her. Charlie had hoped it would help her move past her grief over her mother's death, and it had. But it had also given her a sense of purpose, an identity and ultimately a career she loved.

As they bumped along the crushed seashell driveway now, Julia was pleased to see that the property and its surrounding area looked about the same as when she'd left. Flying in, she'd noticed a lot of new construction, but there was no sign of development here. Preston's five acres of mostly scrub growth were still quiet and private, surrounded as they were by conservation land.

Charlie parked his cruiser beside the front porch and turned off the engine.

"Are you sure my staying here is okay with Mr. Finch?"

"Yep. Absolutely. He said he'd give you a call tonight. You can hear it straight from the horse's mouth. Come on, let's get you settled in."

Julia opened the car door and slid out. The shore was at least half a mile away, yet the breeze that whistled through the wild honeysuckle and bayberry was still saturated with the briny scent of the sea. Overhead, in the orange glow of the westering sun, gulls wheeled and shrieked.

Pulling one of her bags from the back seat, she gave the century-old, cedar-shingled farmhouse a cursory glance. Originally a boxy two-story rectangle with a front porch, it had been bumped out on both sides back in the fifties to enlarge the kitchen and to add a den. A decade later Preston had built his studio, a freestanding addition he'd connected to the house by a long breezeway. That was what claimed her attention now.

"Oh." Her heart sank the way it had when she'd first looked at Charlie. The studio wore a look of neglect, almost abandonment.

It's the window shades, she decided. *Nothing more.* Every one of them was fully drawn, lending the shedlike structure a closed-for-the-season look.

Charlie unlocked the breezeway door. People on the island rarely used their front entrances. "Coming, Julia?"

"Uh, yes." Tearing her gaze from the studio, she followed Charlie inside.

Preston's house hadn't been remodeled since the late sixties. Avocado shag carpeting covered the floors. Dark pine furniture, with eagles and liberty bells on the slipcovers, cluttered the rooms. Still, everything was neat and clean and, Charlie attested, in working order. It would do very well, Julia decided, especially considering the brevity of her stay.

She carried her bags up the narrow boxed-in stairs and put them in the front bedroom, the small closet of which had been emptied for summer renters. The other bedroom was larger and faced the ocean, but it was Preston's and still contained his personal belongings.

Julia's was a simple room with two depression-era bureaus, a nightstand and a double bed covered with a yellow chenille spread. The ceiling sloped cozily to side walls that reached only to her thighs. Two windows faced the road, with views of the hotel rooftops in town three miles away.

She left her bags unopened by the bed and hurried down to the kitchen where Charlie was pouring clam chowder from a deli container into a pot on the stove.

"Oh, that smells great," she exclaimed, taking an appreciative sniff.

"I picked up some fried clams, too. They're in the oven crisping."

Julia sighed in anticipation. "I haven't had real fried clams since...since the last time I was home." She opened the refrigerator and saw that Charlie had stocked it with milk, eggs, butter and juice. On the counter was a box of cornflakes, three bananas and a loaf of wheat bread. Everything she'd need for tomorrow's breakfast. For a whole week of breakfasts!

How would she ever repay his thoughtfulness? she wondered. Certainly she'd take him out to dinner later in the week, someplace really nice, but that would hardly balance things out between them.

When the food was heated, they sat at the kitchen table. The meal, although just takeout, was ambrosial. Julia had two full bowls of the creamy chowder and more than half the clams.

Charlie ate well, too, but she noticed with some concern that he washed down his meal with a scotch-and-water. His choice of drink puzzled her. She couldn't remember his being a hard-liquor fan, but maybe her memory was faulty.

They were clearing the table when the telephone rang. It was Preston Finch, and just as Charlie had predicted, he was calling to reassure Julia of her welcome.

"Actually it eases my mind knowing someone is there," the elderly man said. "And while you're at it, I wish you'd use my car. Sitting in the garage isn't doing the battery any good."

Julia protested, but in the end Preston prevailed. He also invited her to use the WHAR studio any time she wished, in case she got the urge "to do radio as it was meant to be done."

She laughed, thanked him, but respectfully declined. The equipment in the studio was so old she knew that using it would just be an exercise in frustration.

Hanging up the phone, she found that Charlie had set out a brown bakery box of assorted pastries. "Oh, none for me, thanks," she said. "Maybe later."

"Coffee?"

"No. Nothing, thanks." She bit her lip. "You know what I would like?"

Charlie smiled, his tired eyes lighting with some of the merriment she remembered. "After talking with Press about his studio? Yeah, I think I can guess." He hung up the towel he'd been using to dry the dishes and said, "Let's go."

They went through the house, from the kitchen through the dining room to the den and out to the long breezeway, turning on lights as they went. On one side of the breezeway the windows looked out on the driveway. On the other side they looked out on a patio and a lawn. The lawn ended at a field of brambles that rolled on to the sea, or more precisely to the cliffs rimming the sea at this portion of the island.

At the end of the breezeway Charlie unlocked the studio door. "You might as well hang on to these," he said, handing her the ring of keys.

He stepped inside and flipped a switch. A dim overhead light went on, casting a gray glow that didn't quite reach the corners of the structure.

Heart beating in childlike anticipation, Julia followed him into the large main room, which really wasn't large at all except in comparison to the kitchenette and washroom that lay off it. The place smelled of mildew and dust.

Julia's gaze went straight to the console where Preston spun his records, the same console where she'd made her first broadcast.

"Bring back memories?" Charlie asked.

Julia barely nodded as she inched forward. It was a simple device with four fat knobs, instead of the elaborate array of slides and switches she currently worked with. The microphone was a heavy tabletop model, and the two turntables were the same ones she'd used all those years ago. So were the tape players. There was no sign that Preston had even heard of CDs.

She ran her fingertips lightly over the board. They left trails in the dust.

"Is Preston broadcasting at all these days?"

"Yeah, some. But not on what you'd call a regular basis."

"That's sad. I hate to see him retire. He provided something unique."

Charlie shrugged. "What can I say? He seems happy."

For a moment Julia was distracted by the smell of alcohol Charlie emitted when he spoke. It was a lot more obvious here in the small closed-up space of the studio.

Hiding her distaste, she crossed the room and began to survey the albums and tapes on the shelves along the wall. "I don't see a single record that wasn't here the day I left. Glen Miller, Vaughn Munroe, Perry Como..." She was being deliberately facetious. Although Preston favored popular artists of the prerock era, his collection was actually quite diverse. It just wasn't current.

Julia leaned into the doorway of the kitchenette, which ran behind the bookshelves and faced the driveway. "Gosh, nothing has changed. Except everything's older and more run-down."

"Aren't we all!"

She turned, love in her eyes. "Oh, Charlie."

"Would you care to sit?" Looking rather serious, he reached for the old leather chair on rollers at the control board, pulled it out for her and then took a seat near it.

Julia crossed the sand-embedded braided rug and sank into the chair, folding her hands on her lap.

"Sweetheart," Charlie said, "are you okay with...with this funeral tomorrow?"

Julia hadn't thought about the funeral for a couple of hours. Now emotions shifted within her. "Yes," she said, then, "I don't know."

Charlie covered her hands with his and gave them a squeeze. "Are you planning to go to church with anyone?"

She shook her head. "I thought of calling Cathryn Hill...McGrath, I mean, but I haven't gotten around to it yet."

"How about we meet in the parking lot, then?"

"Okay. That'd be nice."

He started to pull back. Julia grasped his hands. "Charlie, I have to ask you about Amber again." She watched his wiry eyebrows slant down toward his nose. "I know you said Amber was upset about her upcoming divorce, but I...I'm still having trouble believing that was why she killed herself. Have you found out anything more?"

Charlie sighed. "Not really."

"But there must be something."

A smile eased its way over Charlie's face. "You haven't changed a bit, Funny Face. Always wanting to know why."

Julia sat up taller. "Me?"

"Uh-huh. You drove me nuts, even when you were just a pint of peanuts. Why are there tides? Why are some dogs brown and some black? Why do people fall in love?"

Julia grinned. "I wasn't that bad, was I?"

"Yep. And here you are again, still asking why, worse than a three-year-old."

The smile faded from her lips. She lowered her eyes because suddenly there were tears burning in them.

"It just happens, sweetheart," Charlie said softly. "It would be nice to think there are reasons for all the bad things that happen in life. It'd be very comforting. But the more bad stuff you go through, the more you see there's no rationale behind it, no plot or rhyme or reason. So you stop asking why—why'll drive you nuts—and you just get on with coping. That's really all you can do."

Charlie probably knew what he was talking about. Being a policeman, he saw bad things happening to good people all the time. Two years ago he'd been a victim himself when Pauline died of bone cancer.

"How are *you* doing, Charlie?"

He caught her meaning. "Oh, every day's a little easier," he said with a nonchalance she was sure he didn't feel.

"Are you still living in the same house?"

"Yep. Maybe I should move, but..." He shrugged.

She nodded understandingly, but inwardly she kept thinking, *He's changed. Not just heavier and grayer. He's changed.*

"Are you keeping busy?"

"Oh, sure." He glanced away evasively.

Julia pressed her lips together and sighed. "I wish I'd come home for her funeral. I loved Pauline. She was a good person."

"And she didn't deserve to die so young and in such pain."

He was right and there was nothing she could think of to say. They fell silent. Through the shade-covered windows came the dull roar of the sea below the distant cliffs. A breeze piped through an unseen chink in one of the frames.

"Well, I should run," Charlie said, glancing at his watch.

Julia got to her feet. "Thanks for picking me up at the airport, and for supper and arranging this place." *And my life,* she thought.

"My pleasure." Charlie opened the studio door and stepped into the breezeway. Night had deepened. Crickets sang loudly in the surrounding thickets. "Are you going to be all right way out here alone?"

"Sure. I love it. I still have to unpack and get acquainted with the house. Maybe I'll even drive around a little, try out Preston's car."

"Oh. Do you want me to drive you?"

"Charlie, don't be silly."

He looked a little offended, and she thought, *He isn't silly, just lonely.*

When he was gone, she locked the studio and went up to her bedroom. She was worried about Charlie. His wife's death had struck him a blow. It was obvious he wasn't coping well.

Julia opened her suitcase and began to unpack.

Funny, but she probably wouldn't have been so worried if she hadn't run into that Ben Grant earlier. She had enough faith in Charlie's ability to eventually pull himself out of whatever he was going through. She also had enough trust in his character to know he'd never let anything, even grief, seriously compromise his job. Growing up, she'd seen his strength manifested in too many ways to count.

But had Ben Grant?

Obviously this newcomer's view of Harmony's chief of police was severely limited. Obviously he was out to get him.

Julia hung the suit she planned to wear to the funeral in the closet. When she moved away, her gaze drifted to the window and the lights of town in the distance, fanning palely into the dark night sky.

The newspaper office used to be in town. Probably still was, she thought, feeling the urge to go down there and give Ben Grant a piece of her mind. But it was Sunday night. The likelihood of finding him in his office was zilch.

She resumed unpacking and tried to get herself into a

more sanguine frame of mind. She had a funeral in the morning, a difficult funeral, and that was all she wanted to focus on right now.

But the scene she'd witnessed at the airport continued to bother her. So did the fact that, as editor of the island paper, Ben Grant controlled the news and had the power to ruin a person's reputation. Charlie's reputation. Maybe even create a circumstance where his job would be in jeopardy.

Julia gazed toward the lights of town once again and her stomach clenched. Something told her this visit home was going to be a lot more complicated than she'd thought.

CHAPTER FOUR

BEN LEFT the *Record* office at quarter to eleven, drove his Bronco up Center Street and around the corner to Church, where, appropriately enough, two churches stood diagonally across from each other, vying for the spiritual business of the island.

Ben turned in at the First Congregational, a simple white-painted structure with a square side steeple and modest stained-glass windows. Harmony lacked the whaling heritage of the other islands in the area; consequently it lacked the grand homes and public buildings that heritage would've provided. Except for a few decades of prosperity in the Victorian era, when vacationing at seaside resorts became the fashion, Harmony's inhabitants had remained simple farmers and fishermen right into the twentieth century. Ben didn't mind one bit.

Pulling into a parking place, he could already hear organ music pouring from the open windows of the church. He turned off the engine and vaulted out of his vehicle—and nearly collided with Julia Lewis. His heart kicked like a spooked horse. He'd been thinking about her a lot since yesterday and for a moment believed his preoccupation had conjured her up.

As his heart settled, he wondered how he could've missed her. She was standing right there alongside his Bronco, leaning against a thirty-year-old Pontiac.

There was another reason he should've noticed her. She

was wearing a suit in a shade of gold that lit her up like a sunrise. Quite a fashion choice for a funeral. Probably a California thing. She wasn't wearing a blouse under her jacket either, just one of those little lace things women used as a nod toward modesty.

Aware that his gaze had stalled there at midchest, he forced it to move on. But the view didn't get any easier. He gulped, taking in the short skirt and the long expanse of shapely leg below it. "Good morning," he said, his eyes still somewhere around her knees. He was fairly surprised when she reciprocated his greeting.

"Hi!" she said. It was an aggressive *hi,* as if he was exactly the person she'd been hoping to run into, and not for any good reason. She pushed away from the car, took a step forward.

Ben recalled the scene at the airport and the anger she'd barely suppressed. He'd had a feeling even then that she wasn't done with him. He glanced toward the church; if he knew what was good for him, he'd keep on walking and save himself a lot of grief. For some perverse reason he remained rooted to the spot. He wondered when he'd become a masochist.

With a rolling shrug of one shoulder, he turned and reached into his car for his sports jacket. "How's it going today?" he asked, slipping his arms into the sleeves. She only nodded, lips pressed tight. "Dumb question. Sorry. I understand you and Amber Davoll were friends."

Ben had left the airport yesterday more than a little curious about Julia. He'd taken a walk to the Water Street Diner after he got home, figuring somebody there would know who Charlie's Funny Face was. It being a Sunday, only one other person was there besides the owner, but both knew Julia Lewis.

Over two cups of coffee and a meat-loaf platter, eaten at

the counter, Ben had learned the basic facts of Julia's life: she was from Harmony, her father had taken off when she was still in diapers, her mother had died when she was a teenager, and she'd lived with Charlie and his wife until she'd left for college. He'd also been told that she worked in radio as a deejay, a revelation that fascinated him more than it probably should have. But the disclosure that struck him as most poignant was that Julia and Amber Loring Davoll had been best friends. Julia had come home for the funeral.

Ben didn't learn much else, and even those facts were sketchy. The diner owner, Asa Hodge, was eager to close up and wasn't exactly encouraging conversation, so Ben wasn't about to start asking a lot of questions. Not in this matter, anyway. That'd only raise speculation. Besides, what was the point? Why did he have to know anything about Julia Lewis? No reason whatsoever, except personal curiosity.

Now, tightening the knot on his tie, he asked, "Isn't that Preston Finch's car?" Permanent residents knew one another's cars.

Julia gave the Pontiac a quick distracted glance. "Yes."

"Is Preston home?" No one at the diner had mentioned anything about Preston.

"No. I'm staying at his place for a couple of weeks, that's all. He's lent me his car, as well." She seemed tense and impatient with the subject.

"Oh. For some reason I thought you were staying with Chief Slocum."

The peach coloring of her cheeks ripened. Her lips worked over gathering words. "About Chief Slocum... "

Here it comes, Ben thought.

But at that very moment a police car turned into the parking lot. Ben wanted to laugh. *Here it comes, indeed.*

Julia noticed Charlie and the tension drained from her face.

"You were saying?" Ben prompted.

"Oh. I was wondering if you and I could talk, but obviously this isn't the right time. Will you be free later? After the funeral?"

"Sure. All I have is work and I can get out of that. That's the good thing about being the boss." He smiled affably, but she didn't smile back. "Would you like to meet somewhere for a drink or coffee, or how about lunch?"

He must've been pushing, although he wasn't aware of it. Her eyes ran up and down the length of him. "No thanks. We'll just…talk."

She walked past him to the parked cruiser, leaving a faint scent of perfume in her wake, something intriguingly spicy and sophisticated. She linked her arm with Charlie's—he was in full dress uniform today—and they both cast sour looks at Ben. He decided that asking if she cared to sit with him probably wasn't such a good idea. Tugging on his earlobe, he continued on his way toward the church.

Best to get his mind back on track, back to the reason he was here. He wanted to pay his respects to the deceased of course, but he was also curious to see who'd shown up for the funeral and how they acted in their hour of grief.

At the door, though, Ben paused and gave Julia Lewis one last over-the-shoulder glance. *Bam!* There it was again, that kick to the heart.

In deep regret he opened the door and slipped inside.

THE CHURCH, which held 250 people, was nearly full. Sitting in the fourth-to-last pew with Charlie, Julia was aware of only one of those 250. Ben Grant was sitting across the aisle one pew back from theirs. His presence was an irritating distraction. She didn't know what business he had here. Had he known Amber? Was he here to pay his respects? Julia couldn't help thinking his reasons had more to do with his newspaper.

She made a conscious decision to cast him from her thoughts and concentrated, instead, on the congregation seated before her. She found Mr. and Mrs. Loring easily enough, sitting in the front row, looking a lot older than she remembered. Actually they looked battered. Pity flowed through her. No one deserved what they'd suffered.

She spotted Amber's husband next, sitting a few rows behind the Lorings. Bruce Davoll was into bodybuilding, and it was his excessively thick neck and bulky shoulders that made him so easy to find. He was sitting with a slender woman with straw-blond hair caught back in a black chiffon scrunchie.

"Who's that Bruce Davoll's with?" she asked Charlie in a whisper.

Charlie quietly snorted. "His girlfriend."

Julia's eyes snapped. "He came to his wife's funeral with a girlfriend?"

Charlie placed a finger over his lips. She noticed a couple of people had turned. Unapologetic, Julia went back to glowering at Bruce.

Bruce was from the island, but because he was a few years older than Julia and Amber, he'd run in different circles. Amber had only gotten to know him later, when she was nearly twenty-two and home for a visit.

By then, she'd already graduated from secretarial school and was employed by a large insurance agency in Worcester. Julia, in her last year at Emerson, still kept in touch with her. They called regularly and once a month spent a day together. She'd thought her friend was happy living the life of a young urban single. She'd thought they'd be get-

ting together for lunch and shopping dates for years to
come.

But one day Amber called unexpectedly and told her she
was moving back to Harmony. ''I'm totally in love,'' she'd
said on a laugh.

Julia could barely remember Bruce Davoll, except that
heavy-metal music had usually blared from his Trans-Am
whenever he drove by, and Charlie had once picked him
up for brawling at the Old Town Tap.

Amber's parents hadn't been crazy about the match, but
seeing there was nothing they could do to change their
daughter's mind, they'd eventually accepted the marriage.
They'd even given the young couple the down payment for
a house.

As maid of honor, Julia remembered the wedding well.
It had been lovely. She had to admit Bruce was a handsome
guy and he and Amber made a stunning couple. However,
she also remembered thinking that Amber was making a
mistake. She'd kept her thoughts to herself, though, pri-
marily because Amber was so happy. And Bruce *did* seem
devoted to her. Too devoted maybe.

Julia recalled a moment during the reception when she
and Amber had stolen away to a quiet table in the lounge
and were talking, innocently enough, about Julia's job with
a small classical-music station in Boston. Not ten minutes
into the conversation, Bruce had come looking for his bride,
surprising Julia with his anger and possessiveness. Amber
belonged at his side on their wedding day, he'd said, giving
Julia a look she could only interpret as jealous.

Amber had laughed, somewhat embarrassed, and started
to protest, but Julia had wanted her friend's day to run
smoothly and so had shooed her back into the reception—
and gracefully bowed out of the picture. And she'd kept

bowing out, because she'd realized Amber belonged with Bruce and to a new life she could never be a part of.

Now, staring at the back of Bruce's close-cropped head, Julia wondered what had caused the breakup of the marriage. Had Bruce left Amber for the blonde sitting beside him? Had Amber come to her senses and realized they just weren't suited?

Was the loneliness and sense of having failed what led her to put a gun to her head one night and pull the trigger?

Finding herself growing too agitated, Julia closed her eyes, drove Bruce Davoll from her thoughts and concentrated, instead, on the soft organ music. After a couple of minutes she felt better and continued to survey the congregation.

"Who are those people?" she asked Charlie. "The ones on the right, third and fourth rows."

Charlie leaned forward, squinted. "Ah. That's the contingency from the bank. Amber's boss. The other tellers."

Julia studied the group, headed up by an impeccably dressed middle-aged man with thick blond hair and a sailor's tan. A couple of the women were sniffling into handkerchiefs.

Gradually she recognized several other people—neighbors, merchants, relatives of Amber's and finally, finally, a few old friends. She broke into a smile. There was Mike Fearing, whom she'd dated briefly, and there, the O'Banyon boys, twins as unalike as night and day. And there, oh, there sat Cathryn McGrath.

Of course she'd expected to see Cathryn here. Cathryn lived on Harmony. But Julia hadn't expected to feel so moved—which was silly, she realized. When you went through school with only four girls in the class, you couldn't help but develop extra-close bonds.

She looked around the church for the fourth wheel of their old group, but apparently Lauren hadn't made it.

The bell in the steeple was tolling now. The organist had stopped playing, and in the silence Julia could hear the pallbearers in the vestibule readying the casket for its entry into the church. Up in the choir loft sheet music turned. Through the half-open windows came the warbling of wrens in the still-green trees. Out on the sound a distant bell buoy rhythmically dinged.

Suddenly the organ started up again, and the elderly woman at its keys launched into a tremulous rendition of "Jesu, Joy of Man's Desiring." The congregation got to its feet as the casket began its slow journey up the aisle. Heart pounding, still unable to believe this was Amber's funeral, Julia turned to watch it pass.

Her gaze never reached its destination, though. It snagged on the tall dark-haired editor standing across the aisle. He was watching her, and as the casket passed, he gave her a small bolstering smile. She spun her gaze away, trying to ignore him, but she already knew he'd become an integral part of this day. Forever after, when recalling it, she would remember him, as well.

The pallbearers positioned the casket in front of the minister's lectern and then took their seats. The congregation did the same. As soon as the organist finished singing, the service began.

It was a simple affair, very low-key. The minister read a few passages from the Bible and the organist sang a few traditional hymns—nothing that would foster displays of emotion, and certainly nothing that would personalize the event. Julia found it all quite odd and disappointing.

If her memory served her right, funerals on Harmony weren't normally like this. People here were close-knit. They *knew* one another, and they made that fact abundantly

clear at funerals. The minister usually gave a eulogy filled
with his own personal memories of the deceased, and that
opened the way for the congregation. One by one people
stood and narrated anecdotes. Sometimes they were sad,
sometimes dull, other times downright hilarious.

And the music…oh, Julia was especially offended by the
choices played today. They were so bland. She could think
of a dozen pieces Amber would've enjoyed more.

The minister gave the final benediction, and then the
pallbearers moved to the casket and began the slow trek
back up the aisle.

"That's it?" Julia exclaimed.

Charlie nodded. "Considering the circumstances, Hank
and Viv requested it be quick. They're not even having
anyone back to the house afterward."

Julia sighed, watching the Lorings follow the casket up
the aisle. Mrs. Loring was leaning on her husband's arm,
just barely holding herself together.

"I guess I can see their point," she admitted. But she
still felt dissatisfied. Amber deserved eulogies. She deserved to be publicly remembered. Without that ritual, the
funeral didn't seem complete.

Charlie stepped out into the aisle and let Julia go ahead
of him. She wasn't surprised when Ben Grant stepped out
of his pew at the same time.

"Chief," he said with a polite nod.

Charlie nodded back but didn't make eye contact. He
took Julia's elbow and guided her through the crowd. "Will
you be okay driving to the cemetery by yourself?" he asked
once they were outside. "We should take separate cars in
case I get called in on something."

"Of course. I'll be fine." From the corner of her eye she
noticed Ben had sidled up to Bruce Davoll and was shaking
his hand. Extending condolences?

Charlie fitted his flat-brimmed hat on his head. "Well, we'll probably catch up later."

"Definitely. How about dinner tomorrow night? My treat?"

Charlie accepted her invitation and was just striding off when Cathryn caught up to her.

"Oh, my God! I thought it was you," Cathryn said, clearly excited but keeping her reaction appropriately subdued. Her cheeks were still moist with tears shed during the service. She wrapped Julia in a hug so tight her arms trembled.

"It's so good to see you, Cathryn," Julia said ardently, hugging her in return. "But why does it have to be under these circumstances?" Stepping back, she dug into her handbag for a tissue.

"Do you have a spare? I'm clean out."

"Here." The two women took a moment to mop up.

"This really stinks," Cathryn said chokingly.

"It sure does." They moved off to the side lawn, out of the way of others leaving the church.

"My God, Jules," Cathryn exclaimed, lips still trembling, "you look like a million bucks! I hate you."

This broke the mood. Julia laughed through the knot in her throat. "So do you, Cath. You never age."

"Oh, go on. I've put on ten pounds with each of my three pregnancies, and don't you dare say you can't see them." Julia had to admit her friend had put on weight. In fact, she was verging on plump.

Pocketing her tissue, Julia noticed that Ben Grant had said goodbye to Bruce and moved on to someone else, one of the tellers at the bank. Julia couldn't help thinking he was mighty busy this morning. Good Lord, was he interviewing people? Here at the funeral? The man was shameless.

"I had no idea you were coming home," Cathryn said, distracting her. "When did you get in? Where are you staying?"

Before Julia could answer, Mike Fearing and the O'Banyon twins joined them. Mike, following in his father's footsteps, had become a Harmony lobsterman. The twins had come over from the mainland where Tyler was an attorney and Wyatt worked in construction.

After hugs and hellos, Julia answered all their questions about how long she was home for and where she was staying. They promised to get together for dinner before she left, and then the three men hurried off to the parking lot.

"I wish Lauren had been able to make it," Cathryn said, watching them go.

"Me, too," Julia replied. "She's in Boston, right?"

"Uh-huh. Working in real estate. I phoned to tell her about Amber, but she must've been away on business or something." Cathryn paused, then said drolly, "Would you like me to introduce you, Jules?"

Julia gave a start. "What?"

"To Ben Grant. You keep looking at him."

Julia was so appalled she blushed. She was not a blusher. "You know the guy?"

"Oh, sure. He's the editor of the paper. I write up the PTA news for him." She gave Ben a wave. "Adorable, isn't he?"

"Adorable" wasn't a term Julia would use to describe Ben Grant. The man had too much dark and dangerous sex appeal.

"He's really sociable, too. He's mingled right in since moving here, joining things. And he's a great cook."

"Cook?" Julia's eyes widened.

"Mmm. A group of us have these rotating dinners, appetizers at one house, entrée at another, you know? And we always make sure to include Ben. That way we figure he'll have to host an occasional course, too."

Julia couldn't help laughing. "Somehow I can't imagine it—him, the whole suburban scene."

"Seems too good to be true, huh?"

"Is he seeing anyone?" She had to ask. Her curiosity was at the bursting point.

"Sure, he sees a lot of people. His dating life is legendary over at the Shear Delight. But so far no one in particular's caught his interest. Boy, if I wasn't married…" Cathryn laid her hand over her presumably palpitating heart and patted it. "Come on. I'm going to introduce you. Something tells me you two would be great together."

Julia dug in her heels. "Cath, I'm really not interested. I was just curious, that's all. Besides, we've already met."

"You have?"

"Yes, briefly. He was at the airport when I arrived."

"Oh. Oh, well, that doesn't matter."

Julia had to hold her friend back. "Why on earth would you *want* to introduce us? You know nothing can come of it."

Cathryn's clear hazel eyes clouded. "I know. You have your life and it's not here. I just worry about you out there all alone." Her words were an echo of Charlie's.

"Thanks. I appreciate your concern, but it isn't necessary. I like having no one to answer to. I've moved five times in the past seven years, Cath. How would I be able to do that if I had a husband and kids? Tell me that."

Cathryn's look remained worried. Julia gave her arm a squeeze. "I'm okay," she repeated, then glanced toward the parking lot where the funeral director was lining up cars. "Come on, we'd better go or the funeral procession's going to take off without us."

HARMONY ISLAND had become home to the first English settlers in the late 1600s, eleven men who'd promised to live in harmony with each other and the native inhabitants—and had, for the most part, except for the winter they passed along their smallpox germs and wiped out the entire native population. Now, walking with Cathryn over the spongy lawn of the cemetery, Julia was only marginally aware of the graves of those first settlers, their simple markers carefully restored by the historical society. She and Cathryn were too busy talking about Amber.

"Did you see her often, Cath?"

"We didn't hang out together, if that's what you're asking. Her life revolved around her job, her home, her family. She had a couple of friends from work she sometimes went out with, too."

"Men friends?"

"No. As far as I know, she wasn't back in circulation yet."

"When you did see her, how did she seem to you?"

"I had no idea she was so troubled. I mean, there were times when I knew she was going through a rough patch, but she seemed…okay. You can't imagine the guilt I feel."

"Oh, yes, I can. I didn't even know she and Bruce were separated." For a moment Julia's chest felt too heavy for her to breathe.

"Pride. That's why she didn't tell you. It was hard for her to admit the marriage had failed." Cathryn sniffed, her face hardening. "And I say thank God it did. Bruce Davoll is an ass, pardon my French."

Julia glanced at her friend. Cathryn was usually so mild-spoken. "Cath, would you be interested in going out for lunch sometime this week? I'd like to hear more about this."

"How about today? It'll have to be my house, though. My littlest one will be home from kindergarten at noon."

"I don't want to put you out."

Cathryn gave her a scolding look.

"Okay, actually today would be great."

They took their places with the rest of the mourners, and soon after that the minister began reciting a traditional committal prayer. Except for his voice and the occasional sniffle, the cemetery was hushed. Julia turned her attention to the casket and tried to think of Amber, but a shroud of unreality still clung to the day.

She let her attention drift to the mourners. To Bruce Davoll, standing stony-faced with his blond girlfriend. Julia blinked in surprise. She couldn't remember the young woman's name, but she remembered her face, those big blue eyes...

Nicole. That was her name. She was the younger sister of Jake Normandin, a guy who'd been in Julia's class. Nicole Normandin. That was it.

"Ashes to ashes..." The minister's voice swelled with the words while he tossed a shovelful of dirt onto the casket.

Julia's gaze drifted from Nicole to Charlie—he'd arrived at church with the faint smell of whiskey on his breath—then from Charlie to the Lorings and on to Ben Grant. Her eyes connected with Ben's for one oddly sympathetic moment before swiftly moving on to the O'Banyon twins, to the bank officer who'd been Amber's boss, to Amber's relatives, to people she didn't know, to Bruce Davoll again.

"Dust to dust..." the minister intoned. Julia looked at the casket.

I don't understand why you died, my friend, she thought. *But sooner or later I'll find out.*

"I guess that's that," Cathryn said. "Short and sweet to the very end."

Julia looked up, disappointed. The crowd was dispersing. Some people were heading to their cars, others were talking to the Lorings.

"I'll see you at your house, Cath," she said, knowing her friend was eager to get home and meet the school bus. "I want to pay my respects to the Lorings first."

Mr. and Mrs. Loring weren't quite done speaking with the previous pair of mourners when they spotted Julia. Mrs. Loring took one look and her brave demeanor crumbled.

"Oh," she said to her husband, "it's Julia." She was already sobbing when she wrapped Julia in a tight embrace. Julia bit her lip, trying to keep her own composure intact.

"Vivien, enough," Hank Loring said after a moment, prying his wife's arms from around Julia's neck.

"I'm so sorry about Amber," Julia said, feeling the inadequacy of her words even as she said them.

"I know you are, I know." Mrs. Loring smoothed Julia's dark hair away from her face, just as one might smooth the hair of a child. Her complexion was mottled, her makeup smeared. "Did you come home just for...for this?" Julia nodded. "Oh, how nice of you. Amber would've been so pleased." Mrs. Loring's lips trembled, her eyes welling again with tears.

"I'll be here for two weeks. If you need anything, please don't hesitate to call me. I'm staying at Preston Finch's place."

"Thank you, Julia, we appreciate it. Do come over and visit."

"I will." Julia's thoughts swirled with platitudes. *Everything happens for a reason. She's in a better place. Each day will be easier than the last.* Anger wiped them all out. She decided to move on.

Turning, she gave the casket a silent blessing, then crossed the lawn, wending her way through the modest granite monuments to the one engraved with the name Patricia Lewis. She said a quick prayer, pulled at some weeds around the stone and found Ben Grant facing her when she straightened. His gray sports jacket was unbuttoned. His hands were hooked on his hips.

"Your mother?" he asked.

"Yes."

"I'm sorry." It was strange hearing condolences so long after the fact. Even stranger, Ben seemed sincere.

"Thanks."

"It must've been tough, losing her when you were so young."

Julia only lifted her brows in a sort of understated shrug.

Ben came around the stone and stood beside her where he could read the inscription. She detected the faintest scent of aftershave, something musky and very male.

"What did she die of?"

"Not sure. It'd been a tough winter. She'd had one cold after another, then the flu and then pneumonia, and she refused to stay home from work long enough to recuperate properly." Julia had tried to supplement their income by baby-sitting, but it had never been enough. "And then one day she just...dropped. Her heart failed her."

The silence of the cemetery blew between them, carrying the scent of the sea mingled with the fragrance of incense and flowers.

After a few moments Ben said, "So, you wanted to talk?"

Julia took a deep breath, casting off the somber subject of her mother's death, and girded herself for the confrontation. "Yes. Thanks for waiting. I need to talk to you about Charlie Slocum and the argument I overheard you having with him at the airport yesterday.''

Ben's expression became unreadable. "Why? What's it to you?''

"I'm an old friend of Charlie's, and if you have a problem with him, I'd like to know about it.''

"To what end?''

"Perhaps I can give you a different outlook on the man, expand the one you've got.''

He gazed at her doubtfully, but said, "Be my guest.''

She swallowed. "Okay. I won't beat around the bush. I know you don't like the way he handled Amber's death, right?''

"That's right.''

"What, may I ask, did you expect?''

He sighed. His face grew serious. "All suicides are supposed to be handled in the same way homicides are. You're aware of that, aren't you?''

Julia nodded, but only half-heartedly. The word "homicide" was still zinging through her head and her heart and her stomach.

"And Chief Slocum didn't do that. He let a lot of the rules slide. I'm not sure if it's because the Lorings are friends—''

"Wait," she interrupted crisply. "What do you mean he let the rules slide? Be specific.''

His eyes swept over her, head to toe and up again. "There was no autopsy. Is that specific enough?''

Julia kept her chin up, still challenging him to tell her something meaningful. "So?''

"I find that unconscionable.''

"I find it perfectly humane. Charitable even. The Lorings are obviously in a lot of pain. As I see it, Charlie was only trying to minimize that pain." She paused. "Or don't you see autopsies as being distressful to the next of kin?"

"I see them as necessary procedures that ensure justice and peace of mind."

Julia refused to back down. "Aren't autopsies the baili-wick of the state? If they'd wanted an autopsy, wouldn't they have come looking for one?"

"Not necessarily."

Julia tossed her hair back over her shoulder. "Sorry. I still don't see it as a problem."

"Okay. How about the fact that the chief gathered very little evidence from the scene, and what he did gather is still sitting at the station? He hasn't examined fingerprints, hasn't sent blood samples to the lab—"

"How do you know that?"

"I checked."

"You checked," she repeated antagonistically.

"Yes." He didn't explain how.

"You know, some people might see Charlie's actions as commendable, as pure common sense. I mean, why bother wasting all that time and money on something that's un-necessary?"

"How do you know it's unnecessary unless you do it?"

She laughed. "But in *this* case, what are fingerprints go-ing to prove? That someone else fired the gun?"

Ben didn't react quite the way she expected. He lowered his eyes, not a hint of amusement anywhere in his expres-sion. She could almost feel the color draining from her face.

"That's absurd! There hasn't been a murder on Harmony in eighty-some years."

"Eighty-three."

She wanted to pop him, the arrogant prig.

"Besides," he said, "I didn't say anything about mur-der."

"No, but isn't that what you were hinting at?"

"No."

"Then what's all this leading up to?" When he hesitated she said, "I'm aware that you've run some unflattering articles about Charlie in the past. Is that what you're gearing up to do again? You're planning to use this case to throw darts at him?"

"Maybe. I'm not sure."

"Well, as a friend of his, I'd object. As a friend of Amber's, I'd be outraged."

"I'm taking that into—"

"If I were her parents, I'd sue!"

"I know."

"Do you?" And before he could reply, "I doubt it. If you ask me, you're just out for a story."

His face dropped. "Excuse me?"

"I think you're one of those unprincipled reporters who doesn't give a damn about anybody's feelings as long as you get a splashy headline. What do you think—this is going to win you a Pulitzer prize?"

His jaw clenched. "I don't need a Pulitzer prize."

"Sure you don't."

"I don't. I already have one."

Julia rocked back on her heels.

"Close your mouth, Ms. Lewis. It's not a flattering expression."

She closed her mouth and tried to regroup. Okay, so the man had won a Pulitzer. That didn't make him infallible. Besides, he might be lying.

"If you're not out for a story, why are you doing this? These are good decent people—Charlie, the Lorings, the people of Harmony. They don't need this crap."

He pushed his hand through his untidy hair and sighed. "The situation...bothers me. That's all I can say."

"Ah, a man of conscience," she mocked. "Well, I happen to know another man of conscience, and let me tell you, you have a long way to go to fill his shoes."

Ben held up a hand. "Can we bring this down a notch?"

Julia didn't want to bring it down even half a notch. She wanted to hang on to her anger.

He went on, "I can see Charlie is someone special to you, and this must be difficult to understand..." She tried to interrupt, but up went his hand again. "This isn't the first occurrence of Charlie's less-than-admirable police work. And, yes, I have run editorials criticizing him before. I've also published every letter that's come in as a result. I try to be fair."

"But how can you make an issue of *this* case, a suicide, for God's sake?"

He sighed. "I don't know. I... Maybe I can't."

Julia let out a relieved sigh. Had she actually made a difference?

"But I can't forget it, either," he added. Her relief fizzled. "I'll continue to ask questions, continue to look for an angle. Charlie Slocum isn't off the hook yet."

"Why?" she asked fervently.

He looked at her levelly, his answer heartfelt. "It's what I do, Julia."

For a brief moment she let herself admire Ben Grant. And regretfully she thought, *Another time, another life...*

Giving her head a small shake, she returned to the issue at hand. "Look, I realize you don't know me from Adam and there's no reason for you to listen to me."

"I listen to everyone."

"Yeah, well, I understand how things here might appear to someone from away."

"Away?" A dark eyebrow arched.

"The mainland. America. I'm not advocating anarchy or

anything like that. It's just, this is a small community. Everybody knows everybody else. Most times we can solve our problems without involving outside bureaucracy. Bureaucracy only slows things down and muddles them up."

Ben tilted his head, eyes narrowed.

"Charlie's a smart man," she went on. "He's had lots of experience, thirty-five years of it, and if he judges a situation to be such and such, you can be pretty darn sure it *is* such and such."

"I'd like to believe you, Julia. I'm sure he was an admirable policeman once upon a time. But the man's lost his dedication, his edge, his…his…"

"Wife," she said angrily.

Ben blinked. "What?"

"He lost his wife two years ago."

"Yes, I've heard that."

"So can't you cut him some slack?" His long sigh and averted eyes told her what he thought. Whatever goodwill she'd managed to muster toward him vanished. "I see. Apparently your stand is, shape up or ship out."

"I won't apologize for it. I think Harmony deserves better."

Julia wasn't smiling when she said, "Well, make sure you keep enough space open on your letters-to-the-editor page."

"Why? Are you thinking of writing in?"

"I might. And make no mistake, I'll come at you tooth and nail."

Much to her consternation, he smiled. It was a terrific smile, melting slowly across his tanned face, warming and transforming it.

"Always welcome," he said.

In silent accord they started across the lawn toward their

cars, parked on the gravel road that wound through the cemetery.

"You were maid of honor at Amber's wedding?"

"Yes." She had no idea how he knew that. But then, she'd never won a Pulitzer prize.

"Did you keep in touch with her?"

"Off and on. Did you know her?"

"Casually. I knew her husband better. We play basketball against each other in the island league." Their footsteps crunched the gravel. Everyone but the undertaker had gone.

"Do you have any idea why she did it?" she asked.

Ben paused by her car. "Funny, I was about to ask you that."

They looked at each other and their gazes held. It occurred to Julia that although he was coming from a different direction, Ben Grant wanted answers to the same questions bothering her.

"Getting chilly," he said.

"Yes." Julia gazed out toward the boundless blue horizon and sighed wistfully. "I wish it wasn't September."

"Mmm, coming all the way from California, you're probably wishing it was July."

"Oh, you misunderstand. Fall is my favorite time of year. It's going to make leaving twice as hard." Quickly she opened the door of Preston's Pontiac. "I've got to run. I have a lunch date with a friend."

She slipped behind the wheel. "I hope you'll reconsider your position toward Charlie," she called out the window.

Ben shrugged apologetically. "I wish I could, but I'd be going against my conscience."

Her hand tightened around the stick shift. "You're wrong, you know. Dead wrong."

This time Ben didn't argue. He just stood on the grassy verge and let her pull away. But when she glanced in her rearview mirror, the look of regret in his eyes spoke volumes.

CHAPTER FIVE

JULIA WAS RELIEVED to be back at Preston's. She'd enjoyed going to Cathryn's for lunch, enjoyed seeing her lovely home and her beautiful children. She'd colored autumn leaves with them and taped their creations to the dining-room windows. She'd marveled over curtains and bed-spreads, sewn by Cathryn herself. She'd sipped amaretto coffee and munched on chocolate-chip cookies and toured Cathryn's rose garden, fragrant with summer's last blooms.

It had been great, but she was really glad to be back and alone with her thoughts. Amidst all that happy domesticity, she had carved out a private moment to talk to Cathryn about Amber, and what she'd learned was pretty disturbing.

"Bruce used to hit her. Did you know that?"

Sitting in Cathryn's cheery kitchen, Julia hadn't been prepared for such a blow. "You're kidding."

"I wish. The big bully." Cathryn must have seen how shaken Julia was. She reached across the table and squeezed her hand. "I didn't mean to upset you. He didn't hit her often from what I understand, and it was never se-vere, and, well, she did take care of the problem eventually by throwing him out."

That didn't make Julia feel any better.

Cathryn went on to relate how Amber used to visit and confide in her back when the trouble started, how she used to ask for her advice. Cathryn had suggested she either leave the guy or get help, but that wasn't the sort of advice

Amber had wanted. She'd wanted to know the secret of Cathryn's happy marriage, how she made it work.

"It was sad really. She even used to ask me for my best recipes, as if cooking just the right dish was going to change things."

Julia couldn't believe what she was hearing. Amber had always been so confident with the opposite sex. Evidently Bruce had a gift for knocking confidence clean out of a woman.

"It was his possessiveness, wasn't it?" she said to Cathryn, remembering the episode at the wedding.

Cathryn nodded somberly. "The first incident I heard about happened after they bought their house and were remodeling it. I'd never seen her so happy or so involved in a project. But then one day Bruce came home and out of the blue accused the contractor of coming on to her. They had a huge fight, Bruce fired the guy and then had it out with Amber."

"Oh, man." Julia sat with her head in her hands, wondering exactly what "having it out" felt like when your opponent was two hundred pounds of muscle.

"It became a pattern with them," Cathryn continued. "A guy couldn't walk on the same side of the street as Amber without Bruce accusing them of having an affair. What was worse, he accused her of inviting the attention. It was all his imagination of course. You know Amber. She was just naturally friendly and fun-loving.

"As time went on, though, I saw a change in her. She stopped coming over, asking my advice. She stopped socializing and became quieter and more subdued. It was to please him, I think, but of course a man like that is never pleased. The last couple of years there was always tension. I could see it in her face."

The only consolation Julia got from Cathryn's tale came

from the fact that Amber had stood up to Bruce on the matter of work. He'd wanted her to quit her job at the bank and work full-time at Davy's Locker, the bar and grill they owned. She was already doing the bookkeeping, but he'd wanted her to start waitressing, too. She'd refused. Eventually that was the issue that divided them.

"The decision to end the marriage wasn't an easy one for her to make," Cathryn explained. "This time last year, whenever I ran into her she seemed confused and really blue. I guess she and Bruce had had some good times along with the bad. But then she started seeing a shrink on the mainland, and the next thing I knew, she'd tossed Bruce out and hired a lawyer to represent her."

Unfortunately Amber's troubles hadn't ended there, Cathryn went on. Bruce occasionally went to the house and harassed her, and they were still trying to hammer out a financial settlement. That was the issue causing the delay.

"But Amber held up well. In fact, after she made that first tough decision to throw Bruce out, she seemed to be doing great. It was like she'd finally woken up and was becoming herself again."

So why did she put a gun to her head and pull the trigger? Julia wondered yet again as she slipped out of her suit and into a pair of jeans. Had Bruce continued to harass her? Was he a nightmare that wouldn't go away? Had Amber seen death as the only escape?

Julia slipped a sweatshirt over her head, then brushed her hair, tying it back at her neck.

Maybe Cathryn's assessment of Amber was wrong. Maybe she hadn't been doing as well as she thought. According to Cathryn, Amber hadn't gotten back into circulation yet. The loneliness might've caught up to her, especially seeing Bruce taking up with Nicole Normandin.

Amber might've had more financial stress than she admitted to, as well.

By the time Julia was leaving her bedroom, her head was pounding with theories. She'd attended Amber's funeral today, but her friend still felt as unburied as ever.

The light was slanting from the west when Julia strolled into the kitchen. The clock over the stove read five-thirty-two. She warmed some tomato soup that she found in a cupboard of canned goods, poured a glass of milk, fried up a giant omelet and buttered some bread. After placing everything on a tray, she made her way through the house and across the breezeway to the WHAR studio. She wasn't sure why, except she felt more comfortable there.

The darkness inside the building was oppressive, though. Before doing anything else, she went from window to window raising the shades. Immediately late-afternoon sunlight poured through the salt-clouded panes.

It felt warm and comforting on her face as she sat down to her meal, but unfortunately the sun also threw a spotlight on the dust furring everything. As soon as she'd spooned up the last of her soup, Julia got to her feet and went back to the house to look for a cleaning cloth. She returned with several, along with a bucket of soapy water.

She cleaned the table first—the damp rag came up black—then the microphone and the board. She tackled the telephone next, the two turntables, the tape players, chairs, windowsills, door frames, everything she could reach. She didn't know why. She just couldn't stand *not* cleaning them.

The sun was going down fast and occasionally she'd stop what she was doing just to watch the ever-changing play of light on the landscape. It was breathtaking. Invariably she'd think of Amber, whose eyes were forever sealed from this beauty, and she'd feel undefinable pain rising. So she'd return to her cleaning and the pain would retreat, at least for a while.

She found a vacuum cleaner and gave the studio carpet a thorough once-over. With the brush attachment she also vacuumed the shelves of records. She thought about doing the washroom and kitchenette, too, but by then her enthusiasm had waned. She returned the cleaning supplies to the house, poured herself a glass of wine, trekked back through the breezeway and reclaimed her seat in the studio.

And what a seat it was. With three side-by-side windows over the console and two to her left, Julia couldn't help thinking of all the walled-in studios she'd occupied since leaving here. Working in such conditions affected the way a person thought.

So did this.

She sipped her wine and watched the sun go down, and gradually the sky darkened. Crickets chirped. Lights from isolated houses glowed through the twilight. Every few seconds the beam from East Light swept the land, then whisked out to sea.

Staring out the windows, sipping her wine, Julia finally acknowledged the reason she'd cleaned the studio. She needed to do something tonight to work off the emotions still warring inside her. No, not *something*. She needed to ride the airwaves.

Before she could talk herself out of it, she crossed the room and stood before the small metal box on the wall that controlled the transmitter. "I must be nuts," she muttered even as her right hand lifted toward a button marked with an up arrow. She pressed it until a "1" appeared on the display. Then she pressed a yellow button labeled "Raise." The needles on the gauges pegged and then dropped. So did her shoulders, in relief. She'd just turned on the transmitter. No noise was added to the night, yet she felt a hum, a vibration, come alive between herself and the tower thirty feet away.

She wasn't done, though. She still had to take a meter reading. Beside the transmitter box were two plastic pockets in which Preston kept his records for the FCC, program logs in one pocket, engineering logs in the other. Julia pulled out a blank engineering-log sheet and a pen, wrote the date, the time in military hours, then checked the gauges and recorded her reading.

With the meter reading done, she returned to the console. There were two clipboards sitting on the windowsill over the table. She reached for one, fitted a blank sheet of paper into it and at the top wrote "Program Log."

Figuring on a three-hour broadcast, she framed her time, noting when to identify the station, when to take the required meter readings, when to air public-service announcements. Satisfied she'd covered all the legal requirements, she put the clipboard back and reached for the other. "Playlist," she printed at the top, her hand trembling slightly. She hadn't broadcast in this freewheeling way since her college days.

She went to the shelves and scanned the spines of the albums. She pulled out one, then another, a few fragile singles, then several tapes and laid them on the floor near her chair. Remembering that she'd brought some tapes with her to listen to on the plane, she ran to the house to get those, too.

The clock read six-forty-nine when she got back. Eleven minutes to the top of the hour. Was she still up for this? Her stomach was beginning to knot. There was nothing to hide behind here at WHAR, no prerecorded jingles, no commercials, no anything.

Not that it mattered, she reminded herself. No one expected the station to be broadcasting tonight. No one would be listening.

She fanned the records and tapes on the floor around her chair, turned them over and read down the lists of selections. It would be nice for the show to have a theme, or at least a mood. But she could see nothing before her but a haphazard hodgepodge. The clock ticked on. Eventually she just closed her eyes and reached. Her hand landed on John Denver's *Greatest Hits*. A soft exclamation fell from her lips. How fitting, she thought. Like Amber, John Denver had also met a sudden death.

Julia scooted her chair closer to the table, slipped the well-worn LP from its jacket and placed it on the first turntable. After writing the selection and artist on her playlist, she put on her headset, set the needle down precisely in the groove before "Country Roads" and turned the fader knob so that the cue light illuminated. She listened to the beginning of the song, then the end, returned to the beginning and turned the record back a half turn.

"Ready or not..." she whispered, watching the clock. Her nerves thrummed. At precisely 7:00 p.m. she turned on the microphone, picked up the Sign-on/Sign-off card and began to read. "This is FM 91.2, WHAR Harmony. WHAR is owned and operated by Preston Finch Inc., a private corporation, and broadcasts on an assigned frequency of 91.2 megahertz, with an output power of 500 watts as authorized by the Federal Communications Commission. WHAR is noncommercial radio maintained by private funding and is an associate of Atlantic Network News. WHAR now begins its broadcast day."

With the legal ID done, she moved right into the first musical selection. Her heart was ticking like a full-tilt water meter. Once that was playing, she readied her next selection, a fragile 78 called "Harbor Lights" from the Second

World War era, a song about partings. That done, she sat back, determined to enjoy the music currently going out over the airwaves.

She'd chosen the John Denver album thinking that it was vaguely appropriate tonight. But as she listened to the song, she smiled in chagrin. Lyrics about roads, roads taking someone home. Maybe her subconscious had caught a theme, after all.

The music faded. "Good evening, Harmony." She'd forgotten to turn on the microphone. Grimacing, she flipped the switch and repeated, "Good evening, Harmony. That was John Denver and his classic from the early seventies, 'Country Roads.' And I'm Julia Lewis sitting in tonight for Preston Finch, who's on vacation. I'll be broadcasting for the next three hours, bringing you all the wonderful eclectic music you've come to expect from WHAR. So, turn the TV off, pour yourself a glass of wine and stay with me awhile."

She started "Harbor Lights" with only a couple of seconds of dead air, and while that record was playing, she filled in five more titles on her playlist.

"The time is seven-twelve on this twenty-ninth evening in September. And a beautiful evening it is, clear skies, a bright quarter moon, October right around the corner. You can smell it in the air, can't you?" Julia was aware that her shoulders were beginning to relax, the knot in her stomach untying. "Coming up next, as a nod to the season, 'Autumn Leaves' by the inimitable Roger Williams."

That selection was playing when she noticed her phone light blinking. She frowned. It had to be a wrong number.

"Hello?" she said uncertainly.

"Hi. I just went out to empty the trash and noticed the red light was on at the top of the transmitter."

The red light! Julia had forgotten. The transmitter wasn't

tall enough for Preston to worry about low-flying planes, so the light wasn't a cautionary measure. It was a courtesy to his listeners. He'd installed it so that it went on when the transmitter did. That way, people could just look out their windows and see if he was broadcasting.

"I don't think I've ever heard you on WHAR before. Who *are* you?"

Julia wondered why her caller asked with such emphasis.

"My name's Julia Lewis," she replied. "I'm filling in for Preston Finch tonight."

"Only tonight?" the caller asked.

"Uh, yes."

"You have a great radio voice."

"Thank you." She smiled appreciatively, even though it was a familiar compliment.

"So I'll ask it again—who are you? And if you're not a pro, why the heck not?"

Watching the timer, she said, "How about I answer you on the air? That okay with you?"

"Sure. The name's Norm. Norm Silvia. Nice talking to you."

The piano piece ended. "I just received a call from a listener—" Julia placed the record in its sleeve "—who wants to know who I am and what I'm doing here behind the mike at WHAR FM. Well, Norm, my name is Julia Lewis, and I've worked as a professional deejay for the past seven years. Before that, though, even before my college radio days, this was my gig. WHAR. When I was a teenager, I had a show called 'Julia in the Afternoon,' and for two hours every weekday I tortured Harmony with the most godawful rock music ever recorded."

Julia slipped a cassette into the tape deck and cued it up while continuing to talk. "Since then I've worked the gamut. Alternative, country, some light jazz, mostly soft rock. Tonight? Tonight's a little bit of everything as I get reacquainted with the music library here. It should be fun. So throw another log on the fire, put your arm around someone special and stay with me awhile.''

Marveling at the tag ''stay with me awhile'' that was emerging from her patter, she segued smoothly into the sixties hit ''Tonight, Tonight'' by the Mello-Kings. The phone light was blinking again.

''Hello?'' This call *had* to be a mistake.

''Julia! Hey! I just tuned in. This is Mike Fearing.''

''Mike! Hi,'' she said to the classmate she'd seen just that morning at the funeral. ''What's up?''

''Two things. First, you sound great, absolutely great. And just for the record, I loved 'Julia in the Afternoon.'''

Sipping her wine, she grinned. ''What's the second thing?''

''I was wondering if you'd play a request.''

''Sure, if it's here. What do you want?''

''Do you have 'Unforgettable' by Natalie and Nat King Cole?''

''Oh, I doubt it, Mike.'' Julia got up and went to the shelves. ''It's too new—for Preston anyway. Don't despair, though,'' she said on a soft laugh. ''I've just spotted the original.''

''Great. Will it take long to air?''

''Nope. I'll make it my next selection.''

She was about to close when Mike said, ''Would you mind dedicating it to someone?''

'''Course not. Who's the lucky lady?''

''Oh, it's nothing like that.'' He hesitated. ''I was thinking of Amber.'' Julia stilled. ''Is that okay?''

''Uh, sure.''

''Thanks. See you around.''

Julia's voice carried a different tonality when she went

back on the air. It was slow and reflective, and she couldn't have made it anything but if she'd tried. "A few days ago I was living in L.A., working at my job, running the usual rat race, uncertain when I'd ever return to Harmony again. I don't have any family left on the island, you see, only a few old friends I thought would be here forever, unchanged, just the way I left them.

"But on Friday I learned that one of those friends had died. Her funeral was today, and that's why I'm here. If you're from the island, you know I'm talking about Amber Loring Davoll.

"I wasn't going to mention Amber tonight. But I just got a call from a listener who requested a song in her memory. So here it is, and I agree with you, Mike. Amber was, and always will be…'' Julia raised the volume and with perfect timing Nat King Cole sang, "Unforgettable…''

The phone was blinking again. Julia was aghast. "Yes?''

"Julia! It's Cathryn! Mike just called me. What are you doing? Never mind answering that. It's a stupid question. Oh, this is so cool! I don't really have anything to say. Just called to let you know I'm listening and enjoying, and now I'm gonna call my mother and my aunt. See ya.''

Julia grinned through the next two recordings.

She was nearing the end of the first hour when the phone rang again. "Yes, may I help you?'' she said.

"Hi. I'd like to request a song, please?'' The caller's voice—male, mature, cultured—intrigued her. "Do you have 'The Lady in Red' by any chance?''

"I doubt it. I'll look, though.''

"I'd be much obliged. That was Amber's favorite song.''

Julia's lips parted on several silent questions. The one she asked was, "Do we know each other?''

"No. I'm quite certain we've never met.'' That was all

he said before repeating, "'The Lady in Red.' I'd be much obliged." Then he hung up.

Julia stared at the phone awhile before lowering it to the receiver.

"Good evening, Harmony," she said after the top-of-the-hour ID. "To the gentleman who called in asking for 'The Lady in Red,' I'm sorry to say I can't find it in the record library. You were right, it *was* Amber's favorite. I remember she even bought a special red dress because of that song. Wore it to one of the wharf dances the Chamber of Commerce used to sponsor—do they still do that?—and got two proposals of marriage and three for something else." Julia laughed, realizing her tension had drained away completely.

"If there's another song I can play for you, give me a call back. In the meantime here's a different tune I remember Amber liking. I'm glad I brought it with me. This is Julia Lewis for WHAR FM. Rock on, Harmony."

She turned up the volume and grinned as "Simply Irresistible" pounded out across the night.

The phone lit up again.

"Hi, Julia? My name's Angie, and I'm a hairdresser at Shear Delight. I'm the person who put the champagne highlights in Amber's hair these last five years."

"Oh, nice to be talking to you, Angie."

"Same here. I usually don't like calling in to radio stations, but this is different, huh?"

It sure was. "What can I do for you, Angie?"

"Nothing really. I just wanted to call and say Amber was a doll. A real doll, you know?"

"I sure do."

"She never passed on gossip like some women I know. Nothing that'd hurt anybody, anyway. It was all harmless and real funny, and personally I'm a mess over her death. I can't believe it.''

"Me, neither.''

"That's all I wanted to say. Oh, and she had great hair.''

Caught between a smile and a sob, Julia bit her lip. "Thanks for calling.''

She wished others had heard the message. If only she'd been able to tape it, play it back over the air.

"Dummy!'' she said, slapping her forehead with her hand. There was a phone channel right there on the board, and it was clearly labeled.

She potted it up and waited. Maybe no one else would call tonight. Maybe she'd talked to every last person on the island who was listening. But in case she hadn't...

BEN WAS TYPING away on his laptop, trying to catch up on work backlogged because of the funeral, when the police scanner on his desk squawked to life. The communication was between the dispatcher and Charlie Slocum, who was out patrolling in his car.

"Chief, Bob Willis from Briggs Road just called with a strange question. Said someone's broadcasting over WHAR and he was wondering if we knew.''

Ben glanced up from his computer screen.

"Somebody's broadcasting?'' Charlie Slocum repeated.

"That's what Willis said.''

Charlie Slocum's gruff laugh lifted from the tinny speaker. "Well, I'll be!''

"You know about this, Chief?''

"That person broadcasting, that'd be Julia. It's okay, Bill. Preston knows.''

As soon as the communication ended, Ben turned down the scanner and switched on his radio. His eyes felt hot in their sockets, his hands clumsy, as they adjusted the settings. He found WHAR just as a song was finishing.

"That was 'The Lady in Red' by Chris De Burgh, and I have to thank Marian Wilson from Barney's Cove Road for bringing that one by."

Ben stood riveted while Julia's voice poured from the radio. It was the smoothest, most melodic voice he'd ever heard, rich as chocolate and deep as sin.

"The time is eight-o-five and you're tuned to 91.2 FM, WHAR, Harmony radio. We'll go to another caller. Yes, what can I do for you?"

"Hello? This is Gray McCord from out Piney Point Road."

"Hi, Mr. McCord."

"You know what I'll always remember about Amber Loring?"

"What's that?"

"I'll remember her riding in my '57 Caddy in the Labor Day Parade."

"That was your car?"

"That's right."

"It was a beauty."

"Thanks. She was a beauty, too, Amber was. Looked like Cinderella that day in her white dress and diamond tiara, and carrying them red roses over her arm."

"She was first runner-up in the state beauty pageant that year."

"I know. I was very proud. We all were, all of us on the island. We never had anyone in the pageant before. She left me one of her roses. I kept it for a while in the glove compartment, but then my wife started griping, so I tossed it out."

Julia sounded as if she was smiling when she replied, "Thanks for calling that in, Mr. McCord."

Ben pulled up a chair close to the radio and sat, leaning in.

Julia delivered the time, made a comment that was downright poetic about the moon shining on the water and started the next selection. Although she didn't announce it, Ben recognized the artist as Kenny G and the number as the theme from the movie *Dying Young*. A chill ran down his back. What was going on over there at WHAR?

He sat through three more selections before Julia had another caller.

"Hi. What can I do for you?" she said. By now, Ben was mesmerized. Julia had a voice tailor-made for radio, late-night radio, sensual and intimate, evoking illusions that she was speaking directly to each listener. It was in such contrast to the Julia he'd dealt with. That Julia had been brisk, distant, distrustful. On the air, though, she seemed to open herself up and let people in.

"Hey, Jules. It's Mike again. Enough of the hearts and flowers already. I've been sitting here listening to all these comments about how great Amber was, and all I can think of is the mischief she could scare up when she wanted to. In particular, I'm thinking of her sassy little derriere mooning the last ferry out of the harbor on Labor Day of our sophomore year. Remember that?"

Ben listened to Julia's musical laughter, feeling it vibrate deep inside him. "I sure do, Mike."

"What I can't remember, though, is how she got all of us out there on the breakwater with her. There must've been a dozen of us."

"I don't know, Mike, but she had a way about her." Julia laughed again. "I just got a mental picture of myself looking down at my shorts tangled around my ankles and thinking, Charlie Slocum's going to kill me."

Ben tried to imagine Julia participating in such a stunt and failed.

"I'm not sure if you know this," Mike added, "but mooning the last ferry on Labor Day has become quite a tradition."

"You're kidding!"

Ben smiled at Julia's delight.

"Nope. Every year it draws more and more people."

"Well, talk about immortality…"

"All this to say, Amber was a lot of fun and the world's a dimmer place without her."

The introductory bars of a song had been playing as a soft undercurrent, and as soon as Julia said, "Thanks, Mike," Cindy Lauper began singing, "Girls Just Want to Have Fun."

Ben sat back, letting out a slow whistle of appreciation for Julia's talent, especially considering the equipment she was probably working with. And that voice! It almost didn't matter what she said, as long as she kept talking.

When Ben's telephone rang, he almost pulled the plug from the jack in irritation. "Yes," he barked into the receiver.

"Mr. Grant, it's Scott Bowen."

Ben's irritation fell away like a loose coat. "Scott, what's up?"

"I thought you'd like to know I called those people you said could help me get an autopsy."

Ben was truly surprised. He'd underestimated the kid. "And?" he asked.

"I've got some news."

When Ben hung up the phone a few minutes later, he wanted to nominate the kid for a medal of honor. A representative from the state medical examiner's office would be landing on Harmony tomorrow afternoon.

"We're quickly coming up on the top of the hour and the end of this broadcast..."

Ben looked toward his radio and felt the first stirrings of guilt.

"A few people have asked if I plan to be on the air any more while I'm home. I honestly hadn't planned on it, but this turned out to be fun, so I guess we have a date, tomorrow evening, same time, same spot on your dial."

From where he was standing Ben could just about make out the small red light of the transmitter three miles away, across the dark undulating hills of Harmony. He imagined Julia sitting at the microphone, pleased with life for the moment. His guilt deepened.

"I'd like to close with a recording made right here on Harmony about a decade ago. The occasion was the Ecumenical Choir's spring concert, but the song is one they perform at graduation every June. At least they used to when I lived here. Till tomorrow, then, this is Julia Lewis for WHAR FM. Good night, Harmony. And to Amber...sweet dreams, my friend."

Ben was surprised by the tightness in his chest as the local choral group began to sing the old spiritual "May the Circle Be Unbroken."

Julia was going to be hurt when she heard the news tomorrow, hurt and outraged. He couldn't imagine her learning about it without warning. He felt obliged to go over there and tell her himself, tactfully. After all, if it hadn't been for him, none of this would be happening.

But how? How did you tell a person who's just laid her best friend to rest that the body is now going to be exhumed?

Julia signed off and then the airwaves went to static. Ben switched off his radio and returned to his laptop. But it was a very long time before he was able to return to work.

CHAPTER SIX

JULIA WAS ON HER BACK on the floor of the WHAR studio, wrapping black electrical tape around some wires she'd just spliced, when she heard a car pull into the yard. She slid out from beneath the table, got to her feet, brushed off her sweater and tights and went to the door. When she recognized Ben Grant's black utility vehicle, her pulse jumped. She refused to acknowledge it as a pleasurable feeling, however.

"What's *he* doing here?" she muttered. The morning had been so enjoyable until now, too.

She'd awakened before seven refreshed and in a surprisingly good mood. She suspected last night's spontaneous tribute to Amber was the reason. Or maybe it was just knowing the funeral was behind her and two weeks of vacation time lay ahead.

Whatever the cause, Julia had found herself humming in the shower this morning. She'd dressed in her favorite hang-around clothes, eaten a breakfast fit for a lumberjack, then taken to the hiking paths that crisscrossed the conservation lands behind the house. It was a beautiful morning, and she'd wandered for a couple of hours, shoulder deep in bayberry and rugosa roses, all the way out to East Light and along the cliffs.

Upon her return she'd found an interesting message from Cathryn on the telephone answering machine. Cathryn had decided to organize a get-together before Julia went back to the West Coast, a combination class reunion and informal memorial service.

"Nothing elaborate," she explained when Julia returned her call. "We can have it here at my place, a leisurely brunch, an afternoon of catching up, swapping brag pictures, maybe even a game of ultimate Frisbee for old time's sake. Somewhere in there we can also take a trip out to the cemetery, you know, for the benefit of those who couldn't make it to the funeral. Then we can cap off the day with dinner at a nice restaurant. What do you think?"

Julia thought the idea was wonderful, and although Cathryn insisted she could handle it alone, Julia was equally insistent that she would help.

"When do you want to do this?"

"Well, when are you leaving?"

"A week from this Sunday."

"How about the day before? A Saturday'll probably be easiest for most people. Or will that be cutting it too close for you?"

"No, that Saturday's fine."

After getting off the phone, Julia had headed for the studio, eager to plan that evening's program. She'd be too busy this afternoon with grocery shopping and later meeting Charlie for dinner. Best to get her music organized before the day ran away from her.

In the bright glare of morning, however, she'd noticed how frayed some of the wires were and before long had gotten happily sidetracked repairing them. She was hardly done with that job, hadn't even started on her program, and now Ben Grant was here.

She remembered the conversation she'd had with him yesterday at the cemetery. She'd thought she might be able to convince him to ease up on Charlie, but it was obvious the man's mind was cast like cement.

Above and beyond that, he simply made her jumpy, but that had more to do with his physical attractiveness than anything else. In any case, she was determined to send him away as soon as possible and return to enjoying her peaceful morning.

Standing at the door, she watched him reach for something on the car seat, slide out of the vehicle, nudge the door shut with his elbow and start walking toward the house, unaware of her throughout. She couldn't help noticing how compact his movements were, how sure and fluid—a man of conviction even in the most minute details of his life.

Julia was so caught up in observing him that she almost missed the bouquet he was carrying tucked inside a florist's paper cone. Surely not for her? She was appalled at herself for suddenly feeling wobble-kneed. How spineless of her. How mindlessly…female.

He looked up and noticed her, and his steps faltered. "Good morning," he said. "How's it going today?"

"What do you want, Grant?" She tried to sound tough and bored and not at all pleased to see his handsome face at her door.

He mounted the one granite step, the glass door between them. "I'd like to apologize."

"For what?"

"I'm sorry we got off on the wrong foot. We may have different opinions on certain issues, but that's no reason for us to create a situation that's going to spoil your visit home." He glanced at the flowers. "May I come in?" When she hesitated, "I won't be long. I've got to get back to the office."

She relented—what else could she do?—and opened the door. But she kept him standing in the breezeway. He extended the flowers to her, a standard arrangement he'd probably picked up at the food market for only a couple of dollars. There was no reason for her attitude toward him to mellow.

"What's this for?"

"A peace offering. I brought you this, too." He handed her a folded newspaper. "This week's edition of the *Record*. It's just hit the stands."

Julia accepted the flowers and newspaper with a firm reminder that this was the same man who intended to skewer Charlie in the press and, in the process, throw a spotlight on her best friend's ignominious death. "Thanks. But gifts aren't necessary."

He sighed, his lips pressed together. She noticed, when he did that, a faint dimple appeared in his right cheek. "No, but I figure they can't hurt. Maybe, if you take a look at the paper, you'll see I'm a fairly decent journalist and not the ogre you think I am."

The urge to glance at the paper was almost painful, but she stubbornly resisted it.

"One more thing..." From under his arm where it had been tucked, he pulled a long tray with a Lucite cover that contained audiotapes. "I listened to your show last night and thought maybe you could use these."

"You heard me?" she asked, feeling suddenly exposed and defenseless. He nodded and she groaned. "I wasn't exactly in top form last night."

"I thought you were terrific." His deep blue eyes glittered.

"Thanks," she said, her gaze drifting to the container of tapes. Of all the gifts a man could've brought her, here was the one she couldn't resist.

"Come on in. Let me put these flowers in water and then I'll take a look at what you've brought."

She led the way into the studio where she laid the flowers

on the table by the control board and then went looking in the kitchenette for a suitable container. She found a drinking glass and filled it with water.

When she returned, Ben was standing over the board, his eyes alive with curiosity and interest. "I've never been in here before. I've been in lots of studios, but never one like this. It's fascinating."

Julia snorted.

"It is," he insisted.

She went to the table, set down the glass and tore open the protective sleeve around the flowers. "It certainly is different from what I'm used to. Here, you're not just deejay, you're engineer, manager, director, janitor—everything." She cut a stem and fitted it into the glass.

"Sounds a little bit like my job. Some days I find myself playing photographer, sportswriter, errand boy. It's very satisfying being so totally involved."

"Oh, I don't know about that." From the corner of her eye, she saw Ben watching her. Her fingers grew clumsy, dropping as many flowers as they managed to get into the glass. She wondered why she was working here at all. She was getting water all over the table. Why not at the sink? What happened to her brain in this man's presence?

"Well, you sounded as if you were having a good time," he said.

She shrugged noncommittally. "It's something to do for two weeks."

Ben squatted down by the tools she'd left on the floor and peered under the table. "What's going on here?"

She regretted bringing him into the studio. Why had she?

"I was just taping a few of the wires."

Ben looked up at her from his squatting position. She was suddenly aware of how frumpy she must look this morning, with no makeup and her hair in a loose sagging ponytail.

"Where'd you learn electrical repair?"

"Here, on Harmony."

"Preston Finch?" He stood up, the folds of his trousers falling neatly into place.

"No. Charlie Slocum." She gathered up the debris of leaves and snipped stems, rolled it in the florist's paper and stuffed it all into the wastebasket. "He believed that if I was going to make my living working around so much electrical equipment, I ought to at least learn the basics."

Ben's gaze traveled over her as if he was gazing at a package at Christmas. "Would you mind if I interviewed you for the paper?"

Her eyes snapped wide open. An interview? Was that the reason he was here?

"Um...yes, I would mind." She crossed her arms.

"But you'd make a great subject. Your job is interesting, *you're* interesting..."

She bit her lip, flattered to the point where she almost gave in.

"I'm sorry. I don't like being interviewed."

"Are you sure? I'd do a good job. I don't mix personal differences with my work."

"That's not the problem."

Ben frowned, tilted his head. "What is it, then? You don't want to contribute anything to *my* paper?"

That wasn't quite it, either. To get him off her back, though, she said, "That's right."

His eyes, those damn all-seeing eyes, narrowed. Before he'd said a word, she blurted, "Look, I just feel better without people poking into my life. I'm—" she cast about for a word "—shy."

"Interesting. Very interesting, considering what you do for a living. Has it always been like that with you?"

"Questions like that are precisely why I don't like to be interviewed."

"Are you sure?"

"Yes."

He sighed. "Stubborn mule!"

She smiled a little. "You got that right. So do you want your bribes back?"

"They weren't bribes."

"Good, because I don't come that cheap."

"Cheap?" Ben laughed as if offended. "I'll have you know that case contains fifteen of my all-time favorite tapes, which, in my opinion, makes them priceless."

It struck Julia suddenly that they were on the verge of actually enjoying each other's company. The realization sobered her.

"Um, would you like some coffee?"

"Sure, if it's made."

Ben sat in the leather chair at the control board, watching Julia sashay off to the kitchen—and wondering why he'd accepted coffee, instead of getting to the point of his visit. *I'm a coward, that's why,* he thought.

"I can't guarantee how it'll taste," she called. "It's been reheated a few times."

"That's okay."

She returned with two mugs and handed him one.

"Thanks." He took a sip and found it…dreadful. Trying not to grimace, he said, "I really did enjoy your broadcast last night."

She was dressed in a long loden green sweater and tights, with thick scrunched-up socks and high-top black shoes, her thick chestnut hair caught back in a ponytail that kept slipping. She looked sporty and scrubbed—an elf—and not at all like her sophisticated radio voice.

"I'll admit it *was* fun. I don't get to choose much of the music I play these days. Actually I don't get to choose any of it at all."

"How come?"

"We use a Top 40 format. All the music comes prechosen and prearranged on prerecorded carts. All I have to do is make sure it gets played at the predetermined times."

Ben found a smile settling deep inside him. He enjoyed listening to Julia. She had a subtle sense of humor and a real way with words. "That sounds brain-numbing."

She shrugged. "I can live with it, considering everything else. I make decent money, have good medical coverage. There's even a retirement plan, although I don't need it. I've got my own."

Ben propped his elbow on the table, rested his jaw on his hand and stared at her, wishing he knew what made her tick. He must've made her uneasy because she added quickly, "That's not the only reason I plan to stick with my present job. The equipment's state of the art, the people are fun to work with, and the audience is huge."

She stared into her coffee mug for a thoughtful moment. "But if the music ever becomes too much of a drag, I...might move on."

"Does that mean there's no one in your life who'd make leaving a problem?"

"A man?"

He nodded and was disconcerted by the amount of pleasure that ran through him when she said no.

"Would you consider moving back home to WHAR?"

She laughed, nearly choking on her coffee. "And what would I do for money? Work as a chambermaid?"

Ben hadn't really been serious about her working here,

but now that he'd mentioned it... "Couldn't Preston pay you a salary?"

"Are you kidding?" She looked at him as if he'd grown another head. "This station doesn't make any money."

Ben frowned, puzzled. "How does he do it, then, pay for the electricity and the license and other expenses?"

"This is just a hobby with him. He has a couple of pensions to live off, plus some inherited money."

"Oh." Ben smiled at her regretfully. "Oh, well, you can't fault a guy for trying." His smile felt strained. It would've been nice being able to hear her honey-smooth voice on local radio, to listen to her artfully chosen musical selections. But he knew that wasn't the only reason he would've enjoyed her presence on Harmony.

"So where would you move if you decided to leave L.A.?"

"I don't know. Wherever a better job opened up."

"Are you telling me you could live anywhere, as long as the job was right?"

"No. Location's a consideration, too. I've learned I don't like the snow in Buffalo or the summer heat in Mobile, and I'm not crazy about really large cities like L.A...." She paused, her frown deepening. "As you can see, I've moved around a bit."

"How about the size of your audience? Does that come into play when you look for a new position?"

She bit her lip, looking so sincere and endearingly serious he wanted to gather her into his arms. It was an urge that troubled him, because if there was anyone he didn't want to be attracted to, it was Julia Lewis.

"I'm not into fame, if that's what you mean. I've never had any desire to go network or syndicated. But I do consider the size of an audience important. After all, it's a reflection of the financial solidity of the station."

Financial solidity? Retirement plans? Health insurance? Ben was beginning to think he understood her, knew what was at her center. Folks had told him about her father's desertion and her mother's early death. But what they'd failed to mention was the financial hardship that had undoubtedly plagued her as a child.

"I hope you won't think I'm butting in where I don't belong, but it seems to me you're letting the tail wag the dog."

"I'm what?"

"Running from city to city, trying to find your ideal life ready-made, instead of digging in somewhere, building what you want and letting the money follow."

Now she looked at him as if he had *three* heads.

"What's made you so insecure, Julia?"

She stiffened defensively as if she meant to refute him, but then sighed defeatedly. "Just the way I grew up, I guess." She gazed out the window, her profile limned in morning light. "Money was scarce. If you haven't already noticed, there isn't much opportunity on Harmony."

"Now there's another point of contention between us. I see opportunity everywhere. Lots of prosperity, too."

Her eyes grew slightly resentful. "Well, it isn't available to everyone. My mother worked at the Gray Dory, two shifts during the summer, one during the winter, and she was lucky to get it. Not too many inns stay open year-round. She worked hard but still had trouble making ends meet. When she died, I promised myself two things. First, I'd never make the mistake of trying to live off this island, and second, I'd never depend on a man. Neither can be trusted."

"As a man and a lover of Harmony, I thank you," Ben said dryly.

"You're welcome," she replied, unrepentant.

"So, you don't foresee marriage in your future?"

She opened her mouth to answer, then paused, looking at him with a narrowed stare. "Why do I get the feeling I'm being interviewed even though I told you no?"

Ben smiled. "I'm just making conversation."

"Okay, I'll make conversation, too," she challenged. "What are *you* doing here on Harmony?"

"Doing?"

"Yeah. Why did you move here?"

"I love the place. I visited it two years ago and decided I wanted to make my life here." He crossed one ankle over the opposite knee and rocked comfortably.

"Just like that?"

"Just like that."

Julia shook her head, causing her ponytail to loosen further. "I don't buy that. You had a life somewhere else, I presume."

"Yes. My family's in Boston—my parents, my sister, my two brothers and their families. We're all very close."

"And you had a good job."

"That's right. At the *Globe*."

"Ben, people just don't pick up and relocate like you did unless there's a reason."

"True. And mine was the newspaper."

"The *Island Record*," she said drolly.

"Yes."

"You chose the *Island Record* over the *Boston Globe*."

"Uh-huh. I've always wanted to own my own newspaper."

Julia's eyes widened. "You *own* the paper?"

He grimaced. "I know, a lot of people think I'm crazy. What can I say? I love it. I love everything about it—the work, the people, being my own boss, the lack of competitiveness."

Julia continued to look at him suspiciously. "Is there something in your past you're running from?"

"No." He laughed softly. "You don't get it, do you?"

"You're happy." She pulled back a little, as if suspecting his sanity. "Here."

"Yes."

"And you're going to live here the rest of your life working on the *Record*."

"I hope so. It might be nice to settle down with someone, too, and have a couple of kids. According to my family, that's what life is all about."

Julia folded her arms tightly, wishing she hadn't gone poking into his life. She'd been curious about him, she admitted, but the conversation had turned too personal for her liking.

"Well, I wish you the best of luck, Ben," she said.

He looked at her dubiously.

"I really do." She pushed away from the table, determined to bring this visit to a polite close. "Well, I should let you get back to the office."

Ben got slowly to his feet. "Do you want to take a look at those tapes first? You might not want to use them."

"Oh, that's right." She turned to the table, lifted the cover. "Let's see…"

Ben came to stand beside her, and as she read down the titles, taking some of the tapes out of the case to examine them more closely, she became uncomfortably aware of his nearness.

"I don't mean to foist these on you…" he said.

"Oh, you're not. These are wonderful. You have great taste."

"You don't have to sound so surprised."

A smile tugged at her mouth.

"There are more where those came from. Feel free to come over anytime and..."

"Oh, no, this is plenty. I'm not going to be here that long." She looked down at her fingers resting nervously on the case. "Besides, I don't know where you live."

"Above the newspaper office." Had he moved closer? His words seemed to whisper just over her ear.

She shivered, blinked a few times to clear her head, but for the life of her couldn't move away. It was as if he'd drained her of her strength. "Oh, that's handy."

"Yes. It's a nice space, but in the summer it can get pretty noisy being in town."

She turned to look at him and realized with a zing of adrenaline that he was indeed standing as near as she'd thought. She couldn't meet his gaze, but she knew he was watching her, every cell of him as aware of her as she was of him. She felt light-headed, unable to think, unable almost to breathe. All she could do was feel the pull, that wordless, timeless urge to meld.

Her eyes lifted to his mouth, to the firmness of that full bottom lip, to the intriguing divot defining the upper one. Suddenly she was fighting the urge to go up on tiptoe and press her lips to his.

His head lowered ever so slightly, but enough to let her know he was thinking the same thing. Reality came back into focus. With a hitch of her breath, she turned her head and stepped to one side.

"Well, thanks f-for the tapes," she stammered. "It was very th-thoughtful of you."

"You're most welcome." He spoke politely, but self-recrimination darkened his expression, as if he was just as sorry as she for the momentary lapse of judgment. "Well, I should go, see what my staff is up to." He started toward the studio door, but before opening it he paused, his expression thoughtful.

"Julia?"

"Yes?"

"I...there's something else I came over here to say. I'm sorry I've taken so long to get to it, but I knew you wouldn't be pleased to hear it."

"What is it, for heaven's sake?"

He scrubbed at the back of his head. "I got word last night that the state has decided an autopsy might not be such a bad idea, after all."

"What?"

"I'm sorry. There's going to be an autopsy," he restated, wanting to be perfectly clear. "Someone from the medical examiner's is going to be here this afternoon."

His meaning sank in and her mood traveled at the speed of light, from puzzlement through understanding and on to outrage. "But we've already had the funeral."

"I know. It happens this way sometimes." He had the audacity to place his hand on her arm. She jerked it away.

"It happens this way sometimes? Don't give me that. How did this come about?"

Ben raised his hands and shook his head, trying to look innocent of the whole matter.

She felt nauseated. "Oh, those poor people," she said, thinking of the Lorings. "And Charlie! How's this going to reflect on him?" Her eyes fixed on Ben. "What did you do?"

"Why are you accusing me?"

"Who else? You're the only person I've run into who's talked about an autopsy." She was beginning to tremble. "Oh, God, and here I was, stupid enough to think you were really just trying to be friendly."

"It wasn't a pretense, Julia," he said sternly.

"Yeah, right." Tears stung the back of her throat. "Wait a minute." She spun toward the table and grabbed up the things he'd brought. "Here," she said, thrusting the case of cassettes at him, although it broke her heart to part with them. He caught the case against his chest. "Take your newspaper, too. And your flowers." When she pushed the flowers at him, water sloshed out of the glass and down the front of his shirt. He caught the paper but didn't take the flowers, whether because his arms were full or he simply refused, she wasn't sure. She thought of throwing them, but then just plunked them back on the table.

"You're making a mistake, Julia. I didn't appeal for this autopsy."

"No? Then who did?"

"I can't say. You're just gonna have to trust me."

"Sorry, I'm clean out of trust for the moment. Now I'd appreciate it if you'd leave."

"I don't want to go with you feeling like this."

"Like what? Angry? How did you expect I'd feel?"

"I wish you'd think this through rationally. I'm sure you'd see it's for the best."

"I think you've said quite enough for one day." With that, she opened the studio door and gave him a hard shove.

"Judas H. Priest!" He stumbled out to the breezeway. "I'm going, I'm going! Why I thought I owed you a personal visit I'll never know." He shoved open the breezeway door, dropping the newspaper in the process, and hurried outside. "You're certifiable, lady!" he called as he stormed off to his Bronco. "Absolutely cert—"

She didn't hear the rest. She'd slammed the door on his tirade. But she did hear the engine roar to life and tires kicking up crushed seashells, and after a while, when the vehicle had gone, the surge of her own angry heart.

JULIA WAS STILL in a temper when she left for the market two hours later. She was in no mood to grocery-shop, but unless she planned on eating out all the time, which she didn't, she needed more than breakfast food at the house.

Unfortunately the quickest way into town took her by the cemetery, and as she was passing the gate, she noticed a small gathering of official-looking people within, along with two police cars, a van and Ben Grant's Bronco. Good grief, the man was everywhere. She rolled to a stop, her hands whitening over the steering wheel. Should she butt in, too?

But what would she do? Go in there and tell them she thought what they were doing was wrong, unnecessary, stupid and a desecration? What would that accomplish against a state mandate? After a few minutes she moved on. When she returned an hour later, the cemetery was deserted.

She put away her groceries, somehow swallowed a tasteless sandwich and went right back out to her car, driven by restlessness and a need to know what was happening. The police station was in town, four blocks up from the harbor. Within minutes she was there, pulling to the curb out front.

"Hi, Madeleine."

The middle-aged woman doing a crossword puzzle at the desk glanced up. "Oh, my land! Julia!"

She broke into a smile. "I wasn't sure you'd remember me."

"How could I forget? How've you been?"

"Very well." Julia couldn't maintain her smile. "Except for this business with Amber."

The older woman made sympathetic clucking sounds. "I know. It's dreadful, isn't it?"

"Madeleine, is the chief in by any chance?"

"No, but I expect him any minute." The woman's expression tightened with concern. Julia could only imagine the sort of day Charlie was having.

"We're supposed to be going out to dinner later, and I just wanted to…touch base with him about the time and such."

"Oh. Well, you're certainly welcome to wait."

"Thanks. Do you think he'll mind if I sit in his office?" She'd always been welcome there in the past.

"I don't see why not."

"Thanks." Julia went past the front desk, down a short corridor and through the deserted squad room to the office she knew was Charlie's. The blinds facing the squad room were closed and the door was shut, but Julia could see the lights were still on inside. She opened the door and walked in.

The room hadn't changed much, except it seemed more cluttered. There were the same bookshelves stuffed with criminology texts and softball trophies; the same battered desk littered with stacks of paperwork; the same commendations on the wall, along with photographs of Charlie shaking hands with various dignitaries. One was a president. He'd gotten a new American flag, though, she noticed.

Julia didn't mean to pry as she prowled the room. She simply had an overload of nervous energy. But as she moved closer to the desk, she realized she'd made a grievous mistake. Her breath utterly deserted her, for there, spread out on Charlie's desk, were a dozen or so photographs of Amber taken the morning she was found.

There were full-length shots taken from the foot of the bed, shots taken from above and from the sides, shots from several feet away and others so close Julia could see the pores of Amber's skin.

Adrenaline raced through her, obliterating all logical thought. All she could do was stare in enthralled horror while her heart threatened to bang its way right out of her chest.

She was still standing there, hand to her mouth, when Charlie blustered in. "Hi, sweetheart. Madeleine just told me—" He stopped abruptly and then muttered a phrase she'd never heard leave his lips before. "You shouldn't be looking at those things." He nudged her out of the way and began to gather the photographs into an untidy pile.

"I'm s-sorry," she stammered. "I shouldn't've come in here."

"No, I should've put things away before I left. It's just been so crazy around here today." He stuffed the pictures into a large manila envelope and fixed the clasp. "Try to put these out of your mind, okay, hon?"

"I will," she said, wishing she could but suspecting they were indelibly printed on her memory.

"Have a seat."

Standing within reach of his breath, Julia once again detected the sour tang of alcohol. *Oh, Charlie. As if things aren't bad enough.*

But she told herself not to judge. For all she knew, he might've been out with the people from the state. They might've gone to lunch and had a cocktail. Still, he was in uniform.

"I heard about the autopsy," she said, sitting in the chair by the desk. "What's going on?"

Deep lines creased his brow, yet he tried to minimize his concern. "It's just a dumb decision made by some horse's patooty up in Boston." He tossed his hat on his desk and dropped heavily into his chair. "It doesn't mean anything. A tempest in a teapot. A week from now, nobody'll even remember what it was about."

Julia sat back, sinking into her thoughts for a moment. She wished she could believe Charlie, but no one, not even "a horse's patooty," would order an autopsy unless he was convinced it was necessary. Why create problems where none existed?

She felt angry and helpless and incredibly bad for Charlie. By now the entire island would've heard about the exhumation. The odds were that at least half would be questioning why he hadn't ordered an autopsy right off.

"Who's behind this? Do you know?"

"Yeah. The appeal came from one of my summer auxiliaries, the officer who was first on the scene." Charlie dragged a hand down his face. In his eyes was the dark hurt of betrayal.

"You mean, it wasn't Ben Grant?"

Charlie looked at her and frowned. "No. Why do you say that?"

She felt heat swirling through her. "It was just…I don't know." She waved it off and moved on quickly. "How are Mr. and Mrs. Loring handling it?"

"Better than I expected."

"Really? Well, that's something."

"So, is this the only reason you stopped by?" Charlie flicked a surreptitious glance at the clock on the wall.

"No. We have plans to go out to dinner tonight, and I was wondering if you were still up for it."

Charlie winced. "Considering all that's happened…"

"That's what I figured."

"We'll do it some other night, okay?"

"Sure. No problem. You let me know when you're available." Julia got to her feet. Charlie walked her to the door.

"How long before the autopsy results come back?" she asked.

"Oh, probably a couple of days. It usually doesn't take long."

Julia slipped the strap of her purse over her shoulder.

"Well, I'm sure it'll all turn out fine. As you say, a tempest in a teapot."

He smiled at her, grateful for her support. Julia couldn't meet his eyes, though, because a part of her wished he'd ordered the autopsy just to be thorough, just for peace of mind, just to silence critics like Ben Grant.

"Take care of yourself, Charlie," she said, giving him a quick tight hug.

"I will," he said. "Now, get going. Go do something fun. You're on vacation."

DURING THE FIRST HOUR of Julia's broadcast that evening, she got ten calls, and while a few of them were simply requests, most callers wanted to talk about the autopsy. Some condemned the M.E.'s office for being a meddlesome bureaucracy. Some praised it for countermanding Charlie. All speculated on the reasons. Julia allowed none of it on the air. She wasn't in the talk-radio business, she politely reminded them.

She was pleased with her program when she signed off at ten. She'd been more organized tonight, her music already chosen and at her fingertips and most of it of a type—lots of Rosemary Clooney and Tony Bennett, Ella Fitzgerald and Frank Sinatra—what Preston liked to call "the American songbook." She'd added the national and world news, too, which she'd recorded earlier off the news service to which WHAR subscribed, and as the night wore on and her music selections grew more mellow, she'd read a few poems from a book she'd found in Preston's den, written by a local author.

She'd been right to keep the issue of the autopsy off the air. What would it have accomplished except to stir up controversy and generate damaging rumors? Of course, it would've provided her with a good opportunity to defend

Charlie, and that would've served Ben Grant right. Somebody needed to counterbalance his paper. But she hadn't,
and she was glad. She'd taken the high road.

After shutting down the transmitter, she put away the
music she'd used, filed her program log, made sure all the
equipment was turned off and went into the house. By
eleven she was in bed, looking forward to the morning and
another hike on the nature trails, followed by a couple of
hours of browsing the shops in town with Cathryn.

Julia closed her eyes. But the contentment she felt was
an illusory thing. As she drifted in that muzzy world between wakefulness and sleep, images from her visit to
Charlie's office rose to haunt her—images of Amber lying
on her bed with that neat little bullet hole in her right temple and blood congealed in her pale blond hair.

And as those images returned, coming clearer and
clearer, Julia realized that her decision not to defend Charlie on the air had little to do with taking the high road or
with any other excuse she'd made. It was more because of
the outfit Amber had been wearing when she died.

She might've worn that faded red T-shirt and those jeans
with a tear at the knee to do housework or to hang out with
friends. But the Amber who'd always taken such pride in
her appearance, especially when she knew others would be
looking at her, that Amber wouldn't have been caught dead
in such an outfit.

CHAPTER SEVEN

BEN USUALLY LOVED Wednesdays. The office throbbed with energy at midweek: phones jangled, stringers dropped in with their columns, computer keys quietly clacked.

This Wednesday, however, Ben sat at his desk tossing paper clips into a Celtics coffee mug and fuming about his visit with Julia the previous day. Meanwhile his article about a sewer-extension proposal languished on his monitor.

The worst thing was he didn't even know what was bothering him. Was it that he disliked being shoved? He'd been shoved before, shoved, punched, even shot at once, and it hadn't bothered him quite this way. Was it her throwing his gifts in his face? Actually he didn't blame her. They *had* been bribes, meant to soften her. Maybe it was simply that he didn't like being the bearer of bad news. But to him the autopsy was good news; only Julia saw it as bad.

He lifted another paper clip, aimed and then paused. He was evading the truth and he knew it. The only thing bothering him was his attraction to Julia, something he couldn't do a damn thing about. The entire universe was stacked against him, including the fact that she was only here for a short two-week stay. After that she'd be heading back to California. It was an impossible situation, and what he was feeling now was unadulterated frustration.

He tossed the clip, but it missed the mug. "Damn." He wanted to pick up the phone and call her. He wanted to be with her, get to know her, every last secret in those big brown eyes. He wanted to hold her, feel her against him, every last luscious curve and swell. He wanted... He wanted entirely too much from Julia Lewis, especially considering how briefly he'd known her.

That was the craziest part of all. How fast he'd been attracted, how fast he'd known they'd be wonderful together. It made no sense, considering everything that stood between them, but when his instincts were this strong, they were rarely wrong.

He was aiming another clip when his phone rang.

"Island Record," he said, relieved to be distracted.

"Ben?" said a breathless voice. "It's Kelly."

Ben sat forward, his frustration momentarily on hold. He'd sent his young reporter over to the police station earlier with orders to hang around the front desk.

"What's up, Kell?"

"It's in," she said. Since the night she'd invited him to her place and he'd turned her down, Kelly's behavior had reverted to strictly professional.

"And?"

"Slocum says he'll have a statement ready at four o'clock."

Ben glanced at this watch. It was two-thirty now. "He's not releasing any information about the report?"

"Not till four. What do you make of that?"

Ben chose to be cautious. "I don't know." But he'd never known anyone to put off favorable news.

"I'm not sure if this means anything," Kelly went on, "but an assistant D.A. arrived a little while ago. He went straight into the chief's office."

Ben's gaze drifted over his staff, busily pulling together their articles for the next edition, benign pieces about harvest suppers, a five-mile benefit race, the annual bird count out on the reserve.

"Something's brewing, Kell. I'll be there at four for the statement. In the meantime keep your eyes and ears peeled."

Ben hung up the phone and pulled his keyboard forward. He'd better get cracking, clean up what was on his plate, because it looked like a lot more was coming. He read what he already had, his malaise blown away by the adrenaline now pumping through him, and then started typing.

He finished the article in less than an hour, read and edited "The Senior Scene," took care of various staff members' problems and still had time to think about Julia. She'd been on his mind throughout, just under the surface of whatever he was doing. He wondered where she was and, more importantly, if she'd heard the news yet.

On impulse he picked up the phone and dialed Preston Finch's number; he already knew it by heart. She answered on the third ring.

"Julia, it's Ben. Before you hang up, just listen for a minute. The autopsy results are back."

Her small gasp of surprise answered his question about whether she'd been informed.

"I haven't heard what's in the report. Chief Slocum's going to have a statement ready at four o'clock. I thought you might want to know. That's all." Before she could sail into him, he hung up.

RED-CHEEKED FROM RUSHING, Julia pushed open the front door of the Harmony Police Station, intent on finding out from Charlie personally what Ben's call was all about. She was surprised to find the lobby crowded, mostly with grumbling town officials. A sense of foreboding ran through her.

Realizing she'd walked into something more formal than

she'd anticipated, she kept unobtrusively to the doorway. Still, she was able to look through the crowd and spot Ben Grant up front. His dark good looks set him so well apart from the other men the contrast was startling. Her foolish pulse fluttered and her face grew warm. For one irrational moment she thought about joining him, but then remembered he was no ally of hers, even if he had taken the time to call.

Besides, he was with someone, a female someone, who kept looking up at him with big moony eyes. From the way they interacted, Julia suspected they worked together. She wondered what else they did together—and immediately rebuked herself for the twinge of jealousy that thought provoked. So she found the man attractive. Big deal. She knew lots of attractive men. This was one she preferred to forget.

He turned at that moment and found her at the back of the crowd. She looked away as swiftly as possible, but not before he'd caught her watching him. Damn.

There was no time to dwell on it, though. The door to Charlie's office opened and a young man in an ill-fitting blue suit made his way through the squad room to the lobby. From the mutterings around her Julia picked up "assistant D.A." Charlie followed him. His face was unhealthily flushed, and his hands shook as he raised them to call the room to attention.

"Thanks for your patience," he began. "I know a lot of you have been calling, wanting to know what's what with the Davoll autopsy, and I'm sorry I couldn't answer your questions sooner, but Mr. Nunes and I and the rest of the department had a lot of, uh…business to get through."

Charlie hadn't noticed her standing at the back of the room. She doubted he'd noticed anyone, in fact. He kept his eyes lowered and fixed on the shirt buttons of the person directly in front of him.

"The medical examiner's report on the autopsy of Amber Loring Davoll has been completed." He spoke carefully, as if he'd been coached. "And based on the findings of that report, I want to announce that the case of Ms. Davoll's death has been—" he swallowed "—reopened."

A buzz filled the room and joined the roaring in Julia's head.

"I'm not at liberty to discuss details of the report at this time," he continued, "but I can say that certain findings indicate the victim may have already been unconscious at the time the gun was fired."

Confusion was the overwhelming reaction. Julia covered her mouth with trembling fingertips, wishing she *was* confused.

Ben's hand went up—of course. "In other words, Chief, someone else shot Amber Davoll?"

Charlie looked exhausted as he admitted, "As of now, the Harmony Police Department is actively conducting a homicide investigation."

Anger, denial, alarm and dismay. Julia heard all those emotions in the voices that rose following Charlie's announcement. She felt them warring within her, as well.

"Chief, what do you mean she was unconscious when she was shot?" Again it was Ben's voice that lifted above the others.

All eyes turned to Charlie, but he waved off the question, repeating he wasn't at liberty to divulge any information at that time. "I'll have more details tomorrow. There'll be a press briefing at noon. If any of you care to come by, you're welcome." Then, ignoring the tumult in the lobby, he retreated to the office with the assistant D.A. and shut the door.

"DAMN!" BEN SWORE.

"I know. I'm bursting with questions, too," Kelly complained.

But Ben wasn't thinking about Chief Slocum's hasty exit. He'd turned, concerned to see how Julia was handling the news.

"Kelly, I've got to run. Will you stick around here a little longer? More information is bound to leak."

"Sure." She looked puzzled. "Where are you going?"

But Ben was already heading to the door. "Thanks, Kell. Catch up with you later."

Ben jogged down the stairs, looking up and down the line of cars parked at the curb. He found the old Pontiac Julia had been driving the other day, but Julia wasn't in it. Reaching the sidewalk, he looked toward the harbor, and there she was, about a block and a half away, walking as if the devil himself was chasing her. Knowing he was succumbing to masochistic tendencies again, he took off after her.

"Julia?"

She didn't stop, didn't turn.

"Julia, wait," he called more loudly, in case she hadn't heard him the first time. She picked up her pace until it was a jog.

"Julia!" Ben caught up with her and grabbed her upper arm, hauling her to a stop. "Slow down."

She spun around. "Buzz off, Grant."

He raised his hands. "Whoa! What did *I* do?"

"You couldn't let it go, could you? You had to come chase me down and rub it in."

"Is that what you're thinking? I'm gloating over this?"

"Well, aren't you? You've been right all along and I've been wrong."

"Thanks a lot." He was surprised by how hurt he felt. "I was worried about you. That's why I came looking for you, nothing else. And just for the record, I'd rather be wrong in this case."

She didn't apologize, but her expression became somewhat less combative.

He touched his hand to her back and started walking again. "How about we go find a place to sit down and have a drink. The Brass Anchor is just up the street."

She moved away from his touch. "I just want to walk this off. Alone, please."

He stepped in front of her, and she'd walked halfway up his shins before she came to a stop. He took her by the arms to steady her balance.

"You spend an awful lot of time alone."

She shrugged out of his grip and gave her hair a flippant toss. "I like my own company."

"But sometimes it's easier to get through troubles like this in the company of others."

She dropped the flippancy and made an effort to be sincere—no doubt just to get rid of him. "I'm fine. I really am."

"Sure you are." Ben lifted a hand to her face and brushed away a tear with his thumb. This time, he noticed, she didn't pull away quite so quickly.

"If you know what's good for you," she said, "you'll let me be. I'm not in the best of moods right now."

"I'll take my chances."

She lowered her eyes, turned and continued walking. Ben fell into step beside her.

He didn't say anything again until they'd turned the corner onto Water Street. Out on the harbor, the masts of dozens of pleasure craft bobbed and swayed at their moorings within the marina basin. Halyards clanked in the breeze. East of the marina, the passenger ferry was berthed at its wide concrete pier, having just returned from its one daily run to the mainland. During the summer there were ten runs a day. On the far side of the harbor, near the icehouses and bait dealers and ships' suppliers, were the docks set aside for Harmony's small fishing and lobstering fleet. At this time of day most of the boats were already in.

"How are you doing?" Ben ventured.

"How do you think?" She wrapped her cardigan closer, folded her arms around herself and walked on, her heels punishing the pavement. "I'm angry, dammit. I came home thinking my friend had committed suicide, and after nearly a week of guilt and recriminations and beating myself up with wondering why, I find out it wasn't suicide at all. I find out all that torment was totally unnecessary."

It was an odd reaction, he thought. Rather inappropriate, too. As odd and inappropriate as the anger she'd directed at him. Or misdirected.

They walked on, past the restaurants and shops and inns of Water Street. A block ahead, jutting out over the sidewalk, swung the sign for the Brass Anchor. He hoped she'd agree to stop in. The way she was shaking worried him.

"That's not why I'm angry, dammit."

Ben hadn't thought so, either.

All at once she stopped, planted her feet, raised her arms, bunched her fists and brought them down in a hard angry chop. "How could he *do* this?" she cried. "How could he mess up so badly?"

"Who?"

"Charlie, of course."

Ah, so now it was Charlie's turn to take the heat of her wrath.

"How could he miss what was right under his nose?" she railed. Tears swam in her dark eyes.

Ben looked around. They were in front of the ice-cream parlor, fortunately closed for the season. "Do you want to sit for a minute?'' He nodded toward one of two benches out front.

''No, I'm too angry to sit. I've got to keep walking or…or I'll implode.''

''You've picked a great place to do it, kid. Main Street U.S.A. But that's okay. Things've been a little dull around here lately, anyway.''

They walked half a block before he asked, ''So do you want to talk about it? Charlie, I mean?''

Julia came to another abrupt halt and for a moment simply spat out hells and damns and a few other words he suspected she didn't ordinarily use.

She resumed walking and talking at the same time, seemingly oblivious to his presence. ''And, of course, because he missed the obvious, the whole investigation is screwed up now. I don't know much about police work, but even I'm aware the first twenty-four hours after a crime are critical. After that, witnesses' memories tend to get fuzzy.''

They'd reached the Brass Anchor, but Ben no longer thought that was the best place for her. She was too agitated. He didn't want to stay on Water Street, either. The diner was located on the next block and at this hour would be full of busybodies. He guided her around the corner, instead. She didn't even seem to notice.

''And then there's the matter of the murderer.'' Her throat closed over the syllables of her last word so that they came out half-moan, half-curse. Ben glanced at her and noticed her lips were trembling again. She pulled herself together quickly, though, moving from grief back to anger, rather like a plane pulling out of a nosedive. ''It's been almost a week. Whoever did it, his trail is so cold by now he'll never be found.''

''Maybe not. Most criminals are pretty stupid. They make mistakes, leave lots of calling cards.''

"But you told me Charlie didn't check Amber's house the way he should have. He didn't collect much evidence."

"Maybe he collected more than I heard about. Maybe something important is still there. Luckily he had enough sense to cordon off the property. The tape is still up."

Just then, Julia happened to notice they were outside the newspaper office. She glanced up at the building, surprised to find herself where she was. Then she looked at Ben and her surprise deepened. "God, what am I doing here? And what am I doing talking to *you*? About Charlie, no less." Her eyes filled again.

"Come on." Ben put his hand on her back. "Let me buy you a drink."

She nodded. "I think I could use one, after all."

He guided her around the building to the wood-plank stairs that led up to his apartment. She looked at him questioningly.

"Special rates," he said.

JULIA WALKED UP Ben's stairs, trying to figure out if she was making a mistake. It didn't *feel* like a mistake. She couldn't see herself walking all the way back to her car in her present mood, on the verge of tears one minute, ready to punch someone's lights out the next. And she didn't know where else in town she could go to pull herself together.

"This is a terrible imposition," she said, watching his key slide into the lock. "It's the middle of your workday."

"End," he contradicted. "And I have an office manager who's perfectly capable of closing up shop. So come in. Make yourself comfortable."

The apartment surprised her. It was a large space with a vaulted ceiling, shiny hardwood floors, white walls and lots of windows. An open stairway led up to a loft with two skylights.

"This is beautiful. The rent must be out of sight."

"No, but the mortgage is." When Ben saw her frown, he added, "I don't pay rent. I bought the building when I bought the newspaper."

"Oh." She looked at him with new eyes. He'd made a heavier investment in Harmony than she'd thought.

"Have a seat while I get us something to drink." Ben touched the back of a sofa on his way to the kitchen. "Or would you prefer coffee or tea?" he called from the other side of the divider counter.

"No, thanks." She wasn't a big fan of alcohol, but at the moment she felt like getting blitzed.

He returned with a tray holding two cordial glasses and a leather-covered decanter. He set the tray on the coffee table, sat beside her on the couch and poured. She didn't ask what it was, just took the delicate stemmed glass and tossed it back. It went down smoothly, then exploded in a fireball that raced from her stomach to her lungs and on up to her head.

Ben's eyes widened. She wondered if she'd just abused twelve-year-old scotch or something.

Slowly he poured again.

"Thank you," she said with an edge of contrition.

"Are you cold? Let me start a fire." Ben was up before she could protest. "These late-September days can get pretty chilly. Come to think of it, today's the first of October, isn't it?"

Sipping her drink, she watched Ben move about the fireplace, laying paper, kindling and wood. He was being very kind, she realized to her utter dismay. Why? She didn't deserve it.

He struck a match and held it to the paper. He waited a

moment while the fire spread, then returned to his seat, sitting back comfortably.

"It's been a hell of a day," he said dryly.

She didn't know why that struck her on such a deep, sad, ironic level, but it did, and the next moment her grip on her emotions had slipped again. The room swam. Her chest ached and a tear slipped down her cheek and hit her wrist.

"Julia?" he asked, concern in his voice.

She turned her head aside, away from him, but it was no use. She couldn't pull herself together as she had before. The ache rose and swelled and consumed her. "Oh, my God," she cried, "Amber was murdered!" She pressed her fingers over her mouth, stopping up the moan that was grinding through her. "Somebody *killed* her!"

When Ben gathered her into his arms, she went stiff with instinctive resistance until he murmured, "It's okay. Go ahead and cry, sweetheart—or hit me, if that's what you prefer to do. No one'll know." Then she wilted. She felt as if a plug had been pulled and all the emotion came whooshing out of her. She buried her face in his neck and surrendered to the sadness and anger swirling inside her. In the circle of his arms she felt safe.

"That's it," he murmured, holding her as tightly as she was holding him. "Let go, sweetheart. Let it all out." And she did.

After a while, when her sobs had subsided and her breathing became calmer, Julia raised her head and noticed the wet stain of her tears and the mass of wrinkles she'd scrunched into his shirt.

"I'm sorry. I've made a royal mess here." She sat up and smoothed the rumpled fabric.

"Don't worry about it." Ben's mouth lifted in that particular slow smile she enjoyed so much.

They were still sitting close, his hands resting at her

waist, hers on his chest. Under her palms he was all muscle and sinew. Suddenly she became painfully aware of every point along her body where they touched. Heat built at those points and spread over her until she was sure she was glowing from it.

She sat back, straightening her sweater and clearing her throat. "Would you mind if I used your bathroom? I need to mop up."

"Sure. Over there. That door off the entrance hall."

"Thanks."

When she returned a few minutes later, Ben was just coming down the stairs from the loft, having changed into a different shirt, a soft chamois in a shade of blue that matched his eyes.

"Feeling better?" he asked, buttoning the right cuff.

She nodded, thinking it was time to go. She didn't belong here in an apartment alone with this man. He was far too appealing, and at the moment she was far too vulnerable. But before she left she needed to apologize.

"Ben, I'm sorry I unloaded on you," she said, embarrassed. "I don't know what got into me."

He came to stand in front of her. He didn't touch her physically, but he might as well have. Just his proximity was enough to make her senses leap. "Give yourself a break, Julia. What you heard at the police station today was pretty shocking news."

She lowered her eyes and nodded. "Yes. Yes, it was. But I feel more rational now. I still have this rage——" she pressed her hand to her chest "——but I can focus it now." She hadn't been angry at Ben or at the anguish she'd suffered when she'd believed Amber's death was a suicide. It wasn't even important that Charlie had made a mistake and let her down. "Someone killed Amber," she continued, "and that person has to be found and brought to justice."

Ben nodded. "That's right. That's what we have to concentrate on now." He searched her face and, apparently satisfied with what he saw, turned and walked into the kitchen.

"Who could've done that to her?" Julia said, wandering over to the divider counter. "My God, she was so... harmless. Who'd want her dead?"

"A lot of people are going to be asking that question," Ben replied, turning on the overhead lights.

His answer was sufficiently evasive to make Julia wonder if he knew something or suspected someone. Maybe she didn't have to be running off just yet.

"Do you suppose it's someone on the island?" she ventured, slipping onto one of the stools. "Someone we all know?" She was only vaguely aware that he'd placed a pot on the stove and removed a large container from the fridge. He opened the container and poured its contents into the pot.

"Maybe. Maybe it was someone just passing through."

"But for it to look like a suicide..." Julia frowned. "Oh Lord, what was she involved in? Could she have been mixed up with somebody sick or dangerous?"

"Possibly." He set a head of lettuce, a tomato and a cucumber on the counter.

"What are you doing?" she said, finally taking note of his busyness.

"Making us some supper."

"Oh, no. I can't stay. I have my show—"

"In two hours. It's just leftovers, Julia. No trouble."

Julia hesitated. Whatever he'd poured into that pot smelled awfully good. "What is it?"

"Fish minestrone. Please, I'd like you to stay."

"Well, okay, but let me help."

"Fair enough. Want to do the salad?"

"Sure."

She went around the counter and set to work. He had a wonderful kitchen: heavy pots and skillets hanging from a rack in order of size, various herb vinegars in tall bottles on a shelf by the stove, even basil and thyme growing on the windowsill.

"No wonder no one thought Amber was depressed," she said after a moment, tearing lettuce over the salad bowl. "She wasn't. Not enough to kill herself, anyway." She reached for the tomato and began cutting it into wedges. "In a way I'm relieved. Does that make any sense?"

At the adjacent counter, Ben was mixing a salad dressing from scratch. "Sure. I barely knew her, but even I wondered if there wasn't something I could've done to help her."

Julia pressed her lips together and sighed, almost smiling. "This is strange, our talking like this."

"Not really. I always had a feeling we'd get along if we gave ourselves half a chance."

"Well, don't get used to it, Grant. I have a feeling I'm not going to like you much once I see how you write this up in your next edition."

"Does that mean you like me *now?*"

"Don't push your luck."

He grinned handsomely. "Did you take a look at the paper by any chance?"

"Yes, I did. It's...all right." Her lips twitched as a teasing spirit infected her. "At least it's very absorbent. I fried some fish today and..." She didn't get the chance to finish before a damp sponge hit the side of her head.

Laughing quietly, they let the subject slide and resumed preparing their meal. Julia's thoughts soon turned serious again.

By the time she was topping off the salad with croutons,

she was frowning. "Poor Charlie. I wish he wasn't caught up in this. I'm not sure he's capable of handling a homicide investigation." Bad enough that he had no prior experience with a crime this serious, but his drinking was dulling his mind and reflexes.

She paused, feeling like a traitor. "I shouldn't've said that." Especially to the editor of the *Island Record!*

But instead of gloating over her admission, Ben merely said, "Maybe he'll step aside and call in the state police." He lifted the cover on the pot and stirred up a cloud of fragrant steam. "How firm are your intentions to stick around for two weeks?"

"Fairly firm. Why do you ask?"

"Something tells me the mainland press is going to be all over Charlie very soon. It won't exactly be his shining hour. He might want to handle it without you around."

"Are you trying to get rid of me, Grant?"

She'd thought they were bantering. She'd thought everything was fine and safe. But then he came up to her, put his hands on her waist and, standing too seductively close, said, "As far as I'm concerned, you can stay here forever."

Her breath locked and her mind went blank. But then he moved off, casually taking bowls and utensils to the table, and she realized he'd just been flirting with her, maybe even teasing. Feeling profoundly foolish, she helped him set the table.

Before sitting down he put on some soft music. She was chagrined to realize it was one of the tapes he'd offered her yesterday. Visions of her ousting him from the WHAR studio returned to torment her.

"I owe you another apology," she said, watching him pour a crisp Riesling into her wine goblet.

"For what?"

"Accusing you of being the moving force behind the autopsy. I've heard it was one of Charlie's summer cops."

Ben filled his own glass slowly, his eyes avoiding hers. "Well, I did help him a little," he admitted, trying to rein in a smile.

"Oh. Then I take my apology back." Julia knew she should've been angrier, but she liked his honesty. She was beginning to like *him*, as well.

"By the way, you're still welcome to my music collection."

"Thanks. And I will take you up on the offer." She finally tasted the soup. "This is wonderful. Cathryn told me you were a good cook, but I didn't take her seriously."

He shrugged. "It's just a hobby."

"Some hobby. How did you pick it up?"

For a long while they talked about pleasant but inconsequential matters, enjoying the food and the music and each other's company. But eventually Julia's thoughts returned to the murder. She looked across the table and would've bet Ben's thoughts had turned that way, too.

"What do you know about Bruce Davoll?" she asked experimentally.

Ben turned his wineglass by the stem, staring at it with a thoughtful frown. "I don't much like his style of playing basketball. Lots of elbows in the ribs. But otherwise we get along. What do *you* know?"

"Cathryn told me he used to hit Amber."

Ben nodded. "I heard that, too. Did Cathryn say anything about the issues holding up their divorce?"

"She said they hadn't reached a financial settlement yet. I didn't get any details, though." She looked at Ben, one eyebrow raised.

"As I understand it, the big issues were the house and the bar. Bruce and Amber owned everything jointly."

"Hmm." Julia held her wineglass to her lips.

"What are you thinking?" he asked, eyes narrowed.

"Seems to me Bruce had a lot to gain from Amber's death." The ticking of the clock on the mantel filled the taut silence.

"Are you saying you suspect Bruce Davoll of murdering his wife?"

Julia shrugged. "He has a motive."

"But you need a lot more than a motive to suspect him of her murder."

"There *is* more. There's his history of abusing her."

Ben mulled over her statement, then shook his head. "The shooting was too controlled, too neat. Bruce would've wanted to use his hands."

"I've thought of that, too. But, dammit, he's the only person I can think of."

They sat for a while without speaking, watching the firelight glinting off the silver and glassware, their thoughts on possible suspects and motives.

Finally Ben glanced at his watch. "I don't mean to cut this short, but you do have a radio show to do."

"You're right. Let's clean up these dishes."

Ben got to his feet. "Forget it. I have a dishwasher for that. Right now we have to go get our cars. Remember?" He'd left his outside the police station, too.

The evening lay quiet and still on the island as they walked to the station. It was painful to think that this time tomorrow the story of a murder on peaceful Harmony would be running over half of New England.

"Are you going to call the news in to the mainland?"

Ben frowned up at the stars. "That's what I should do."

"It's too late to make the six o'clock news."

"But it can make the eleven."

Julia sighed, wishing he'd refrain but knowing he couldn't.

She walked on, carefully avoiding touching him, because when she did, it became difficult to think clearly.

"Doesn't it kill you to be working on a weekly at times like this? You're sitting on an exclusive."

"I've thought of that." He smiled wryly. "But, no, I don't regret anything." They'd reached her car. Ben stared across the street at the light pouring from the windows of the police station.

"Will I see you at the press briefing tomorrow?" he asked.

"I'll be there." She opened her car door and placed the case of borrowed cassette tapes on the seat. But when she attempted to get in, he put his arm in her way.

"Wait." He turned her around so that they were standing toe-to-toe. Her breath fluttered out of her.

From almost the moment they'd met she'd been aware of a special chemistry between them, and tonight that chemistry had been steadily heating up. She'd tried to ignore it, but it had been there, in every lingering glance, every casual touch of his hand, every soft syllable of conversation.

It was there now.

He said, "I've been thinking about Charlie and how disappointed you are with him."

Julia's shoulders collapsed with the release of tension. Ben only wanted to talk about Charlie? "Yes? What about it?"

"You can do what you want, Julia, but it seems to me the chief's got enough going against him. If ever he needed a friend, it's now."

She looked at Ben in amazement. Would he never stop surprising her or giving her reasons to like him? "Thanks for reminding me.'' She glanced toward the station, but Charlie's car wasn't in the lot. "Maybe I'll take a ride by his house before I head home.''

"Good.''

Apparently that was all he had to say, so Julia moved to get into her car again.

"Wait,'' he said again, and again her heart quickened.

"What?''

"Do me a favor tonight while you're doing your show?''

She relaxed once more. "What is it?''

"Lock your doors.''

"I will, but I doubt there's any reason for alarm.''

"I know. Lock 'em, anyway.''

"I will. Good night, Ben. And thanks again for supper.'' She turned and started to get into the car.

"One more thing...''

She sighed and turned around. "What now?'' But the words were still on her lips when Ben lowered his head and kissed her. She was so surprised she didn't move, and after a moment she didn't want to. He was a wonderful kisser! His lips were warm and smooth and moved over hers with perfect sensual slowness and just the right amount of pressure. No, not just a wonderful kisser; he was quite possibly the very best she'd ever known.

"Now you can go,'' he whispered.

She opened her eyes slowly, and they filled with the vision of his handsome face, smiling down at her. She tried to say something, but her brain had turned to mush.

"Good night,'' he said, giving the tip of her nose a playful brush with his index finger. "See you tomorrow.''

JULIA ALMOST FORGOT her intention to visit Charlie. But as she drove through the night, a reviving breeze blowing in her open window, her body cooled and her mind eventually cleared.

She found the chief sitting at his kitchen table in the dreary light cast by the bulb over the stove. A bottle of vodka and an old-fashioned glass were keeping him company. He didn't get up to answer the door, so, seeing him there through the window, she just walked in.

"This isn't a good time to visit," he mumbled. His gaze never lifted from the table.

"Well, this is the time I've got." She yanked out a chair and sat. She might not have been so angry if she hadn't caught him drinking, but now that she had, all her previous outrage came surging back.

"You heard the news?" he asked.

It took effort to give him a simple yes.

"Thought you did. Someone said they saw you at the station."

Julia moved the bottle aside so she could see him better. "I'm sorry I didn't stick around. I needed a little time to myself."

"I'm the one who's sorry. What I let happen…" His expression became pathetically weak. "For over thirty years the people here've trusted me, and I go and pull a bonehead stunt like this." He lifted the glass and tipped it back. "The worst thing is, I thought I was doing the right thing. I still *want* to do the right thing, but something's happened to me. I'm just not functioning the way I used to."

Julia folded her hands carefully on the table and unclenched her jaw. "Okay, Charlie, enough of the self-pity. It's beginning to turn my stomach."

He looked up, startled.

"Sure, what happened is bad. You didn't look into a suicide the way you should have, and now it's come back a murder. But that's in the past. The question now is, what do you intend to do about it?''

His watery eyes lowered again. With difficulty he admitted, "I intend to resign."

Julia drummed her fingers. "I've never known you to be a quitter."

"It's best. Someone more qualified'll come in, take over."

"So you're just going to throw in the towel, dump a distinguished career and go out in disgrace?"

He dropped his head to his hands, fingers plowed into his gray hair. "What else can I do?"

Julia stared at him, disheartened and furious and ready to sail into a lecture. But suddenly she heard Ben's words echo in her heart. *If ever he needed a friend...* What was she doing? Anger wasn't the answer. Neither was ordering him to shape up. That was like telling a crippled man to dance.

She came around the table and took the seat next to his so she could put her arm around his shoulders. "Charlie, it's your decision. Of *course* you can resign. And please know I'll love you no matter what you do. I just think you're selling yourself short, that's all."

He lifted his head out of his hands and patted her arm. "I know you mean well, honey, but what you don't understand is, I've never tackled a homicide investigation before."

"I know, but there's a first time for everything. That's what you always told me. Right at this very table, too."

He started to pull away, stubbornly resistant. She gave his shoulders a bolstering squeeze. "You can do it if you want to. It's just a puzzle, Charlie, and puzzles can be solved. You talk to people who knew Amber, you go through the house with a fine-tooth comb, you send stuff to the lab. Hell, *you* know what to do. The trick is to take it one step at a time. That's another thing you told me whenever I felt overwhelmed. One step at a time, and before you know it, all the pieces'll fall into place. You'll see.''

He sat back, his breathing calmer. Encouraged, she continued, ''I'll help you any way I can. I'm going to be here another week and a half.''

Lines creased his brow, and he lowered his eyes again, embarrassed. ''I wish you weren't. I hate you seeing me like this.''

''Tough. I'm staying, anyway.'' She had the pleasure of watching him smile.

''I don't know what to do, sweetheart. God knows I'd love to be the one to close this case.''

Julia wanted to make the decision for him. Resigning now would forever taint his future. It would change how people thought of him, how they interacted with him. It would change how he thought of himself, as well. He didn't deserve that.

''You're going to have to make that decision for yourself. One thing I will say, though—you've got to lay off the booze, Charlie. It may make you feel good for a while, but it's frying your brain and weakening your body. It's probably pulling you down emotionally, too.''

She'd never seen Charlie blush before, really blush, but he did now.

She took one of his hands in hers and gave his knuckles a kiss. ''You're still only in your fifties, Charlie. I expect you to be around for at least another thirty years.''

He chuckled, shaking his head.

''It's not a joke. Yes, Pauline is gone, but for you this could be just the beginning of a whole new life. But you've got to start taking care of yourself.'' She held his hand to her cheek. "*Please* take care of yourself. I need you, Charlie. You're the only family I've got."

He turned his head and looked at her a long while, his eyes bright with moisture. "One step at a time, huh?"

Julia bit her lip and a smile rose from a well of hope deep inside her. "That's all anyone can expect."

CHAPTER EIGHT

JUST AS BEN PREDICTED, the mainland media landed in force the next day: crews from two TV stations, as well as reporters from four papers. Julia walked into the small lunchroom at the police station where the press briefing would be conducted and couldn't believe her eyes. Or ears. The chatter was deafening.

"Julia!"

Hearing Ben call her name, she scanned the crowd. He waved to get her attention.

"Hi. I saved you a seat," he said.

"Thanks. I don't believe this mob."

"And to think, you scooped them all." He tapped the silver bauble dangling from her right ear, setting it to swinging.

Julia tried not to smile too smugly. "I did, didn't I?"

During her broadcast the previous night, her phone had rung incessantly. People had been shocked at and worried about the rumors spreading that Amber had been murdered. They wanted to know if it was true, and if so, what was being done about it.

Julia hadn't planned on mentioning the day's events on the air, but she'd soon come to see it as an obligation. She knew the truth—she'd heard Charlie's announcement first-hand—and she had the means of disseminating that truth.

For a while she'd thought the best way to go about it was by adding a conventional news item after the world and national report. She'd even scribbled out a rough draft. But in the end she'd scrapped the formality—it seemed too cold and evasive, considering how close the subject was—and she'd simply conveyed the information in a personal conversational style.

Ben had called as soon as she'd put on a record. No hello, just, "What are you trying to do, Lewis, show me up?" His voice had been warm and teasing, instantly bringing to mind the intimacy that had blossomed between them earlier that evening.

"Trying?" she'd teased in return as she pictured his face on the moonlit clouds outside her windows.

"Ooh, you witch."

"Hey, I have a right. I'm the media, too." It was at that moment that the realization had sunk in: being on-air daily, she *was* the news-bearing medium on Harmony. Being a weekly, the *Record* was only the island's paper "of record," chronicling news, rather than breaking it.

When their teasing had finally abated, he'd said, "I won't keep you. I know you're busy. But before I go, two requests. First, would you like to have lunch with me tomorrow after Charlie's press briefing?"

She'd hesitated, not wanting to encourage him or complicate their friendship any further. On the other hand, lunch would be a good opportunity to get that idea across. "Okay. Lunch sounds good. What's your second request?"

"Could you play something for me?"

"Sure. What would you like to hear?"

"'I've Got a Crush on You,' by Linda Ronstadt."

Even now, Julia warmed uncomfortably when she remembered the way he'd spoken, his lips close to the telephone, each soft syllable sending shivers over her scalp. Oh, yes, they really had to have a talk.

But obviously this was not the time. Charlie had entered

the small room and was taking his place at the podium. His eyes were puffy and his shoulders drooped. Julia wondered if he'd gotten any sleep at all. She sent up a fervent prayer for him to get through this ordeal with his dignity at least somewhat intact.

He opened by thanking the press for taking time to come out to the island and promising to answer all their questions, provided they didn't jeopardize the investigation. Then he went over the basic facts of the case: the victim's name and vitals, when she was found, how she was found, and that she'd probably been murdered between 9:00 p.m. and midnight. He also slipped in that her death had been considered a suicide until the autopsy results came back.

"Now I'll take questions," he said. He'd omitted detailing *how* that autopsy came about, but Ben knew. Would he bring it up? Julia wondered. Would he put Charlie on the spot? Give the press another juicy facet to the story?

His hand went up, along with every other hand in the room. Charlie's gaze roamed the crowd and, to Julia's horror, came to rest on Ben. She could barely breathe. Charlie knew what Ben was capable of. That awareness was in his eyes, yet he didn't move on. "Mr. Grant?" he said.

Julia was astounded by his stupidity. He'd walked right into it, eyes wide open. And then she realized it wasn't stupidity at all, but courage. That quiet moment of decision had tested his mettle, and it sealed her respect for him forever.

"Chief Slocum, yesterday you said that certain findings of the autopsy indicated the victim might've been unconscious at the time she was shot. Could you elaborate on that statement, sir?"

If Julia had been surprised by Charlie's courage, she was flabbergasted by Ben's charity. And charity was the only thing she could read into his choice of question.

The same thought was running through Charlie's mind, too, it seemed. For a moment he struggled to hide a smile. "Yes, I can. Traces of a drug called—" he glanced at a limp index card "—flunitrazepam were found in the victim's body." Hands went up immediately, but he kept talking, anticipating the question. "Flunitrazepam is one of those substances that's being called a date-rape drug. 'Roofies' is what they're called on the street. Flunitrazepam is illegal in this country but easily smuggled in through Mexico or South America where, I understand, it's legally prescribed for severe sleep disorders. It's a very powerful sedative, colorless and odorless, and therefore easily slipped into a drink. In recent years, sad to say, date-rape drugs have become more and more available, especially on college campuses."

A reporter from a Providence paper called out, "Was the victim sexually assaulted?" Julia had been agonizing over that herself.

"No," Charlie answered.

She sat back, relieved but confused.

"Did she have *any* sexual contact prior to her death?" asked a different reporter. Again, Charlie said no.

"Sir, can we assume, then, that the drug was used merely to tranquilize the victim so there'd be no struggle when she was shot, thereby making it look like a suicide?"

"That's one scenario," Charlie admitted cautiously.

"Chief Slocum, where did the gun come from?"

"It belonged to the victim. According to a statement made by her father, she bought it because she lived alone. She kept it by her bed."

No one questioned why she had a gun, given the low crime rate on Harmony. Julia suspected it was because of Bruce.

"Was there any sign of forced entry?" another reporter asked.

"No."

"Would you conclude, then, that the victim knew her killer?"

Charlie hesitated just long enough for Julia to know the answer. Of course Amber knew her killer, and her killer knew her, knew she was struggling with a messy divorce, knew she'd gone through a spell of depression and had prescription drugs in her medicine chest, knew she kept a gun by her bed. Knew she was a seemingly good candidate for suicide. It all fit together perfectly.

"I'd rather not comment on that right now. That would be speculation on my part, and I don't want to start any unfounded rumors."

Ben asked the next question. "Did any of the neighbors see anyone in the vicinity around the time Ms. Davoll was killed? Any suspicious vehicles?"

"Unfortunately there aren't too many neighbors on that street. It's a wooded area and the houses are far apart. In short, to answer your question, no, no one saw anything."

"Have you had any cases involving date-rape drugs on Harmony before this?" someone else asked.

"No. None."

Ben raised his hand again. "Do you know where the drug came from?"

"No, but my department is looking into it aggressively."

Julia envisioned his department, that mighty force of two, and wasn't encouraged. Like Charlie, neither officer seemed prepared to handle a crime of this magnitude. For one bleak moment she wondered if Amber would ever be avenged.

"Who saw the victim last, Chief Slocum?"

Charlie scratched his head. "If I knew that, I'd have this case solved." Ironic laughter rippled through the room.

Ben leaned toward Julia and spoke close to her ear. "He's doing well, the old son of a gun."

She nodded, aware that matters could easily have been quite different. "Ben, I have to ask it—why didn't you go after him?"

Ben shrugged casually. "That issue is nobody's business but Harmony's. I'll get him later."

Julia let her gaze roam over Ben's face, taking in each engaging feature. She really liked him. It wasn't just a case of physical attraction. She liked *him*, his outlook on life, his intelligence, his compassion and humor—to say nothing of his cooking—and that scared the living daylights out of her.

"To answer that question seriously," Charlie was saying, "Ms. Davoll spent her last evening with her parents. She left the Atlantic Trust at around five, went home and changed out of her office clothes, fed her dog, walked to her parents' house up the road and had dinner with them. At around eight-thirty she left for home, saying she was going to watch TV. Nothing in their conversation indicated Ms. Davoll was in any danger."

Julia finally raised her hand and asked what was on everyone's mind. "Do you have any suspects, Chief?"

Charlie gave her a private smile. "No, but we're collecting leads, talking to a lot of people, and evidence found at the scene has been sent to the state lab for analysis. Something is bound to surface soon."

He fielded a few more questions and then the briefing was over. He retreated to his office, leaving the various news teams to disperse.

Out on the steps Ben surprised Julia by curling his hand

over her shoulder and quietly asking, "How are you do-ing…you know, after hearing all those details?"

She took a breath. "Surprisingly okay. I think the brief-ing actually helped. It made Amber's death more of a puz-zle, more an objective problem."

"Good."

"Are you still up for lunch?" she asked.

"Yes, ma'am."

"Do you have any particular place in mind?"

"I did." He gave her an amused glance. "But you look like you want to suggest something." He opened the pas-senger door of his Bronco and she climbed in.

Once he was behind the wheel she asked, "Would you mind Davy's Locker?"

At her naming Bruce Davoll's bar, his expression dropped. "Why there?"

"I hear they make a nice thin-crust pizza."

Ben didn't even give her a token smile. He turned to face her, his right arm resting on the back of the seat. "Knock off the fooling, Lewis. You don't want to go there."

She pushed her hands deep into the pockets of her blazer, frustration bunching her shoulders. "Aren't you even a lit-tle curious about Bruce's reaction to all this?"

"Nope. You're not still considering him as a suspect, are you?"

She bit her lip, stared at the dashboard, then let out a breath that released her shoulders. "I don't know. Maybe."

"I thought we went over that last night."

"I know, the crime was too neat." She turned. "But the husband or boyfriend is always the first suspect."

"Then I'm sure Chief Slocum knows that and is doing something about it."

"You're sure of that, huh?" Julia caught his eye, then looked away guiltily.

Ben closed his hand over her shoulder. "Julia, it's not up to you to take up Charlie's slack."

She stiffened. "I'm not."

"No? Then why do I have the feeling you want to go over there and play girl detective?"

She slid him a doleful look. "Girl detective? Why not just pat me on the head and tell me to go play with my dolls?"

"God save us," Ben muttered. "I didn't mean anything by it. It's just…what are you going to do—walk in there and say, 'Hi, Bruce. Ben and I were just discussing the possibility you killed your wife, and we'd like to get your input'?"

Julia wiped a hand over her smile. "Give me a little credit for intelligence."

"You'd better use some intelligence, lady, because Bruce Davoll is no one you want to mess with."

Julia sobered under the fierceness of Ben's scowl. "I know."

Ben turned and stared out the windshield. "So, do you still want to go there for lunch?"

"Yes. I have heard good things about their food."

Ben turned the ignition. "Okay, Davy's Locker it is. But behave, Julia."

BRUCE DAVOLL made most of his money on the summer crowd, the younger end of it, to be precise. His place was fortuitously located across the road from the public beach, and from June to Labor Day, morning to the wee hours, its two-level outdoor deck teemed with tanned and buffed bodies in various stages of dress and sobriety. The music was loud, the food salty and fried, and nobody looked too carefully at ID.

In the off-season the patio tables got put away, and Davy's Locker reverted to being just an ordinary neighborhood bar and grill.

Although it was called Davy's Locker, Bruce had ignored the nautical decor left behind by the former owner and imposed his own, which ran to sports. He'd refurbished the pool table, hung up a couple of dartboards and installed a big-screen TV, which he locked in to a sports channel. In summer he strung up a volleyball net on the sand, and in winter he skippered a team in the island's all-ages, all-abilities basketball league. Ben played against him on a team ingloriously called the Yogurt Shoppe-shooters.

When Ben and Julia showed up, Bruce was restocking the bar while moving to the beat of something by Guns N' Roses. No other customers were there. Ben was still uncertain about the wisdom of bringing Julia here. His instincts told him Bruce hadn't killed his wife—he'd seemed just a little too dazed at the funeral—but on the chance that he had, Ben didn't want Julia asking a lot of questions and drawing attention to herself.

"Hey, Bruce," he called from the door.

Bruce looked up, his eyes darting in momentary apprehension from Ben to Julia before reverting to their usual chilling flatness. He nodded, expressionless.

"Is the kitchen open yet?"

"Ten, fifteen more minutes." Bruce hoisted two full cases of beer onto a shelf without even a grunt. As usual he was wearing a T-shirt a size too small, revealing every muscle in his torso. His short sandy hair was gelled so that his scalp showed through, reflecting the lighted Coors sign revolving overhead.

His eyes slid toward Julia again. Apparently he decided

it was in his best interests to join the human race. "Hey, who you got there, Ben?" He smiled a little. Being the proprietor of a popular pub, he was called upon to smile quite often, but Ben had never been able to let down his guard in Bruce's presence. It probably came from playing ball against him.

Ben curled his hand around Julia's waist and urged her forward. He could feel her tensing with each step; whether because of this place or his touch he wasn't sure. Maybe a combination.

He'd known as soon as he'd kissed her last night that he was eventually going to hear about it. In fact, he'd known before he'd kissed her. Stepping up their relationship had been a mistake. He and Julia had no future. He knew it. She knew it. Still, he'd kissed her. He'd been unable not to. And since then, all he'd wanted to do was kiss her again. In place of that he'd been replaying the moment over and over in his mind, remembering the pleasure of it, remembering the surprise.

Although he was pretty sure she'd felt it, too, he knew she regretted it. He'd heard the reserve in her voice when he'd called her later. He also knew she was going to confront him today.

The logical thing, of course, would be to let go and back off. The responsible thing would be to forget her. But Ben didn't want to be logical or responsible. He wanted to pursue Julia in spite of the fact that she was leaving soon. He wanted them to let nature take its course and enjoy whatever they could in the short time they had.

Faced with this dilemma, he'd ignored the issue, hoping Julia would let it slide, as well. But he knew it was only a matter of time.

"Hello, Bruce." Julia reached over the bar to shake his hand.

"Julia," Bruce said. "I saw you at the funeral."

"Yes. I'm sorry I didn't have a chance to talk to you that day, to extend my sympathy."

Ben hoped his surprise wasn't showing. Considering what Julia knew about Bruce's relationship with Amber, he figured she was gagging on her words.

"That would've been a switch," Bruce said. "Somebody offering *me* sympathy."

"I know, you and Amber were getting a divorce, but seven years have to count for something. And for whatever it's worth, I'm sorry about your loss."

"Thanks. What can I get you?" He dealt out two napkins faster than a Nevada croupier. It was easy to think Bruce was slow because of his bulk. Easy to think he was stupid, too. Having guarded him in a few games, Ben knew how dangerous those assumptions could be.

"A club soda for me," Julia said, slipping onto a stool.

"Sam Adams," Ben said.

Bruce reached into a cooler behind the bar. "I had no idea you two knew each other."

"We don't," Julia said impishly.

"That's not from lack of trying," Ben added with a laugh.

"Well, watch out for this one," Bruce warned Julia, placing her drink in front of her. "He's got some pretty slick moves."

"That right?" She gave Ben a playful once-over.

A woman came out of the back room just then—Nicole Normandin, Bruce's longtime waitress and supposedly his current girlfriend. She was dressed in a black miniskirt and a black V-necked sweater appliquéd with shiny gold leaves. She went right to work, spraying tables and wiping them dry, but every once in a while her eyes lifted, checking out Ben and Julia.

"It's a shocker, this latest on Amber, isn't it?" Julia said, lowering her voice.

Oh, hell. Ben struggled not to wince.

"About her death being a murder?" Bruce said.

Ben moved his foot along the brass rail until it rested against hers and pressed. She ignored him.

"Uh-huh. Isn't it awful?"

"It sure is." Bruce shook his head, but his expression had closed up even further, revealing nothing of his true feelings.

Julia sipped her soda and eyed him over the rim of her glass. "Actually Ben and I just came from a press briefing at the police station and there's more."

"Oh, yeah?" Bruce picked up a damp rag and began wiping the bar, his hand moving in deceptively casual circles.

Julia began to tell him about the drug that the autopsy had uncovered. She spoke calmly enough, but under the bar, out of Bruce's view, she was twisting her napkin into a tighter and tighter wad. Ben surprised himself by draping his arm over the back of her stool and stroking her shoulder with his thumb, just to remind her he was there.

Bruce reacted to the news about the drug with the same shallow expression that had greeted her earlier remark. "Yeah, I heard about that, too. The police chief was in here this morning, early."

Julia's back straightened. "Charlie? He was in here?"

Bruce grunted, and Ben thought, *Well, I'll be damned!*

"What did he want?" Julia asked.

"Oh, the usual. If Amber had said anything to me lately. Did she have any enemies." Bruce tossed the damp rag into a sink and wiped his hands on his shirt. "I wish I coulda been more help, but I really had nothing to give him. Nothing."

Ben didn't like the way Bruce suddenly looked at Julia.

"Well," she said, her voice betraying a slightly nervous tremor, "I just hope whoever did it is caught soon." She lifted her gaze and made a sweep of the room. "I like your place. I've never been in here before. It's really nice."

Bruce loosened up a little and even smiled. "She's my baby!" he said, slapping a hand over a Budweiser tap.

"And it's obvious you take good care of her." Julia swiveled her stool and scanned the tables. "Does it matter where we sit?"

Ben breathed a whole lot easier.

"No. Anywhere. I'll go see how the kitchen's doing." Then Bruce called, "Hey, Nicky, you got customers."

JULIA CHOSE A BOOTH as far from the bar as she could get. She couldn't abide being near Bruce for another second. She'd wanted to grab him by the chest hair—or somewhere even more painful—and tell him she knew exactly how he'd treated Amber during their marriage and he wasn't going to get away with it. But she'd kept her cool and now was glad she had.

"Well, what do you think?" Ben asked, settling into the bench opposite her.

"Hmm?"

"You came in here to check out his reaction..."

"He's holding a lot back, not reacting normally to the situation, and I can only wonder why."

A flash of gold alerted her to Nicole's approach. The waitress placed two menus on the table and with a tense smile said, "Hi. Would you like to hear what today's specials are?"

Apparently Bruce's taste in women ran to a certain type. Like Amber, Nicole was exceptionally pretty, with long blond hair and big blue eyes. However, unlike Amber, Nicole's looks bordered on hard-edged.

She seemed to care a great deal about her appearance. Her makeup was meticulous, if a little heavy, and her hair was painstakingly arranged to look sexily tousled. Her clothes were neat and good quality, and her earrings were shaped like leaves to match the leaves on her sweater. Julia noticed that her maroon nail polish was the very same shade as her lipstick. She would've bet anything that Nicole had painted her toenails to match.

With a start Julia realized Ben was looking at her. "Did you just ask me something?"

"Yes. Are you still interested in pizza?"

"Yes."

"You can skip the specials, then," he said to Nicole.

Nicole pulled out a pencil and pad from her pocket. "What kind of pizza will it be?"

"Linguica?" Julia said, referring to the Portuguese sausage that was a local specialty. "Is that okay with you?"

Ben nodded. Nicole wrote out their order and started to turn.

"Wait," Julia said on impulse.

"Is there something else?"

"You don't remember me, do you?"

Nicole frowned. "You look sort of familiar."

"Julia Lewis. I went to school with your brother."

"Oh." Something in Nicole's manner gave Julia the feeling she'd known who she was all long. Was it the fact that she didn't ask which brother? She had two, Julia recalled.

"You're the one on the radio, aren't you?"

"That's right."

"I listened to you last night. I wasn't working, and some

of the customers in here were talking about you, so I tuned in. It was nice. Real nice."

Julia had the feeling Nicole would've preferred the Top 40 show she did in California.

"Thanks. Tell me, how is Jake doing these days?"

"Good. He's living in Galilee over in Rhode Island. Working on a trawler for a big seafood company. At least he was last time we talked."

"Married?"

"No. Divorced."

"Do you happen to know his address or phone number off hand?"

Nicole tapped her pencil against her lower teeth, frowning. "Sorry," she said after a moment.

"Would you mind if I called you at home for it?"

"I guess not." She looked at Julia with deeper interest. "You want to get in touch with Jake?" Her eyes flicked toward Ben, assessing his reaction.

"Yes. A friend and I are planning a get-together a week from Saturday, sort of a class reunion. With me living so faraway, we might not get the chance again for a long time."

Ben's surprised interest made her realize she hadn't told him yet.

"Sounds nice." Nicole smiled.

"I think so, too."

Just then, Bruce returned from the kitchen and gave Nicole a hard sidelong look. Immediately she began to move, straightening the utensils at Julia's place. "That pizza will take about fifteen minutes. If there's anything you need in the meantime, just give a holler." With a tight smile she turned and hurried off to the kitchen.

Julia let a moment pass before leaning forward and whispering, "Did she look intimidated to you just now?"

"Yes, a little."

"I hope she knows what she's doing, dating Bruce." Julia sipped her soda, surprised by her concern, but the woman had looked so tense. "Are they living together?"

"Bruce and Nicole? Nah. They still keep their own places. He's converted a couple of rooms upstairs. She rents a small house out on Old Harbor Road."

"Is that because the divorce wasn't final yet?"

"I'm not sure. I get the feeling they're just not that serious. From a few remarks Bruce has made, I'd say it's mostly a physical relationship."

"He talks about it?" She wrinkled her nose. "How long have they been an item?"

"Oh, a couple of months. But rumor has it Nicole's had the hots for him a long time, even when he was still with Amber."

"That must've been interesting." Julia went still.

Ben, who was tipping back his beer mug, noticed the change in her demeanor and gave her a narrowed look. "What?"

"I just thought of somebody else with a reason to want Amber out of the way."

Ben set down his mug, looking half amused, half exasperated. "Will you get serious!"

"I am." Julia turned fractionally, trying to see where Nicole was. "I wonder where *she* was last Thursday night."

Ben's face tightened. "Don't even think it! If you want information, go ask Charlie. He's not supposed to discuss cases with civilians, but seeing it's you, I'm sure he'd make an exception."

Julia was taken aback by the vehemence of his response. "What's the matter?"

His gaze traveled over her, from her eyes to her hair to

her mouth and back to her eyes again. His anger gave way to something softer. "Sorry. I know I have no right to tell you what to do, but I can't help worrying about you."

Julia looked down at her paper place mat. "I appreciate your concern, but it's not necessary." She bit her lip, realizing his concern was part of a larger problem, one she'd vowed to address today. "Ben, we've got to talk."

He sighed in resignation, slumping in his seat. "About what?"

"Last night."

"Just to make sure we're on the same page, are you talking about my kissing you?"

"Yes." She swallowed, her throat suddenly parched. Now that she'd launched the uncomfortable subject, she could only wonder why. "Ben, I'm not looking to start anything at this time in my life. Romance is at the very bottom of my list of priorities. And even if it was something I wanted, it certainly wouldn't be with someone on Harmony. I thought I explained all that to you already."

Ben rubbed his jaw slowly, thoughts tumbling behind his eyes. "This may come as a blow to your ego, but it was just a kiss, one kiss, not a marriage proposal."

She felt her cheeks warming, betraying how deeply shaken that kiss had left her—and how foolish she felt now, seeing how lightly he'd taken it.

"I'm well aware of that, but all sorts of things start with a kiss, one kiss," she mocked. "And in a week's time a lot can happen."

Ben grinned. "One can only hope."

"You're impossible."

"No," he said, his tone serious again. "I just know that something unusual's going on between us, and we owe it to ourselves to spend whatever time we've got exploring it."

His candidness was unexpected. So was his admission of how deeply he felt. Julia curled her fingers over the edge of the table to steady herself. "I'd be lying if I said I didn't feel the attraction, too, Ben. But that doesn't mean we have the green light to act on that attraction."

"Why not? We're both adults, both unattached."

"Just what are you proposing?"

"I have no plan, Julia. I'm as guileless as a babe." He reached across the table and took her right hand in his. "I merely thought we should let instinct guide us and see what comes of it."

With a pain in her heart she didn't understand, Julia shook her head. "I can't."

"Because you're leaving in a week?" He stroked her palm with his thumb.

"Yes, that's a big part of it."

He thought about that for a moment, then, raising his eyes hopefully, said, "Have you considered what a glorious week it would be?"

Julia's breath shuddered. "Please. I don't have room in my life for the emotional complication."

"I'm not trying to complicate your life."

"Then stop pressing the issue."

Ben tilted his head, studying her, weighing his options. "Sorry. I can't make any promises."

"Ben!"

"Okay, okay." He smiled. "I'll stop pressing. The ball's in your court now. The next move we make, it'll be all your doing. How's that?"

"Fine. That guarantees there won't be a next move."

Ben laughed, a deep rumbling sound that touched something vital inside her. "Pretty sure of yourself, aren't you?"

"You bet," she said. But she wasn't, especially when he

was looking at her the way he was now, those intense blue eyes of his peeling back all her defenses.

Fortunately Nicole returned from the kitchen then and handed Julia a small piece of paper with her phone number on it. "I get off early tonight. You can call me anytime after eight."

Julia thought about asking Nicole if she always got off early on Thursdays, but in the natural light pouring through the tall windows the younger woman suddenly looked painfully thin, sad and hardly the murder suspect Julia had envisioned a moment earlier.

"Thanks." Julia slipped the paper into her purse. When she turned back to Ben, she deliberately shifted the conversation to the class get-together she and Cathryn were planning, and the subject of their mutual attraction was dropped.

JULIA CONVINCED Charlie to come on her show that evening from seven-thirty to eight-thirty, the idea generated from the number of calls she'd gotten on previous nights regarding Amber's death. At first he balked, out of nervousness mostly. But he'd been approached so often that day by citizens wanting information that he decided going on the air and quelling their curiosity was worth a bout with performance jitters.

Julia organized the first part of their hour in a question-and-answer format, with all the questions selected beforehand. She kept it conversational and positive, which went a long way to setting a comfortable tone when Charlie began taking questions from listeners.

Julia rode that second portion of the show on a river of adrenaline. She wasn't recording and screening calls tonight. There was simply no time or opportunity for that.

Calls were simply going out over the airwaves live as they came in. So were Charlie's responses.

Fortunately no one said anything *too* inappropriate. A few mild curses, but those didn't concern her. She was more concerned about the fear that was coming across, now that people realized there might be a killer in their midst, that it might be their neighbor or someone they'd just brushed shoulders with at the post office. She was also attuned to a subtle lack of confidence in Charlie's ability to handle the case. Sometimes, such as when they asked if outside help was coming in, it wasn't even subtle.

Julia didn't want to breed panic on her show; that was just the opposite of what she'd hoped to accomplish by having Charlie on. And she certainly hadn't planned on exposing him to criticism. But as she looked out at the darkening sky through her windows, she couldn't help feeling some of that fear and lack of confidence herself.

"Let me take this opportunity to remind you," she said during a lull, "that you can call Chief Slocum anytime if you think you have some information that'll help. You should definitely call if you noticed any unusual activity last Thursday night. It may not seem significant to you now, but who knows, it just might be the missing piece the chief needs to see the complete picture."

Julia gave the number of the police station, assuming listeners knew they should call him there, but when the phone rang a couple of minutes later, she realized the caller had misunderstood.

"I usually put my dog out around ten o'clock and let him run for an hour," the woman said. She hadn't identified herself except to say she lived on Settlers Neck Road. "That time of night I figure he won't bother anybody. And, anyway, we have woods behind our house. That's where he usually goes, sniffing out rabbits and such. That night, though, he came running back within minutes, yelping. He'd been sprayed with something, Mace or pepper spray, maybe ammonia. The only thing I can figure is that he met up with someone on the walking trails back there. The trails are the only way to get through those woods, they're so choked with brambles. But I ask you, who'd be out walking the woods at ten o'clock at night?''

Julia had the presence of mind to thank the woman and remind others to call the police station, not her, with their information. But it was too late. Her skin was already crawling. She didn't need to pull out a map to picture the stretch of woods the caller was referring to. They were the same woods that ran right behind Amber's house.

CHAPTER NINE

"UNFORTUNATELY THAT'S ALL the time we have with Chief Slocum tonight," Julia said, even though the clock read only eight-twenty. "I want to thank the chief for taking time out of his busy schedule to be with us."

"Thanks for having me," Charlie said, looking terribly relieved.

"And now we'll swing over to our regular programming. This is Julia Lewis for WHAR FM. I'll be here till ten o'clock, so put another log on the fire and stay with me awhile."

She started a record, took off her headset and sank back in her chair with a long smiling sigh. "You done good, Charlie."

He clutched the back of his neck. "I'm trying."

"I know you are." She sat forward. "How's the investigation really going?"

"Slow."

"What do you make of that last call?"

Charlie waved a hand in impatient dismissal. "That was just Dottie Carrolton. Most likely the only thing her dumb old dog ran into in those woods was a skunk."

Julia smiled. "I heard you were over at Davy's Locker this morning talking to Bruce Davoll."

"Well, of course I talked to Bruce Davoll. I've talked to damn near half the people on this island. Can't you hear how hoarse my voice is?"

Her smile broadened. Charlie really *was* trying.

"You don't have to tell me anything confidential, but I would be interested to know if he has an alibi for last Thursday night."

Charlie sighed. "He was at the Locker until eleven, and there are witnesses to testify to it."

Charlie's response proved her suspicion that he'd been there questioning Bruce as a suspect.

"But it's possible Amber was killed after eleven. Anytime up to midnight, right?"

"Right. Maybe even later. But Davoll says he went straight to his girlfriend's after closing up and was there all night."

There was enough hesitation in his manner to put Julia on alert. "Was he?"

"*She* swears he was," he said, unintentionally disclosing the fact that he'd questioned Nicole, too. "There are holes in the story, though. Davoll's car was parked outside the Locker all night, for instance."

"How do they explain that?"

"They claim the battery was acting up, so Nicole picked him up in her car and drove him to her place."

"Do you believe them?"

"I'm a cop, sweetheart. I don't believe anything, but until I have proof..." He just shrugged. "Hey, I've got to run." He clapped his hands to his knees, made a motion to rise, but didn't actually get to his feet. He seemed to have something else on his mind. "I'm really sorry this has happened," he said. "I wanted to spend time with you while you were home, do things, go places. But this case is eating up every minute."

"That's okay. I understand. And don't you worry about me. I have plenty to keep me busy."

"I noticed you with Ben Grant this morning. What's that all about?"

"I don't know, Charlie." Julia's shoulders slumped with a sigh. "I don't know."

"Well, hell, that doesn't sound good."

She tried to smile reassuringly. "Don't worry. Nothing's going to happen. I know he's no friend of yours. Besides, I'll be leaving in a week. What's the point?"

"You sound as if you regret that fact."

Her gaze drifted to the windows over the console, to the distant lights of a ship moving with infinite slowness on the dark sea beyond. "What if I say I do?"

She expected Charlie to call her a fool. "I'd say life is never simple."

She breathed out a quiet laugh. "No, it isn't."

"I really gotta go." This time Charlie did get to his feet.

Julia got up, too, and walked him to the door. "Do you want to go on again tomorrow night?"

"Not on your life." He chuckled. "You can call the desk tomorrow, though, get an update and report it yourself if you want."

"Okay, I will. Take care, Charlie." Julia gave him a hug. "And try to get some sleep."

"I will," he said, although he probably wouldn't. "Lock this behind me."

Julia stood at the door long after the taillights of his car had winked out of sight. Nights were so incredibly quiet here on Harmony compared to the ones she'd become used to in Los Angeles. And dark. Streetlights were few and far between on the roads at this end of the island. And here on Preston Finch's property, a hundred feet in from the road, with all those fields and conservation lands surrounding it, the night was positively inky.

Ordinarily Julia liked the peace and solitude, but after

that last call, she would've preferred a little more civilization around her. She couldn't shake her awareness that there were hiking trails here, too. Walking them had become a morning routine for her.

Of course they wound through a different tract of land than the one the caller had alluded to, land that was more shrubbed than treed, but someone could still travel them at night undetected if he wanted to. She wished Charlie had taken the call more seriously.

Predictably her thoughts strayed to Ben. All she had to do was pick up the phone and within minutes he'd be here, keeping her company. As he'd said, the ball was now in her court.

But would it end with him simply keeping company? He was right when he said something unusual was going on between them. She'd never known such a strong affinity to a man in so short a time. Never known such a strong affinity, period. Before they knew it, they'd be in over their heads, and then where would that leave her? Up a creek with a broken heart, most likely.

With a determination that took all of her strength, Julia put Ben from her mind and returned to her control board, eager to lose herself in her work.

CLOUDS ROLLED IN on a cool northeast wind the next day, threatening rain. In spite of that, Julia laced up her walking shoes and as usual attempted to go for a hike. What wasn't usual was that she decided to walk the paths through the woods Dottie Carrolton had spoken of. Usually she stayed on the trails near her house.

She drove to the nearest trailhead but was stopped by a guard at the entrance. The woods were closed off today, the guard said, but he wouldn't explain why. Julia didn't

know what to make of that, but her confidence in Charlie
went up several notches.

As long as she was already out, she decided to run the
day's errands. She stopped by the bank to get a cash ad-
vance on her credit card, then visited the food market and
post office. She was embarrassed to admit that she also
drove by the newspaper office. Twice.

Ben hadn't called last night. She'd half expected he
would, since he'd called almost every other night. But he
hadn't and she'd gone to bed like a child without supper,
feeling cranky and hollow and just a little sorry for herself.

She'd thought a good night's sleep would cure her of her
restiveness, but this morning she'd awakened with Ben still
on her mind and the hunger to see him even greater.

Driving by his office, she tried to concoct a reason to
drop in. Although she would've died before admitting it,
she loved being with him, loved the way he made her
feel—alive, tingly, euphoric.

And that was precisely why she drove right on by.

Julia was about to head home when her thoughts turned
to Nicole—the final item on today's to-do list. She'd given
Nicole a call last night as promised, but no one had answered.

She spotted a phone booth on the corner of Center Street
and School, pulled over and looked up Nicole's house number in the directory. Of course the most sensible thing
would be to go home and call again. But the truth was,
Julia wanted to talk to her face-to-face.

Nicole's place turned out to be a dollhouse-size Cape
Cod cottage tucked under a canopy of white pines. Dry pine
needles matted the yard. Julia went to the back door, hes-
itating before knocking. She wasn't in the habit of visiting
people unexpectedly. But Harmony was different from
other places. People were less formal here and dropped in

on each other all the time. She raised her knuckles and gave the door a few raps.

After a considerable wait the door opened, but only a crack. Nicole peered out, wearing a green silk kimono, with a towel wound around her head. Without makeup, she looked younger and softer than she had yesterday. "Yeah?" she said.

"Sorry to disturb you, but I was just driving by and remembered we never did connect last night." The door opened a little more. Nicole was frowning as if she couldn't recall why she and Julia would want to "connect."

"I asked for your brother's phone number?" Julia reminded her. Glacial blue eyes ran the length of her. Julia suppressed an unexpected shiver and added, "If I could get that from you now, I'd really appreciate it. I won't take any more of your time. I can see you're busy."

"Yes, I am. With the hours I work at the Locker, I depend on my mornings to get stuff done." Nevertheless she opened the door wider. The kitchen Julia stepped into was old but well kept, although the smell of cigarette smoke hung in the air.

Nicole did indeed seem busy. Dishes soaked in the sink. A pair of sneakers, freshly washed, were drying on a radiator. A jar of jewelry cleaner, buffing cloths and several gold chains littered the table. And in the living room beyond, stacks of neatly folded laundry sat on the coffee table.

Nicole didn't invite her to sit even though the table and chairs were right there. Instead, she clopped across the room in her green satin mules, went directly to the phone and looked up her brother's number in a small book. She wrote it on a heart-shaped pad of paper, then returned.

When she handed the paper to Julia, the sleeve of her

robe rode up, revealing a yellowing bruise on her forearm. "Thanks," Julia said, barely able to get the word out.

Nicole reached around her to open the door, clearly in no mood to entertain, which was perfectly understandable. Still, Julia didn't make any motion to leave. She didn't know when another opportunity would present itself.

"Nicole, would you mind if I stayed another minute?"

Nicole glanced over her shoulder at the wall clock and sighed eloquently.

"It's important," Julia added. "It's about Bruce."

Nicole went very still. "What about Bruce?"

Julia took Nicole's arm by the wrist and raised it, exposing the bruise again. "This," she said.

Nicole looked confused for a moment, and then understanding dawned. She yanked her wrist free. "I bumped my arm while I was clearing a table at work."

Julia didn't want to argue. That would only put Nicole more on the defensive. But she couldn't let the matter slide, either. "I'm just concerned about you, Nicole. I know what Bruce was like with Amber, and abusive men don't change."

"Bruce doesn't hit *me*."

"Maybe not, but I can't help thinking it'll just be a matter of time."

"You don't know what you're talking about. Bruce loves me."

"He loved Amber once, too."

"Sure, and she didn't appreciate what she had." Nicole's face hardened with self-righteousness. "She flirted with everything in pants, sometimes even with Bruce right there. I saw it myself. God knows what she did when he wasn't around. A man's got his pride, you know."

"So you're saying he had a right to hit her?"

"No, but I understand why he did it, and I'd never be like that. Never."

Julia sighed, feeling helpless. Obviously Nicole was wearing blinders and didn't appreciate her efforts to remove them.

"Listen, Nicole, I know you don't want to hear it—you're obviously in love with the guy. But watch out for yourself, okay? He could be more dangerous than you realize."

"What do you mean?"

Julia's palms began to sweat. "Well...when you think about it, if there's anyone who would profit from Amber's being dead, it's Bruce."

"That doesn't mean he killed her. He couldn't have killed her. He's just a big softie at heart." She paused, her eyes jigging back and forth. "There's no way anybody can pin anything on him. He was with me last Thursday night. I've already told that to the police. We both have."

"You and Bruce were together *all* Thursday night?"

Nicole gave Julia a vindictive look, her dislike turning darker. "Yes," she said unblinkingly. "All night. So you see, at about the time your friend Amber was killed, Bruce and I were hitting the sheets."

Julia was sure the comment was aimed to hurt, and it did.

"I guess that sounded pretty crass, but I'll be honest, there was no love lost between me and Amber. I mean, I'm sorry she died and all, but I'm not sorry she's out of Bruce's life. She wanted it all—the house, the truck, the boat. But the thing that really got to Bruce was the Locker. She couldn't've cared less about the Locker, yet she wanted it. And you wanna know why? To spoil things for us. That's why. She didn't want us to have anything. No, there was no love lost between me and her. Maybe now Bruce'll be able to find some real happiness.''

''I didn't realize you two were that serious.''

''Of course we're that serious.'' Offended, Nicole reached for the doorknob. ''I'm really gonna have to ask you to leave now. I have stuff to do.''

''Well, thanks again for your brother's phone number. I'm sorry for taking so much of your time.''

Nicole opened the door.

''Nicole, do you have any idea who might've wanted to kill Amber?''

''None whatsoever.'' Her eyes were as blank as wiped slates.

''Well, if you do hear anything, you will call Chief Slocum, won't you?''

Nicole sighed.

''And if you need someone to talk to,'' Julia added meaningfully, ''I'll be around awhile. Don't hesitate to call.''

''Okay. Thanks,'' Nicole said hurriedly, and shut the door in Julia's face.

THE AFTERNOON DRAGGED. Julia organized the evening program, then in desperation for something to do, drove out to Cathryn's and helped her plant spring bulbs while her five-year-old daughter, Bethany, zoomed around the yard on a miniature bike with training wheels. Cathryn extended an invitation to dinner, but Julia declined, feeling she'd imposed her gloomy self on her friend quite long enough.

''You'll come to dinner tomorrow night, though,'' Cathryn said, walking Julia to her car. ''And you might as well know I won't take no for an answer.''

Seeing that the following night was Saturday, the loneliest night of the week, Julia accepted. When she went on the air tonight, she'd simply make an announcement that there wouldn't be a show tomorrow. After all, she wasn't obliged to broadcast every night. She wasn't obliged to broadcast at all. The show was just a lark. Even so, she was developing a strange sense of responsibility toward her audience.

The evening finally arrived, bringing with it a cold rain. Julia sat in the studio playing her music, watching the rain slanting in the beam of an outside light above her windows and finally feeling a measure of contentment, as she usually did when she worked. Still, something wasn't quite right.

An hour went by before her phone rang. She picked it up, expecting a caller with a music request, but hoping it would be Ben. Her heart warmed at that thought.

But as she listened to what the caller had to say, her smile faded. It wasn't a musical request and it wasn't Ben. It was another piece of information regarding Amber, and this one left her dazed.

BEN WAS TAPPING OUT an article on his laptop, listening to Julia's show, when the phone rang. "Yes?" he said.

"Ben, it's Julia."

His heart skittered. He'd been thinking about her all day, wondering what excuse he could devise to call her or drop by to see her. But foolishly he'd handed over the reins of their friendship to her, and he wasn't about to go back on his word.

"Hey there," he said, trying to sound as if his heart wasn't thumping through his chest. "What's up?"

"I can't talk long. I'm doing my show. But I thought you might want to know what I just heard."

Ben stretched the phone cord to its limit as he walked to

the window and looked toward the transmitter. Because of the rain, he couldn't see its red light.

"Do you know anything about an affair Amber might've been having?" she asked breathlessly.

"An affair?" His eyebrows shot up. "Like, with a married man?"

"Yes."

"No! She was having an affair?"

"That's what a caller just told me."

"A caller? Who?"

"Sorry, I can't say."

Ben frowned. "Have you told Charlie?"

"Not yet, but I plan to as soon as we get off the phone."

"Hmm." Ben paced, questions crowding his thoughts. "Who was she having an affair with? Someone I might know?"

"Look, I'd rather not talk about this on the phone."

The words "Why not?" were on the tip of his tongue when he suddenly caught them back. A smile began to warm him from the inside out.

"What are you doing tonight?" she asked in a small voice.

Ben punched the air with a victory fist. "I'll be right over."

It was a dark night, rain obscuring the stars and moon. But both the house and the WHAR studio streamed with light.

"Good girl," Ben muttered as he climbed out of his vehicle.

She had the door open before he could knock. "Hi."

He struggled with the urge to scoop her into his arms right then and there. "Hi."

Her eyes, those gorgeous brown eyes with their intriguing flecks of gold, met his and then quickly lowered. "Come in."

Ben followed her into the studio, watching the sway of her hips under her long red sweater, which she wore with a calf-length black skirt printed all over with red poppies. Just looking at her made him smile.

"I'll just be a minute," she said, sitting at her control board.

Ben straddled a wooden chair beside her, rested his arms on the top rail with his chin on his fist so he could watch her every move as her voluptuous voice went out over the airwaves.

"The thermometer outside the WHAR studio this rainy night reads sixty degrees," she said, "and the barometer is holding steady. But skies are supposed to clear by morning, with temperatures rising into the low seventies by the afternoon. So if you're planning an outdoor activity tomorrow, hang in."

She lifted a clipboard. "Let's see what we've got for announcements. Ah, yes. Lillian Dumont from over on Billings Road says she still has two pups left out of her litter of beagles, so if you're interested, give her a call. The number's 2927." She put down the clipboard and did something mysterious with the knobs on the board. "And now here's a classic from the velvet fog himself, Mel Torme."

By the time she took off her headset, Ben was in something of a velvet fog himself. "You're very good at that, you know."

She smiled, blushing. "Thanks. Want some coffee?"

"No. I want to hear about Amber. What's this about an affair?"

Julia swiveled her chair toward him, folded her legs under her and arranged her skirt. "The person who called me is...someone who worked with Amber at the bank. She asked me not to divulge her identity, so if you don't mind, I'm just going to call her Jane Doe, all right?''

"Of course.''

"Anyway, she said she was a friend of Amber's and knew for a fact she was seeing their boss, Jeff Parker.''

"Jeff?'' Ben let out a long low whistle through his teeth.

"You know him?''

Ben nodded. "I play ball against his team, the Atlantic Trust.''

Julia smiled a little, enough to catapult his heart into the stratosphere. "Is there anybody who doesn't play basketball here?''

"Hey, there isn't much to do during the winter. Basketball, politics, church suppers...''

"Having affairs,'' Julia added on a groan, then she dropped her head into her hands. "I can't believe Amber was involved in something like that!''

"And with Jeff Parker yet! I'll be damned. He must be forty-five if he's a day.''

"Yes, but he's a well-preserved forty-five,'' Julia said with an admiration that annoyed Ben irrationally. "And he's very good-looking.''

"He's also very married,'' Ben reminded her.

"That's what my caller said. Three kids he adores, a big new house on Settlers Neck Road, and a wife who'd turn his life into a living hell if she ever found out he was cheating on her.'' Julia turned toward the console, cued up a tape and turned back.

"Was there a chance the wife was about to find out?'' Ben asked.

"Seems so. Jane Doe overheard Jeff and Amber arguing in his office last week. They were whispering, so she didn't catch everything they said, but it appeared he was trying to end the relationship. Amber was upset and threatening to go public with it if he did."

They looked at each other a long while, passing messages with their eyes, reluctant to speak them and make them real.

"Damn," Ben finally said. "Jeff seemed like such a nice guy, too. The perfect family man."

"To say nothing of his standing in the community. Isn't he head of the Chamber of Commerce?"

"Yup. He's on half a dozen other boards and committees, too, including at church. That's probably why his wife never found out about the affair. Couldn't keep track of his whereabouts."

Lights went on in Julia's eyes. Her back straightened. "Who says she never found out? Maybe she did. Maybe she's the one we should be suspecting."

Ben did—for about two seconds. "Hell, now you've got me doing it, jumping to conclusions just on the basis of motive. Motive's only part of the picture, Julia."

"Yes, I know, but as motives go, you have to admit the Parkers have dandies, especially Jeff. His wife's the one with the real money. He does okay at his job, but she can buy and sell him ten times over. Her lawyers'd clean his clock in a divorce settlement. The big ammunition, though, would be the kids. She'd probably take them back with her to Michigan, where she's from."

"How do you know all this?" Ben asked, no longer able to resist touching Julia's hair. He fingered a silky strand, then tucked it behind her ear.

"Jane Doe, the teller."

"Jane Doe, the gossip, is more like it," he said, giving the tip of her nose a playful brush with his index finger.

"No, I don't think so." Julia's source was a single

mother in need of keeping her job. She wouldn't jeopardize it just for the kick of gossiping.

"Did you get to call Charlie?"

"Yes."

"And what did he think?"

"He seemed surprised." Julia rubbed at the frown between her eyebrows. "He said he'd look into it, but...I don't know. Sometimes I wonder if maybe I made a mistake encouraging him to pursue this investigation. Maybe everybody would've been better off if he had turned it over to state investigators."

That was the course Ben would've preferred. In fact, he'd begun writing an editorial making that point for this week's issue of the *Record,* but then he'd sidelined it, figuring Charlie needed more than a couple of days to prove himself. If nothing developed by next week, though, the piece would definitely run. The people of Harmony couldn't afford to have any more time wasted.

Ben chose to keep this to himself, however. Despite what he thought of Charlie, he hated to see Julia's faith in the man shaken. She'd always trusted him, even when she'd trusted no one else.

"Mind if I pick out some music?" he asked, changing the subject.

"No. Be my guest."

Ben got up and went to the shelves of records. Julia turned her chair to watch him.

"I don't know why Jane Doe didn't call Charlie herself. I told people not to call here."

"It's because of your voice. The way you talk, the things you talk about. You make everything sound intimate and personal. People feel they know you." He glanced at her over his shoulder. "You must've heard that before."

Julia looked away. Yes, she'd heard it, but it had never felt quite the way it did now coming from Ben.

Ben pulled out an LP in a faded jacket and placed it on the table beside her. It was Johnny Mathis's *Heavenly,* a record that was almost forty years old and still one of the most romantic Ben had ever had the pleasure of hearing.

Julia bit her thumbnail when she saw it. "Do you want any particular cut from this?"

"Nope." He turned his chair around to face hers and sat. "They're all good."

He watched her place the record on the turntable, her hands trembling ever so slightly, her image reflected delicately on the rainy windows over the table. She pulled her chair closer, switched on the mike and for the next dozen heartbeats became Julia, the voice in the night, the stuff dreams are made of.

She chose the title cut, and after it began and she'd turned off her mike, Ben took her chair and swiveled it to face him. Her mouth dropped into an oval of surprise.

"So, is that the only reason you asked me over, to tell me Amber was having an affair?" He wanted her to admit there was more. He wanted her to say it, to make her feelings clear as day.

Julia stared at his chest. "I...I also wanted to ask if you think we should do something about it."

"No, you've done enough already, telling Charlie. Bow out of it now."

She nodded pensively, although whether or not she was agreeing with him was still a matter of debate. She felt strongly about Amber, and it was only natural for her to want to be personally involved in finding the murderer.

Ben leaned closer, moving his hands higher on the arms of her chair. "Anything else?"

She frowned, biting the corner of her lip.

"Well?" he prodded.

Why *had* she asked him over? Julia wondered. Was she nuts? She could have told him everything she knew about Amber's affair over the phone.

"I also wanted to continue that discussion we started yesterday at lunch."

"Which discussion?"

She wished Ben would back off. She felt hemmed in, surrounded by him, the way he was holding on to her chair. "The one about our seeing each other. After giving it some thought—" her voice quavered "—I've come to the conclusion it would be silly for us not to. I have eight whole days left here after tonight, and, well, we do seem to enjoy each other's company." She folded her hands in her lap to keep him from seeing how they trembled. "As long as we remember I'm leaving at the end of those eight days. What I'm asking is, do you think we can keep our friendship, um, contained?"

"Contained. You mean like an oil spill?"

"Yes." She lifted her eyes to his and found them smiling. He took her hands, raised them to his mouth and kissed each wildly pulsing wrist. "Was that contained enough for you?"

"Yes, that was fine," she said with barely any breath.

"And how about this?" he whispered, taking her by the arms and gently drawing her forward. She considered resisting, but after those kisses to her wrists, she didn't think she had enough strength.

They met as if in a dream, softly, his lips touching hers, hers accepting, neither asking more than a sharing of warmth before he pulled back. Chaste though the kiss was, it left her weak and wanting more.

His left eyebrow lifted. "How was that?"

"Will you please stop asking? I'm beginning to feel foolish."

Before she knew what was happening, he'd hauled her to her feet and wrapped her in a close embrace. Her breath whooshed out of her as she saw the smoldering intensity in his eyes. Lord, what had she done, giving him permission to stop asking?

The next moment she got her answer. His mouth descended on hers in a kiss that was nothing like the first. It coaxed, it seduced, it demanded. It spoke to her of need. She was abashed to find herself responding in kind, meeting Ben's intensity with her own.

"Wait," she gasped, pushing at his chest to put some space between them. Her heart was racing. "The song." She looked toward the turntable. "It's almost over."

With a sigh of frustration, Ben released her. She sank to her chair, trying to gather her wits, but when she gazed at the board, it was as if she'd never seen such a thing before.

Oh, yes. She reached for the tape she wanted to play next, but it slipped through her fingers and clattered to the floor. When she moved to pick it up, she only made things worse by kicking it out of reach. Time ran out. She fumbled with switches and knobs, aware that Ben was quietly moving from window to window, pulling down the shades. She lifted the needle off the record clumsily, making a scratching sound.

"Th-that was Johnny M-Mathis with the title cut from his, uh, all-time bestselling album, *Heavenly*," she stammered, as Ben came to stand behind her. When he lifted aside her hair and pressed his lips to her neck, she gasped. She prayed the sound didn't carry over the airwaves but feared it did.

His sigh skimmed over her cheek, warm and soft. His

teeth nipped at her right earlobe. She shuddered, losing her breath along with her powers of reasoning.

She gazed at the clock, thought about announcing the time. Gazed at the thermometer. Everything in front of her fuzzed over as Ben trailed openmouthed kisses along her neck to the hollow of her collarbone.

''Th-that was such a beautif-ful cut, why don't we just p-play another.'' She dropped the needle onto the record with another discordant scratch. Then, with a languor that was sure to perplex her audience, she drawled, ''This is Julie Lewis for WHAR radio.'' She turned, looking up at Ben like a drowning woman. ''Stay with me awhile.''

CHAPTER TEN

NO SOONER HAD JULIA switched off the microphone than Ben swung her chair around and kissed her. He was still standing over her, bending to her, and as they kissed, the chair tipped back precariously. She hardly noticed. She felt weightless, and if the chair fell over, she was sure she'd just keep floating in place.

"Oh, Lord," Ben said on a husky laugh, his lips still brushing hers, "this just keeps getting better and better." His gaze skimmed her face with the wonder of it.

"Ben," she whispered, running a finger down his cheek to the corner of his mouth.

He lifted her from the chair and drew her into his embrace once more. As the heat of their bodies melded, the emotion behind his eyes changed, moving from wonder to desire.

Julia curled one hand around his neck and drew him down to her, down to her kiss, down to her acceptance of this mysterious unbidden attraction between them. She sighed as their lips met, and the sigh turned to a moan as the kiss intensified.

All the while the music played on, weaving an atmosphere of romance. It was like a fantasy, she thought—the music, the rain drumming on the roof and a man so handsome that gazing at him made her weak—a fantasy she'd never seen herself a part of before.

And as the music played on, Ben grew bolder, each caress, each kiss sending surges of desire through her.

Julia didn't consider herself an innocent, although by modern standards her experience was probably modest. She'd had a brief affair with a young man in college—mostly out of curiosity, she realized in retrospect—and then there were Brian and David. But none of those relationships had been very satisfying. Until now abstinence had been an easy choice.

She hadn't known about *this,* she thought, this aching heaviness in her breasts, this heat burning deep inside her. Ben left her mouth and whispered kisses down her neck. She tilted back her head, arching into his touch, lifting herself to him. She heard his sharp intake of breath as his hand slipped under her sweater and closed over satin and lace, first one breast, then the other, circling, kneading, making them ache all the more.

"Julia, sweetheart," he said in a hoarse whisper, "there must be someplace more comfortable we can do this. I can't stay on my feet much longer."

She searched the studio through a passion-induced fog. Chairs. There was nothing in the studio but chairs.

His teeth nipped at her lower lip. "I don't suppose you want to leave."

"I can't. I have another hour."

With a grunt of frustration he ran his hands down her sides to her hips and pressed her to him. She almost puddled at his feet.

"Come here," he urged. He sat in her leather chair, drew her onto his lap and they resumed kissing. Before long they were both lost in the urgency rising through them.

The album was into the fifth cut when Julia became aware of a car rolling quietly into the yard. At the same time she also realized that she and Ben had somehow become rearranged. Her legs were now straddling his hips. Her skirt was rucked up to her thighs.

"Oh, no," she whispered, hearing the car engine idling. Ben dropped his forehead to her shoulder and tried to catch his breath. "You expecting someone?"

"No." She felt too lethargic to move. Nevertheless she struggled until she'd put a few inches between them and swung herself free.

Standing, she brushed her hair back with her fingers and fumbled under her sweater with the clasp of her bra. But then she heard the car slip into gear again and start backing up. She inched into the kitchenette and peeked out the window. It was a police cruiser. Charlie's.

Embarrassment flamed through her. It was obvious that Charlie had recognized Ben's Bronco and decided to leave. She wondered what he thought was going on in here. If he'd been listening to the radio, he'd heard the same album playing, song after song. She usually didn't do that.

What *had* been going on here? Julia wondered, touching her swollen lips and feeling the first stirrings of regret.

Ben came to stand behind her, lightly placing his hand over her shoulder. "Chief Slocum?" he asked.

"Mmm." She felt as though she'd somehow betrayed Charlie.

Ben turned her around, but she wouldn't look at him. He tipped up her chin, frowned as he scanned her face, then sighed. "You want to forget about what we were just doing?"

She swallowed with difficulty and nodded.

Stepping back, he sighed again, the grinding sound in his chest one of frustration. "That's okay," he said ruefully. "Contained, remember?"

She almost laughed. What a stupid idea. Had she really thought what she and Ben shared could be contained?

"Come on." He took her hand and urged her back into the studio. "I think your audience may've heard enough of Johnny Mathis for one night."

Ben stayed with her through the remainder of her show and beyond, just keeping her company. After she'd turned off the transmitter, they moved into the house, where he showed her how to operate the fireplace in Preston's living room.

She got out cheese and crackers and a bottle of wine, and as the fire blazed, chasing the dampness out of the drafty old house, they talked about themselves: their childhood, their schooling, their hobbies, their favorite books and movies, their pet peeves. The conversation seemed endlessly fascinating, and before either of them realized it, the brass ship's bell on the mantel was ringing 2:00 a.m.

Julia walked Ben to the door feeling there was still so much more to learn about him. But it was late and she was pushing her luck. Although they'd kept the late evening's activities limited to conversation, memories of what had happened earlier were always there.

"What are you doing tomorrow?" he said as he slipped on his jacket.

"Tomorrow..." She paused to collect her thoughts. "Tomorrow night I'm supposed to be having dinner at Cathryn's. Other than that, I'm not sure."

"How about coming kayaking with me? I have a double seater."

"Kayaking?" She eyed him dubiously.

He smiled. "It's easy. I guarantee you'll love it."

"You do, huh?" Actually the way he was looking at her, Julia would've agreed to hanging by her heels over a pit of vipers.

"It'll get your mind off what's been going on around here lately, too."

"Okay, but give me the morning to myself," she said, suddenly remembering she had a few things to do, including calling Jake Normandin.

"Sure. Come to think of it—" he laughed in chagrin "—I need the morning, too. How could I forget?" He looked at her in a way that made her feel she was to blame.

"What's on your plate for the morning?" she asked, confused by her desire to know what was happening with him every minute.

"Gotta go to work. Usually the paper's ready to go to the printer by Friday afternoon, but because of the unexpected news this week, we're running late. The front page needed to be redesigned, new articles had to be written, space found for some added pictures—that sort of thing. As a consequence, work's spilled over into Saturday."

Front page redesigned? New articles? Pictures? Julia wondered what sort of splash Ben was aiming to make out of Amber's murder.

"Don't worry. You'll like the results. One of my reporters has written a great profile of Amber, with quotes from several people who knew her, including some old teachers. She scrounged up some good pictures, too. Amber as a beauty queen. Amber at the last Fourth of July parade. Another staff member is putting together a piece on the history of crime on the island, with a centerfold spread of old photographs borrowed from the historical society."

"And what are *you* adding to the effort?" She still felt uneasy with the idea of a special edition.

"I've written the hard news, the lead article."

"I see. And are you including the delay in the autopsy?"

He didn't mince words. "Yes. I don't know any way to get around it, Julia. It's a vital part of the story."

Her heart sank. Ben lifted her chin, his October-blue eyes reaching into hers. "Relax. I was careful not to lay blame on anyone. Right now Charlie needs a reprieve, not another battle to fight.''

She eyed him guardedly. "How much of a reprieve?"

"Oh, I don't know. Another week maybe, then I'll take off the gloves."

He hadn't withdrawn his hand from her chin yet. Julia was consummately aware of his fingers lightly tracing the slope of her jaw. She also knew he wasn't much interested in talking about the paper anymore. Other thoughts were shining in his eyes, thoughts of kissing her, and before long she, too, was lost in similar thoughts. But she knew it wasn't a good idea. One kiss would lead to another, and before either of them realized it, they'd be involved in something they'd regret for a long time to come.

She took a deliberate step away from him and folded her arms. "So what time should I be ready?"

Reading her body language, Ben sighed in resignation. "How about noon? And don't have lunch. I'll pack us a picnic."

"Okay."

His gaze flicked over her one last regretful time. "See you tomorrow."

JULIA PHONED Jake Normandin early the next morning. On the second ring a familiar husky voice said, "Jake here."

"Jake! Hi, it's Julia Lewis."

The line was silent for a moment. She imagined he was trying to place her. "Julia!" he finally said. "Hey, how the hell are ya, babe?"

"Great. Yourself?" She tried to picture what he looked like these days, with ten years added to his burly build and open good-natured face.

"Can't complain."

For a while they talked about their work and where they

lived and the tragedy of Amber's death, and then, after they'd touched on everything the way old friends do, Julia explained the reason for her call.

Jake thought a get-together sounded like fun.

"Who else is coming?"

"So far, of the nine of us we've got five firm yes's— me, Cathryn, Mike Fearing, Tyler O'Banyon and Barry Devine. The others are still trying to clear their schedules."

"What's the plan again?"

"Well, Cathryn is hoping people can get here by Friday night. That way we can gather at her place the next morning for brunch and spend the entire day together. Spouses and dates are, of course, welcome."

"Sounds good. Sure, count me in."

"Great. Think of it as a chance to visit with your sister, too. You might even be able to bunk in with her, save yourself the cost of a hotel room."

Jake was quiet a moment. "Yeah, maybe, though Nicole and I aren't on the best of terms these days."

Julia knew the polite thing would be to let the matter lie, but curiosity wouldn't let her. "What happened?"

"Nothing really, except that I don't speak to my kid brother anymore, and she's mad at me about that. She always had a soft spot for Chris. They're just a year apart."

"What happened between you and Chris?"

The line seemed to vibrate with Jake's long sigh. "The kid turned stupid after he moved off-island. Got into trouble and came to me to help him out. And of course I did."

"Anything serious?" she asked hesitantly.

"Serious enough. Grand-theft auto, breaking and entering. Then one day he shows up on my doorstep, saying he's reformed and looking for a job. So I get a buddy of mine who owns a fishing boat to take him on as a deckhand. It was a good job, at sea three or four days a week, in port the rest, good money. But Chris, genius that he is, found a way to blow it.''

''How'd he do that?'' Julia asked, too involved in the story now to be concerned about prying.

''Drugs. There are a lot of 'em floating around the waterfront. Big problem these days. I got sick of bailing him out for possession. The last time I did I told him he was on his own. I was cutting him loose. That was almost two years ago. So far I've stuck to my word.''

''And is he okay?''

''I don't know. He's moved down the Cape, bought a little boat. Some of the guys say he's still fishing. But if you want more details, you'll have to ask Nicky.''

Julia twirled a strand of her hair around her finger. ''I saw her the other day.''

''Nicky?''

''Uh-huh. She's dating Bruce Davoll.''

''Yeah, I heard. Another one who's turned stupid,'' he muttered. Julia assumed he was referring to his sister.

''I think I might've offended Nicole by letting her know I was worried about her. You know, for dating Bruce. I told her I'd be available if she ever needed help.''

''Why'd you do that?''

''I don't know. I just felt bad for her. She seems so vulnerable, all alone here, with no family on the island.''

''I appreciate your concern, Julia, but Nicky's tougher than she looks.''

''I hope so. Bruce is a mighty big guy.''

Jake sighed again. ''All right, I'll give her a call, make sure she's okay. That make you feel better?''

''Infinitely.''

As soon as they'd said goodbye, Julia called Cathryn to tell her to add Jake's name to the guest list.

''That's great. I always liked Jake.''

"Mmm," Julia agreed, thinking how strange it was that three siblings, raised in the same home by the same parents, had turned out so differently.

She was about to close the conversation and get on with her chores when Cathryn said, "Before I hang up I should mention one thing."

Julia knew just from Cathryn's tone that she was grinning her I-did-something-clever grin. "What's that, Cath?"

"I invited Ben to dinner, too. He's going to pick you up around quarter to six."

As Cathryn's words registered, Julia felt a strange sensation. She couldn't pinpoint exactly what it was, but something inside her seemed to shift—like a fuzzy focus becoming clear or a tilted horizon straightening. *Now* the evening would be right, it seemed to say.

"Is that okay?" Cathryn asked after a stretch of silence.

"Sure, I don't mind." Julia's calmness was deceptive. Beneath it she was shaken. She'd never felt such a sense of well-being and completeness at the mere mention of a man's name.

"Okay. I'll see you at six, then," Cathryn said.

"Yes. Take care." Julia hung up the phone. Afraid to think about the implications of the last minute, she moved immediately on to her next task.

BEN FLEXED his aching shoulder muscles under the warm spray of his shower and sighed luxuriously. He couldn't remember the last time he'd enjoyed a Saturday so much.

He'd picked Julia up at noon, then driven to Cook Pond, where they'd spent the afternoon in the kayak gliding through the marshes and tributaries and secluded off-shoot ponds. The weather had cooperated beautifully, too. Blue sky. Warm autumn sun. No wind.

They'd come ashore on a protected stretch of sand, enjoyed a picnic lunch of pasta salad, chicken and wine, and almost fell asleep in the sun.

Julia told him she'd never done anything like kayaking at Cook Pond before. She'd ice-skated there a few times when she was a girl, but that was all. Ben had delighted in introducing her to the sport. His biggest delight, though, came from watching her expressive face as she discovered the treasures that kayaking there revealed: the flora on the boggy shores, the egrets and herons high-stepping through the shallows, the migratory birds winging over the reeds.

Ben had dropped her off just an hour ago so that they could shower and change for dinner, but already he missed her.

He stepped out of the shower and toweled himself dry, then took his razor out of the cabinet over the sink and prepared to shave for the second time that day.

He and Julia had been careful to keep their behavior restrained, as she'd asked. The only tricky stretch had come after lunch, when they'd lain back on the blanket, basking in the warm fall sun. He'd kissed her, but he'd wanted to do a lot more. Lovemaking was out of the question, though. She'd told him that point-blank. When they parted, she wanted it to be with as few regrets as possible.

But as he looked at himself in the mirror, he wondered if he was capable of lasting another week. He'd already decided his biggest regret would be that they hadn't made love while they had the chance.

He finished shaving, brushed his damp hair, then moved to the bedroom to dress. Still restless and having time to spare before picking Julia up, he decided to make the call that had been on his mind intermittently all day.

He sat on the bed, reached for the phone and punched in Scott Bowen's number.

"Scott? Ben Grant."

The young cop sounded winded and explained he'd just been lifting weights. Otherwise he seemed pleased enough to hear Ben's voice.

Ben congratulated him for pushing for the autopsy, especially considering how it had turned out.

"Wasn't that something," Scott said, sounding amazed.

"You're gonna be a good cop, Scott," Ben said. "You have good instincts."

"Thanks. So what's up?"

"What do you think of the drug the autopsy turned up? Do you have any idea where it came from?"

"I wish I did. I saw a lot of drugs on the island this summer, but mostly it was pot, coke, that sort of thing. Nothing like roofies."

Ben scowled. "I must be running in the wrong circles. There're a lot of drugs here?"

"In the summer, yeah. Especially this past summer. More than usual."

"Island people?"

"Nah. Mostly vacationers, kids on the beach who come over on the ferry, people on their boats in the harbor."

"Scott, how would a person like me find out about roofies? Who's selling them. Where they've cropped up recently. Who's been arrested."

"You might ask a person like me."

"Could I?"

"Sure. I don't know the answers right now, but I could make a few calls, maybe search the police computer files." He paused. "Why do you need to know? Has old Lard-butt deputized you or something?"

"Or something."

The kid laughed.

"Actually I'm just impatient," Ben said. "Trying to hustle this investigation along."

"Well, if you stumble across anything important, make sure you pass it on to the right people."

"I will. I'm under no delusions that I'm anything but a reporter."

"Good. You'll live longer that way."

"My thoughts exactly."

"I'll get back to you as soon as I can."

"Thanks a lot, Scott."

IT WAS A WEIRD SENSATION for Julia, visiting Cathryn and Dylan with Ben.

Cathryn had started dating Dylan when she was just a freshman in high school and he was a senior. Against all odds, they remained a couple throughout his four years of college and were married the summer after he finished. They'd settled on Harmony and, in the years that followed, bought a house, gave birth to three beautiful children and established a prosperous landscaping business. Cathryn and Dylan were as married as married could get, and sitting at their table with Ben, Julia felt the forces of couplehood pressing down on her, molding her in the McGraths' vibrant reflected image.

It was Ben's presence that did it. Had she come alone, she wouldn't have had any problem. She would've just been herself. But as soon as she'd walked through the door with Ben, she'd seen the don't-you-make-an-adorable-couple gleam in Cathryn's eye. Cathryn hadn't said a word, but the look was there, and from that point on Julia knew that everyone, right down to five-year-old Bethany, was thinking of them as Ben-and-Julia.

Julia resisted it. They were not a couple. They were two separate individuals who just happened to hit it off while she was home for a short visit. When she left that would be the end of it. Maybe they'd phone or write each other for a while, but eventually time would wear away whatever ties bound them, and even the writing would stop.

The trouble was, although Julia resisted the idea of couplehood, she couldn't rout it out. Especially when she saw how well Ben fit in with Cathryn and Dylan.

He knew them of course. After purchasing the newspaper building he'd hired Dylan to prune a damaged tree on the property. He and Dylan had struck up a friendship during the job, and from there it had been an easy step to socializing with the movable-feast crowd.

But he didn't know Cathryn and Dylan's children, and the way he'd charmed his way into their hearts—and video games—within fifteen minutes of his arrival only showed what a family man he was...or might be one day. When Cathryn made a remark to that regard, he shrugged and said he'd had practice with his nieces and nephews.

After dinner the men helped clear the table and then went down to the basement rec room with the boys to play a game of table hockey, while Julia and Cathryn oversaw Bethany's bath. Even from the bathroom, though, male voices could still be heard, cheering and howling.

"Men!" Bethany said, pressing her lips in mimicry of adult exasperation as she sat in four inches of water topped by three more of bubble-bath foam. Puffs of foam decorated her shoulders and chin and curls.

Sitting on the floor by the tub, Julia burst out laughing and had all she could do not to hug the child, soapsuds and all. The impulse was disconcerting. But then, she'd been feeling it all evening. Maybe she was just changing with age. Younger, she hadn't given children much thought. But with little Beth sitting on her lap during dessert and calling her Auntie Julia, she'd been one big lump of maternal feelings.

"Auntie Julia," the child said now, "are you gonna marry Ben?"

Bethany's query came out of nowhere and had Julia stammering. "Uh, gee, no, honey."

"Why not? Don't you like him?"

"Well, yes, I do. But I live faraway and he lives here."

"Oh." Bethany scooped up a mound of bubbles and clapped her hands, sending them spraying. "Can't you move here?"

Julia looked at Cathryn for help, but Cathryn seemed just as eager as her daughter to hear Julia's answer.

"No, honey. There's no work for me here."

Bethany slid down into the water until the bubbles tickled her chin. "*Ben* could work, like my Dad, and you could stay home and take care of your children."

Julia felt an ache she didn't expect. Her children.

Barely missing a beat, she pulled herself together. "But I like to work."

"Better than you like Ben?"

That question had Julia stymied again.

Cathryn came to her rescue. "I think it's time you stopped bugging Auntie Julia and got out of that water. You're as shriveled as a little old raisin."

The five-year-old swished around some more, procrastinating. It took a threat of no bedtime story to finally get her out.

"Sorry about the third degree," Cathryn said on the way down the stairs after Bethany had been tucked in.

"That's okay. She's not old enough to understand."

"I don't know about that." Cathryn gave a doubtful shrug. "Out of the mouths of babes..."

They crossed the living room and entered the kitchen. Cathryn stood at the top of the basement stairs and called down to the boys, saying they had fifteen more minutes.

"Care for another cup of coffee, Julia?" she said, lifting the pot from its warmer plate.

"Sure." Julia took the mug Cathryn handed her, a frown pinching her brow. "Cath, doesn't it ever worry you, being totally dependent on Dylan financially?"

Cathryn pulled out a chair and sat down opposite Julia. "As I see it, he's just as dependent on me. It's an equal partnership. Do you realize how much it would cost him to hire someone to do everything I do? And even at top dollar, nobody would do as good a job, because I work out of love."

Julia stared at Cathryn, whose life had been as sheltered as hers had been unsheltered. *But what if he left you?* she thought. *How would you pay the mortgage and put food on your table? And what would happen to your kids while you were out trying to make a living?* She couldn't bring herself to say it, though. Couldn't put that fear in her friend.

"I guess I just can't imagine it for myself. I remember how difficult things were for my mother. I can't shake the fear of being hung out to dry."

Cathryn's apple-cheeked face became drawn with concern. "Not all men are like your father, Julia."

"But enough are. The divorce rate is fifty percent in this country."

"Yes, but some of those divorces are initiated by wives."

"Which just goes to prove you can't trust love." Julia paused, realizing how negative she sounded. "I'm sorry. Here you are, soundly married, and I'm bad-mouthing everything that makes your life so wonderful. What a jerk."

Cathryn held her mug to her smile. "I'm not offended. I'm just sitting here wondering why you're so defensive tonight."

Julia felt transparent. She tipped her head forward, hoping her long hair would conceal the flush in her cheeks. "I do like him, Cath."

"Well, heck, that's obvious." She chuckled.

"It's scary. I've always been a confirmed single. Sure, I enjoy the company of men, and I've even had a couple of long-term relationships. But I've never had the slightest urge to live with one of those men, never mind marry one."

"Until now?"

Julia's cheeks burned hotter. "Oh gosh, no. I didn't mean that." Why had she said it, then? she wondered. "No. I've only known Ben a week. Of course I'm not thinking that far ahead."

"But you are falling in love with him, aren't you?"

Julia frowned. Falling in love? Is that what was happening to her? She'd thought it was just a strong physical attraction.

"Don't look so distressed." Cathryn laughed. "It's really not so bad."

Fortunately the four males came pounding up the basement stairs just then and the uncomfortable subject was put aside.

Ben and Julia stayed at the McGraths' till nearly eleven o'clock. With the delicious food and warm hospitality, it was a place that was hard to leave.

"They're a nice couple," Ben said, driving away.

Julia only nodded.

"Nice kids, too."

Again just a nod.

After a while Ben said, "Something wrong?"

"No. What could be wrong?" Except that she'd begun to wonder what it would be like to live that life herself. She'd begun to toy with the idea of her being someone's wife, someone's mother. Moreover, she was beginning to feel actual longings for those things: the joy of holding her own child, the thrill and comfort of slipping into bed with a man who'd be there in the morning, tomorrow and next month and forty years from now.

Julia passed her hand across her damp brow and tried to gather her composure. Now was not the time to start examining her life or creating new priorities. She was obviously under the spell of all that domestic bliss she'd encountered at Cathryn's. A good night's sleep, a little distance, and she'd be back to her normal cynical self.

She'd have to put some distance between her and Ben, as well, because Cathryn was right: she *was* falling in love with him. When she thought of children, they were *his* children. When she imagined sharing her life with a man, Ben was the only man who came to mind. Which was crazy of course, considering how short a time they'd known each other. She was acting no saner than a lovestruck teenager who writes the name of a boy she hardly knows over and over in the margins of her notebook.

Ben parked the car in front of the breezeway and came around her side to open her door. The night was clear and quiet, the moon full and shining on the water like a spilled bridal veil. A perfect end to a lovely day.

She unlocked the door, but didn't step inside. If she did, if he followed, she might not have the willpower to send him away. She turned to say good-night on the doorstep.

"Thanks for coming by for me tonight." She didn't realize she was squeezing and twisting the strap of her shoulder bag until Ben took her hands in his and brought them to his lips.

"My pleasure," he said, his breath warming her knuckles. Slowly he drew her to him, enfolding her in his arms. Because she was on the step, their eyes were on a level.

"What are you doing tomorrow?" His voice was low and husky, his gaze heavy-lidded.

With Ben pressed so intimately against her, Julia couldn't think. Tomorrow? What was tomorrow?

"How about a long lazy brunch at the Surf Hotel?" he asked, his lips feathering over her right temple. "They make the best crepes in the world." He kissed her ear. "With wild blueberries." He kissed her neck. "And fresh cream."

Her answering whimper had nothing to do with the menu he was describing and everything to do with the way his lips were brushing her jaw. She whispered, "Yes," and he whispered, "Good." But the words were smothered as his mouth closed over hers.

The kiss was incendiary. When they finally broke apart, Julia was breathing so rapidly and shallowly she grew light-headed. And she wondered how this marvelous disaster had happened. Why now? Why him?

"Maybe we should take this inside," he whispered.

Inside? Oh, she wanted to, but even if she and Ben had no impediments to a relationship, she would've thought they were moving too fast.

He held his breath, pulled his head back to focus on her. "What?" he asked warily.

"Maybe we should just say good-night."

His exhalation seemed to come from his toes. He unclasped his hands from around her back and stepped away.

"I'm sorry," she said, her throat dry. "Again."

He shook his head. "We're not teenagers, Julia. It's been a long time since I had to make do with necking on the porch."

Illogically his statement hurt. "Oh, really. I didn't realize you made it a policy to sleep with everyone you took out."

"That's not what I said."

"That's how it sounded."

He pinched the bridge of his nose, closed his eyes. When

he opened them again, he seemed calmer. "Okay, you're right. Maybe we should end it here."

"I just don't want either of us to be hurt."

"I understand." He tried to smile, but it was clearly forced.

"Are you still up for brunch?" she asked hesitantly.

"Sure." He looked aside, the corners of his mouth tight. "I'll come by for you at ten."

A moment later he'd driven away.

JULIA HAD JUST TURNED OFF her bedside light when she heard a car slowly making its way up the driveway. She sat up, her heart quickening. Was Ben returning? Why would he do that?

She slipped out of bed, threw on a robe over her nightgown and hurried down the stairs. But when she reached the front door, she realized it wasn't Ben's Bronco. She could tell by the height of the headlights. As it pulled up in front of the porch, she saw it was a different kind of vehicle entirely, not a sport utility at all but a Saab sedan.

She clutched the neck of her robe, wishing she'd pulled on some clothes. She felt vulnerable dressed as she was. Alone as she was. Especially when Jeff Parker, Amber's married lover, emerged from the automobile.

CHAPTER ELEVEN

JULIA FELT A CHILL shoot up her spine. What was Jeff Parker doing here at this hour of the night? What would he be doing here at any hour? They didn't know each other personally.

Standing with the inner door open, she darted a glance at the aluminum storm door in front of her. It was unlocked. Her head pounded as her fingers fumbled, trying to slide the small latch into the lock position. It seemed corroded in place. With enormous effort she finally got it to move. That done, she slowed her breathing, consciously working the nervous ripples out of it the way she'd taught herself when she'd first gone live over the air.

Parker hadn't seen her yet. In fact, he hadn't quite gotten out of his car yet. Half in, half out, he wrestled with a tan windbreaker, apparently trying to put it on. After several unsuccessful attempts, he gave up and tossed it across the seat.

Julia wondered what was the matter with him. Was he hurt? But then he was out of the car and straightening to his full height, which was considerable, and Julia noticed him sway. He clutched the car, one hand on the open door, one on the roof. After a moment he turned, carefully, and started for the front-porch steps. The car door remained opened, a warning bell dinging somewhere in the lighted interior. He'd probably left his keys in the ignition.

While he climbed the stairs and carefully crossed the

porch, Julia looked over her shoulder to gauge the distance to the phone. He raised his knuckles to rap on the door and then frowned when he realized that she was looking out at him through the glass. His eyes narrowed and he said with exaggerated care, "Miss Lewis. I'm Jeffrey R. Parker, vice president of the Harmony branch of Atlantic Trust and Savings."

"Yes, I know," Julia said. "What do you want?"

She wondered why she wasn't more alarmed, why she hadn't dashed over to the phone and called Ben or Charlie yet. Curiosity maybe. She did want to know why he was here. Besides, she'd handled drunks before, even aggressive drunks, and in his current state, Jeff Parker didn't seem too much of a threat.

Still, she was alone, it was night, and her assessment of him might be wrong.

"I've got to talk to you," he said too loudly.

"It's awfully late, Mr. Parker."

He wagged his head. "Gotta talk. Right now!"

Despite his condition, Julia could understand why Amber had been attracted to him. He was tall and well-toned, with sun-tipped sandy hair and a deep golden tan enhancing his patrician features.

"What about?" she asked.

"What about? What th'hell do you think about? 'Bout Amber, of course. Amber'n me." He leaned his head back as if Julia had gone out of focus, then narrowed his eyes again to bring her back.

Julia debated playing ignorant—for about two seconds. She wouldn't evade the issue. "If you're referring to the fact that you and Amber were having an affair, yes, I know what you're talking about."

"Damn right you do. An' you're the one who tol' Chief Slocum, too." He paused, obviously thinking about what he'd just said. When he looked at her again, it was with a clarity of vision that made her breath hitch.

"Chief Slocum spoke to you? About you and Amber?"

He dipped his head in an exaggerated nod. "During bank hours, too. Customers out front, people who know me, know my wife." Parker gave the door handle a couple of clumsy tugs. When it didn't open, he swore under his breath.

Stay calm, Julia told herself. *You have to get to the bottom of this.* "What makes you think *I* told Charlie?"

"Because no one else knew. Amber and I were es-es-tremely discreet." Something in his tone tugged at her memory. She'd spoken to Jeff Parker somewhere before— or heard him speak. And then it came to her. He was the caller who'd requested "The Lady in Red" during her first show last week.

"If you were so discreet, how in the world did I find out?" she asked.

Parker looked uncertain for a moment, but then said, "Ah!" as if he'd just noticed a thought scurrying across his mind. "Amber wrote you a letter. I saw it myself on her kitchen table. I tol' her to rip it up, but she said she couldn't stan' you not knowing about us. You were her best friend, she said, and she wanted you to know how happy she was. Besides, you were so far away who would you tell? I said no. I said it over and over, don't send it. But she didn't listen."

Julia was about to tell him the truth of the matter when she remembered she couldn't. Her source was an employee of his who'd asked to remain anonymous.

She shrugged. "I guess there's no point in denying it."

He stared at her, his lips pressing until they were colorless. "Well, I just want you to know that what you did was low."

It took her a moment to figure out he was referring to her sharing the news with Charlie.

"What *I* did?" She pressed her fingertips to her chest. "You're the one who had the affair."

"That's nobody's business, you hear me?" His eyes again seemed too focused for comfort, and again, Julia reassessed her idea that Jeff Parker, drunk, was no threat. A vein was throbbing at his temple and his hands had tightened into fists. "Not yours, not Charlie Slocum's, not even my wife's. Nobody's."

He shook one of his fists so close to the door she feared the glass might crack. "You tell anybody else or say one word on that damn radio program of yours, an'…an' you'll regret it the rest of your life."

Barely breathing, Julia inched back a little. "Is that a threat, Mr. Parker?"

"You better believe it."

She did. "I think you should leave now, unless you want to be here when the police arrive."

"You leave the police out of this. I'm warning you."

He started to go but then turned back. "I mean it. You shut your mouth. You've done enough damage."

Then he made his way down the steps to his car. Julia was too shaken to worry about him driving drunk. Besides, for someone who'd obviously overindulged, he had remarkable control. That thought rattled her most of all.

After he was gone, Julia went through every room in the house, bolting windows and turning on lights. Unable to go back to bed, she sat on the sofa in the living room with all the window shades drawn and again contemplated calling Charlie or Ben.

But it was late, and what would she say? Jeff Parker had shown up at her door drunk? That wasn't exactly a crime. Besides, what did she expect Ben or Charlie to do? She'd already handled the matter. Parker was gone and she was fine. Fine, she told herself, sitting on the edge of the couch, her fingers digging into the cushion, her senses attuned to every little sound outside in the night.

She jumped when the telephone in the kitchen shrilled. Her heart sped. It was after midnight. Who'd be calling her at this hour? Was it Jeff Parker again? *Please, please don't let it be Parker,* she thought as she reached for the phone.

"Yes?" she said, trying to sound assertive.

"Julia?"

She sagged against the wall. "Ben!"

BEN HELD THE RECEIVER to his ear and frowned. Julia had said his name the way a person might say, "Thank God!"

"Hi. I'm sorry to be calling at this hour. I really don't have an excuse..." How could he explain the reason for this call when he didn't understand it himself?

He'd been restless after dropping her off. Restless, sexually frustrated and verging on a melancholy the roots of which he didn't comprehend. He'd come home, made himself a drink, then stretched out on the couch with the dullest book he could find.

Evidently he'd fallen asleep, because the next thing he'd known, the book had slid off his chest and thumped on the floor. He'd opened his eyes and sat up, his thoughts immediately on Julia, and while that wasn't unusual these days, tonight his thoughts were also full of uneasiness.

He'd gotten up, stretched and started for the stairs, intent on going to bed. But then it had come again, that queasy intimation that all was not well over on Peggoty Hill. Worse, that Julia was in some sort of danger.

He'd tried to dismiss the feeling, but it dogged him, and before long, he was dialing her number—and hoping he wasn't making a fool of himself.

"Did I wake you?" he asked.

"No, I was just…just sitting here, um, reading."

Just sitting. Reading. Great. Now what was he supposed to say?

"This is really funny," she said before he could come up with a response. "I was thinking of calling you, too."

The back of Ben's neck prickled. "Any particular reason?"

"Mmm. I had company after you left."

The prickles turned to spears of alarm as Julia went on to tell him about her visit from Jeff Parker. By the time she finished, he was sure his blood pressure was sky-high.

"I'm coming over. You're not spending the night in that house all alone."

"Don't be silly, Ben. He won't be back. He's probably gone home and passed out on his front steps."

"Did you call Charlie?"

"No. What am I supposed to say? Jeff Parker came over drunk and upset?"

"Yes. And he threatened you."

She sighed. "Okay, I will."

"When?"

"Tomorrow morning?"

"No. Tonight, right after we get off the phone." He knew she was going to resist. "And if you don't, I will."

"Oh, all right!"

"Good. And while you're doing that, I'll be on my way over."

"No."

"Julia, for crying out loud, stop being such a pain in the rump. We're not talking about someone who's a simple nuisance. This guy could've killed somebody, and now he's angry at you."

She was quiet a while, barely breathing. Why had he

said that? Did he really believe Jeff Parker was capable of murder?

"It really is unnecessary, Ben, but okay, if it'll make you feel better."

"It will. See you in a few minutes."

JULIA PLACED TWO CUPS of hot cider on the small kitchen table, then sat down opposite Ben, all her movements graceful in spite of the tension in her face.

"So," Ben said, "did Jeff say anything else?"

Julia picked up her cup and held it to her lips. "No, and I could kick myself now for not drawing him out. I could have done it, too—he was drunk enough. I could've asked him all about the affair, how it began, how it ended, how he felt about Amber's death—all sorts of things. But instead, I panicked and told him to leave or I'd call the police. Dammit! I blew a golden opportunity."

Ben reached across the table and bracketed her hands, the mug between them, with his. "You did exactly the right thing. I wish you hadn't opened your door at all."

She frowned, still regretful. "That's what Charlie said when I called him."

Ben ran his fingers over the backs of her hands. He'd thought they'd be roughened from their afternoon on the water, but they were as smooth as the moonlight sliding in the window behind her.

"Speaking of Charlie, what's he going to do about Jeff's visit? Did he say?"

Julia pulled free of his hold and sat back. "He isn't going to do anything overt. He doesn't want Jeff to know I reported the incident. For my safety, he says. He's going to keep an eye on him, though."

Ben was unsure whether Charlie was showing prudence or just a lack of backbone, Jeff Parker being who he was.

"When Charlie questioned him earlier, did he say where he was the night Amber was murdered?"

Julia nodded. "He claims he was going to a meeting of the preservation society but got a flat tire on the way. He didn't have a spare, so he had to walk home for a pump. By the time he got rolling again, the meeting was over and he just decided to pack it in. Of course nobody actually saw him doing any of this. But he swore to Charlie that's what happened."

"I don't suppose Charlie has any other evidence to implicate him."

"If he has he didn't mention it. I doubt he has any, though. When Jeff was here, he wasn't angry about being considered a suspect. He was just concerned about news of the affair spreading."

"Well, maybe that's all he's guilty of, an affair."

"Yes. Maybe."

Uncertainty hung thick in the air between them, however.

Julia dropped her head into her hands and groaned softly. "Poor Amber. She always had such lousy judgment when it came to men, even when we were kids. I was always trying to talk her out of one foolish crush or another. Usually in the summer. She fell in love so easily in summer." Julia lifted her head and sat back, meeting Ben's interested gaze.

"I have no doubt she was deeply in love with Jeff Parker. Even in the condition he was in tonight, he showed a certain gentility. He has money and class. He's a respected authority figure, a family man, devoted father. Coming off somebody like Bruce, Amber must've seen him as a prince."

"Maybe he was."

"Maybe. For a while." Julia's face tightened as if in

pain. Ben knew she was wondering if Amber's prince had also been her murderer.

"She could get so mixed up at times. I wish—" Julia bit her lower lip.

"What, Julia? What do you wish?"

"That we hadn't lost touch." She swallowed.

"Why did you?"

She stared at her hands for a long while. "Oh, you know. Amber had her life here, her family, her marriage. I wasn't a part of that anymore."

Ben wanted to continue probing. He felt she'd just let him see a glimpse of what lay behind all that protective armor she usually wore. But she didn't give him the chance.

"Oh, by the way, I told Charlie you were coming over," she said, obviously intent on moving on.

"You did?"

Julia smiled as she nodded. "He didn't want to admit it, seeing how it was you, but he was relieved I wouldn't be spending the night alone."

Ben chuckled. "Charlie and I might turn out to be friends yet."

"Don't count on it. He said to tell you to watch your step, or there'd be hell to pay."

"And if I don't watch my step, are you going to tell on me?"

"Absolutely."

Ben made an exaggerated production of falling back as if wounded.

Smiling, Julia finished her cider and stood up. "I'm going to bed. I'm still wired, but staying up's not doing me any good."

Ben scraped back his chair. "And where should I sleep?" He tried to keep the question unencumbered by straying thoughts, but that was impossible. Talking with

Julia here in this cozy kitchen late at night, huddled at a table that had probably seen generations of couples sitting in just such a way, he couldn't help wondering what it would be like if they *were* a couple, if he *could* climb the stairs with her and slip into her bed and not have to worry about tomorrow.

"You can use the sofa in the living room. I'll get you a pillow and a couple of blankets."

"There isn't a second bed?"

"There is, but—" she smirked "—since you insist on playing bodyguard, I think you should stay on the ground floor, where you can be near the action if anyone tries to storm the castle."

He hated to admit it, but she had a point.

She started for the front hall. "Oh, by the way, the bathroom's upstairs. It's the only one in the house."

Ben nodded. "Just leave the blankets in the hallway, then. I'll get them when I go up. I'm going to check the grounds first."

Julia yawned. "Thanks. Good night, Ben."

Ben went outside and walked around the house, checking the cellar entrance and all the doors and windows. Then he examined the area around the garage, the toolshed and the old barn. As he walked, his eyes constantly lifted and studied the rolling moonlit landscape and all the scrub growth that stubbled it, from here to the ragged edges of the cliffs in the distance. At regular intervals the beam from the lighthouse flicked over him, then swept out to sea.

He walked around the house a second time, mostly to give Julia time to get settled, maybe even fall asleep before he went in. He didn't need the temptation of her being awake when he climbed the stairs.

On the back side of the studio he paused, leaning against the rough cedar shingles under the windows Julia looked through while she did her show. It was an awe-inspiring view, although a little too lonely for his taste. There was barely a human marking in sight, just the lighthouse to the east and a couple of points of light on the ocean that were probably ships.

For a moment he wondered what went through her mind as she sat at her board looking out over this landscape. She claimed she liked it here, and when she said it, she usually used the same defensive tone as when she claimed she liked her solitary self-sufficient life. Unmarried. Uncommitted to any one community or group of friends. Unattached to any one job.

But Ben wondered.

I wish we hadn't lost touch...

And then it hit him. Julia was a fake, a great big phony. She wanted love and human connectedness so badly it scared the bejesus out of her. It didn't take a genius to figure out the reason, either. Wasn't one's childhood always the reason? With a father who'd abandoned her and a mother too busy to pay attention, little wonder her distrust of intimacy ran so deep.

Only in her work did she make an exception. Ben looked up and could almost imagine her voice a visible thing, like a beam of light, traveling through the empty night, reaching out to touch others. Broadcasting. Casting herself into the darkness. It connected her. It filled the void.

And he was glad. At least she had that. Still, he couldn't imagine her going her entire life that way, and he wished she wasn't so afraid to connect in a more personal way.

A skittering in the bushes scattered Ben's thoughts. He pushed away from the wall, his shoulders tensed. The shadow came first, long and menacing under the full moon, then the culprit himself—a wild rabbit, who hopped onto the lawn and started to nibble the grass.

Ben shook his head. When he started jumping at rabbit shadows, it was clearly time to call it a night.

Once inside the house, he locked the front door, went into the living room for his gym bag, then climbed the stairs, trying not to disturb Julia. She'd left the hall light on, but the light in her room was off.

The next-to-top stair squeaked, followed by a corresponding mattress squeak. He paused, listening, and when he heard no further noise, continued on past her door and the pillow and blankets she'd left outside it.

He thought he was extraordinarily quiet using the bathroom, but when he was creeping past Julia's room again, he heard the mattress give again.

"Ben?"

His heart banged out a cadence that seemed to say, *Oh no, oh no, oh no.* "Yes?"

She didn't respond. He lifted his hand toward the doorknob but didn't quite touch it.

"Ben, could you open the door a minute?"

Dreamlike, he watched himself do so. The light from the hall penetrated the dark room, angling across the pine floor, the foot of the bed, the far wall.

"What's up?" He forced himself to speak lightly.

At the shadowed end of the bed she pulled herself to a sitting position, holding the blanket to her chest. She was wearing something pale and satiny with thin straps. "Was everything all right outside?" She sounded worried.

"Yes. Why do you ask?"

"You took so long."

"No, everything's fine. Relax and get some sleep." Congratulating himself on his self-discipline, he started to back out of the doorway.

"Ben?"

He could hear his blood surging. "Yes?"

"Come sit for a minute?" she asked timidly.

He hesitated. Two hours ago she wouldn't let him in the house and now she was inviting him into her room?

She patted the bed beside her. "I promise I won't try to compromise your virtue."

He smiled in spite of his misgivings and walked in. "Something in particular on your mind?"

"Not really. My thoughts've been racing, keeping me awake. Maybe if we talk awhile…if it isn't too much bother."

Ben circled the bed, pried off his shoes, propped a pillow against the headboard and eased onto the mattress beside her, careful not to touch her as he stretched his legs atop the wool blanket.

"So what would you like to talk about?"

"Oh…tell me why you called. You never did get around to explaining."

Listening in the thin moonlight, unable to see much of anything except featureless shapes, Ben suddenly realized he was hearing Julia's radio voice, that red-satin sound that could so easily provoke him to thoughts of intimacy.

"No reason really," he admitted with reservation. "I'd been sleeping and awoke suddenly with a feeling something was wrong here, a feeling you might be in danger."

Julia braced herself up on an elbow, frowning. "You're kidding, right?"

"No."

"You get these…feelings often?" She looked at him, and even in the shadows he could tell she was rethinking her opinion of him, putting him in a "possibly weird" slot.

"No, this is the first time I can recall."

"Hmm." Julia lay back, frowning up at the ceiling. "It was probably just coincidence. You've been thinking about Amber's case a lot lately and telling me to lock my doors."

"Yes. I'd probably just been having an anxiety dream."

"Probably. Still, it's flattering, your worrying about me like that. Thanks."

Ben wanted to touch her. He wanted to stroke the smooth white arm resting across her waist. He wanted to gather her silky hair in his hand and hold it against his cheek.

Instead, he folded his arms, tucked his hands under his armpits where they couldn't get him in trouble and cast about for something else to discuss.

She beat him to it.

"If you really want to know, I can't get my mind off Amber."

"Ah."

Julia turned on her side, drawing up her knees. She was quiet for a moment, tense, squeezing the sheet under her chin. "Jeff Parker said something to me tonight that's been bothering me."

"Something beyond those threats he made?"

"Yes. He said Amber wrote me a letter telling me all about their affair."

Ben heard a strange tightness in her voice. He lifted his hand, paused uncertainly, then gave a what-the-hell shrug and placed it on her head. She sighed, grateful.

"I feel so awful," she whispered. "She wanted to tell me what was going on in her life, but it seems she never mailed the letter. Maybe it was because Parker told her not to, but I can't help wondering if it was because of me, because I'd drifted away."

Ben stroked Julia's hair. "I don't think you should feel guilty about that. You had to move away because of your work."

"I know. But...but she still considered me her best friend. I wish I'd known. I feel I let her down. I didn't do it intentionally. I just didn't think I was that important. I didn't think…'' Her voice was growing thicker.

"Think what? That someone could still love you that much?"

Even in the dark he saw the sheen of tears in her eyes.

"I guess I'm feeling a little sorry for myself tonight, too. Because I've been lying here wondering who I—'' she blotted her eyes with the sheet "—who I consider a best friend, and I realize I don't have one. Not that I'm complaining. It's my own fault that I don't. But still, I can't help feeling very alone all of a sudden—'' her voice was breaking up "—and sad for myself and sad for Amber and…oh Ben, will you please hold me?"

Julia couldn't believe she was asking a man for comfort. A part of her was mortified. But when Ben pulled her near to lie against him, her embarrassment dropped away. This was Ben, not just some man. She curled around him, her arms tight and trembling, and tried her best not to cry.

"You're not alone,'' he whispered, folding her closer. "Not alone.'' His beard abraded her cheek, but it felt wonderful. Real. Human. Gradually her breathing became less racked, her heart less heavy.

No, she wasn't alone, she realized. Ben was with her, and it was exactly what she'd wanted all along. She'd wanted to be closer to him, wanted to give in to the attraction, but fear of being hurt had fought her every step of the way. Tonight, however, she'd faced another kind of fear, the fear of remaining alone in the world, and it had defeated the first.

She sat up and, bracing herself with one hand on the headboard, tenderly placed a kiss on Ben's lips. "Thank you,'' she whispered.

"For what?"

"For waiting."

She knew he hadn't expected that. He jerked a little, stopped breathing, his eyes spearing hers. "Does that mean..."

She nodded.

He began to smile cautiously. "Are you sure?"

Julia was smiling, too, when she said, "Positive."

His eyes took on a devilish glint. "I'm warning you, I won't show any mercy. I'm going to make it a night you won't forget."

She laughed. "I was sort of counting on that."

"Well, then..." He wrapped her close again, and the next moment she was lost in a kiss that surpassed anything she'd ever experienced, anything she'd ever dreamed. It was endless and lush and intoxicating, and before long the world beyond faded from her perception entirely. The only thing real in her entire existence was Ben. The only thing that mattered was that he keep kissing her this way.

All of a sudden Ben broke the kiss. "What?" she asked, disappointed. He didn't answer but swung to his feet and gave the bedcovers a hard yank. They skidded to the floor.

"There, that's better," he said.

Under her long nightgown she shivered, but it wasn't so much from a chill as it was from the thrill of watching him standing there watching her, his eyes glittering, his smile growing wider and warmer.

"You are so beautiful," he said slowly, enunciating each word with meaning.

She placed a hand at the base of her throat, feeling her vulnerability in every beat of her heart.

He lowered himself to the bed and lay alongside her. "Much better," he repeated, his hand skimming unimpeded from her shoulder down her bare arm to her hip, where it stayed, a subtle sign of possession.

"Before we go any further, sweetheart, there is one thing we need to discuss. Are you on any sort of birth control?"

Julia shook her head. "You wouldn't happen to have any, uh…"

"Condoms?" Ben placed a light kiss on her forehead. "As a matter of fact I do. Not that I presumed anything was going to happen. I was simply hoping you'd change your mind one of these days. I wanted to be prepared if you did."

"No need to make excuses. I'm glad you're prepared." Julia curled her hand around his neck and applied the slightest pressure, but it was enough to let him know she considered the subject sufficiently discussed.

After a few moments he'd resumed kissing her. This time his tongue joined the kiss, tracing the sensitive inner curve of her lips, then sliding deep, circling, coaxing, awakening new wells of pleasure in her until, mindless, she was doing the same to him.

"Ben." His name was a breath of surrender on her lips as he trailed his kisses along her jaw. "Ben," she whispered again as he moved his hand from her hip upward, his fingers flexing, bunching the soft satin. Her breasts grew heavy and achy, and when finally he touched her there, her back arched off the bed.

"So beautiful," he whispered. "God, Julia, you dazzle me."

No one had ever spoken to her that way. How good it felt. How needed it was.

Emboldened, she said, "Sit up," and when he did, she unbuttoned his shirt, laying it open and running her hands over his hair-coarsened chest. He gritted his teeth, causing Julia to know another new sense of feminine power.

Quickly he undid the cuffs and shrugged off the garment.

Then he slipped off her nightgown, sending it sailing across the room, a billow of moonlit satin.

Although the room was dim, she knew he was aroused. Not only could she see the evidence in the fit of his jeans, she smelled it in the scent of his skin as she placed a kiss just below his heart.

Standing up, he unfastened his belt, broke open the snap of his jeans, but didn't go any further. Instead, he reached for her, sitting on her heels in the middle of the bed, and gave her a kiss that was strangely, beautifully tender. "Are you sure, Julia? I feel I should ask one more time."

Raising herself on her knees, she wound her arms around his neck and looked him hard in the eye. "Ben, take off the damn pants."

That was the last chance he gave her to joke. The pants came off and, oh, he was perfect. Broad at the shoulder, flat of stomach, strong in the thigh, every inch streamlined and smooth.

Julia ran her hands across the slope of his shoulders, over his shoulder blades and down to the small of his back. He swallowed, making an effort to hold still as she explored him—back, hips, thighs.

Suddenly shy, she looked up into his half-closed eyes, her own asking for his help.

With a gutteral cry, he wrapped her in his arms and tumbled back onto the bed. They were entwined before they even hit the mattress, oblivious to everything but the passion driving them together.

She ought to feel more frightened, she thought. She'd never been so close to a collapse of her defenses with a man. Yet she wasn't. Paradoxically she felt safer at this moment than she'd ever felt before. *He* made her feel safe. Safe to be sensual. Safe to be free.

He was a wonderful lover, patient and giving. He spent

an eternity kissing her mouth and another eternity loving each breast, and just when she thought she might die from the unreleased tension, he slid downward and shared another intimacy with her, one she'd never experienced before and hadn't expected now. The heat that flashed through her was so sharp and enfeebling she gasped.

"Did I hurt you?"

"No. I..." She arched as he touched her again. "I can't..." she cried out helplessly, on the verge of release.

The next moment it was Ben who was driving into her. "Ben!" she sobbed, feeling herself coiling tighter, the pleasure-ache between her legs climbing to a peak.

"Look at me, Julia."

She opened her eyes and met his, their intimacy deepening to a level that was almost spiritual. For a split moment she thought her heart would break, first from the pure joy of knowing she and Ben were together like this sharing the deepest secrets of their bodies, second from the pain of knowing that once she left Harmony she'd never find anyone like him again.

A moment later she climaxed and all rational thought was bleached out in the blaze of it. Ben held her there a few incredibly searing moments, then pushed her over the top. With a harsh cry, he came with her, watching her all the way, and when the last spasms of pleasure had finally abated, he toppled to the mattress beside her, utterly drained.

For a long time neither of them moved. There was no sound but their labored breathing and the thudding of their hearts.

"My God!" Ben whispered as the world began to come back into focus. He rested his hand on her cheek and tipped his forehead to hers. Side by side, they stared with astonishment into each other's eyes.

Julia was beyond speech. There were no words for the sense of completion she felt. She reached for the tangled sheet and drew it over them, and soon they drifted off to sleep.

CHAPTER TWELVE

THEY NEVER DID MAKE IT to brunch.

Ben and Julia had spent the night making love, with only intermittent reprieves for sleep. Their passion for each other seemed a voracious thing, quenched for a while, only to rise again and again, and yet again.

Sunday morning found them asleep in each other's arms, exhausted, amidst a tangle of sheets. They slept past noon, past the ringing of the phone when Charlie made his ritual checkup call, past the pealing of church bells beckoning islanders to service, past everyone and everything outside themselves. They were oblivious to the world, lost in a wondrous peace of body and mind and soul.

Even when they did finally awake, neither seemed in a hurry to get the day started. They lay for a long time, their voices desultory as they discussed what to have for breakfast—or lunch, as the clock would prefer to have it—Ben lightly tracing the curve of Julia's spine, Julia making figure eights with her fingernail in the dark hair on Ben's chest.

They decided to make do with coffee for a while, as if food no longer mattered. Ben brought up a tray and they shared a cup while watching the bathtub fill. Then they spent another hour soaking away the stiffness and aches incurred during their long night of lovemaking.

Lazing in the tub, her calves slick alongside Ben's thighs, Julia marveled at her uninhibitedness. She'd never shared

a bath with a man before. Never been loved in the ways
Ben had loved her, either. So many new experiences for
her, experiences she'd thought would tie her in knots of
self-consciousness, but they hadn't. Rather, there had been
an untying, a loosening of the emotional constraints that
had been with her for so long she'd come to think of them
as normal.

Ben shampooed her hair, another first for her. Julia
washed his back. They talked, they sang, they splashed, and
then they had to wipe soap out of each other's eyes. And
they didn't get out until the water cooled.

Once they were dressed, they descended on the kitchen
and cooked up a mound of scrambled eggs with cheese,
bacon and toast, opened a jar of cinnamon applesauce,
brewed more coffee and took it all outside to the warm
sheltered patio on the southeast side of the breezeway.

Midafternoon saw them hiking the trails through the nature preserve adjacent to the property. With makeshift
walking sticks in hand, they talked incessantly, seeking to
know all the nooks and niches of their lives.

They walked along the cliffs, hand in hand like high-
school sweethearts. Ben held her fast while they peered
over the edge to watch the surf crashing on the rocks far
below. Then, sitting at the base of the lighthouse, Julia told
him tales of shipwrecks and the ghostly galleons that sometimes appeared over the shoals where they'd sunk.

And all along the way, they paused constantly to snap
pictures, each taking a turn to photograph the other, neither
talking about the desperation to preserve this perfect day,
to record forever the way the sunlight fell across her cheek,
the way the wind lifted his hair.

Dinner was a porterhouse steak snatched from Ben's refrigerator when he dashed home to get fresh clothes.
Broiled to perfection, it was served with wild rice and salad,

crusty French bread and a merlot he'd been saving for a
special occasion.

Then it was off to the studio for Julia. She'd considered
skipping the show tonight and spending the three hours
with Ben, instead. But on Friday when she'd told her audience she'd be skipping Saturday's broadcast, she'd promised to resume on Sunday. She had a commitment.

Even that turned out to be fun, with Ben in the studio
helping her pick the music. They had a good laugh when
halfway through the show someone called in complaining
that all their selections tonight were slow and romantic.
They realized the caller was right, but instead of reforming,
they immediately proceeded with Tony Bennett's version
of "Fly Me to the Moon"—and another first for Julia,
dancing in the studio.

Later that night, after she'd said good-night to her listeners and turned off the transmitter, after she'd talked to
Charlie and assured him she was all right, long after she
and Ben had climbed the stairs and made love, when she
was lying in the curve of his arm, feeling him in every cell
of her being, Julia remembered those moments when they'd
danced, and tears filled her eyes.

It had been one of the most beautiful experiences of her
life. Swaying to the dreamy music, wrapped in Ben's arms,
Julia had felt she'd truly entered the lyrics, that she was
flying to the moon, playing among the stars. With her lips
against his shirt collar, his against her hair, they'd whisper-
sung the words to each other, words about a romance that
was everything they'd ever dreamed about.

But as the record had approached its end and Julia anticipated the last line, she'd lifted her head off Ben's shoulder and placed her fingers over his lips, and he'd known
tacitly they weren't to say the words "I love you," ever.

Now, lying in his arms, Julia closed her eyes, and tears

soaked her lashes, but whether from the joy of the experience of dancing with him or from the pain, she couldn't have said.

MONDAY, AND REALITY, came too soon. After Ben dragged himself off to his apartment to shower and dress for work, Julia straightened the kitchen, changed the sheets on the bed, did the laundry and then drove into town to the police station to get an update on Amber's case. A couple of callers the previous night had asked her how the case was progressing, and she'd been embarrassed to admit she didn't know.

Charlie was in his office talking on the phone when she arrived. "Thanks a lot. You've been a big help," he said before dropping the receiver in its cradle. He looked up, smiling jubilantly.

"What?" Julia asked, cautiously expectant.

"Close the door, sweetheart."

She did, then sat in the chair by his desk. Charlie took one look at her, and whatever was on his mind was momentarily forgotten. She flushed, wondering what he saw. Were the past thirty-six hours shining in her eyes?

"That Grant fella, is he behaving himself with you?"

"Oh, Charlie..." She glanced aside. "Yes, he's behaving."

"Anything happens between you two, it's got no future. You know that, don't you?"

Julia was in no mood for a lecture. She was being hard enough on herself as it was. "What about that call?"

Charlie sniffed. "This is for your ears only, y'hear? It's not to be passed on to anybody. I shouldn't even be telling you..."

"I hear you, I hear you."

"Okay." He shifted his weight. "I did some checking

into Jeff Parker's background and came up with something interesting.''

Jeff Parker. She frowned. The incident with him at her door seemed like eons ago.

''The guy started out in insurance after college, a big firm in Hartford, Connecticut. And while he was with that firm, there was an investigation for fraud, somebody over-charging clients for premium payments and skimming the excess. Nobody was ever found guilty, but he was one of the people investigated.''

Julia hoped her disappointment wasn't showing. What did a twenty-year-old case of insurance fraud have to do with Amber's murder?

''Second job he had, he was a salesman for a stockbro-kerage in New York. Actually that was his third job, but I'm not counting the five months he put in as a shoe sales-man.''

''And what happened during his stint at the brokerage?''

''Another investigation. Commodities fraud. Again no-body was convicted—these cases can be hell to prove—but the fraud was generated from his department.''

''Hmm.'' Charlie was beginning to get her interest.

''After that he went to work with Atlantic Trust. Worked three different branches in the Boston area before coming here.''

''And?''

''While he was at one of those branches, there was a case of funds being diverted electronically to a private ac-count.''

Julia sat up, perched on the edge of her seat. ''And?''

''No, he wasn't investigated,'' Charlie said disappoint-ingly. ''The only suspect in that case was his supervisor, and he was convicted. But Parker sure had a hell of an opportunity to learn some new tricks, didn't he?''

Julia frowned. "Charlie, do you suspect something's going on over at the bank we ought to know about?"

"I don't know. Could be just a coincidence he worked in some crooked places, but I'm going to request a bank audit, anyway."

Julia was thoughtful a moment. "You think it's possible Amber might've stumbled onto something Jeff Parker was trying to hide?"

Charlie shrugged. "It's a theory."

A theory Julia didn't have much faith in. Business fraud was everywhere. Just because Jeff Parker had worked at firms that had been investigated didn't mean he'd been involved. Nor did it follow that anything illegal was going on at the island bank or that Amber had been killed to cover it up. Charlie was running on speculation.

Julia did find consolation, however, in the fact that he was pursuing the investigation more aggressively than she'd imagined he would. She wished there was some way she could open people's eyes to the effort he was making. She knew they were still grumbling over his calling Amber's death a suicide. Somehow the matter had trickled over to the mainland, as well. Articles questioning his competency had appeared in two newspapers. Even Ben was planning to run something soon. Time was ticking down for Charlie. If he didn't show some significant results soon, no amount of effort on his part was going to save him.

"Anyway," he said, "I thought I'd tell you about Parker just so you'd be more careful and steer clear of him."

"Hey, he came looking for me."

"I know, and if I wasn't worried about retaliation, I'd've gone after him right then, Saturday night. Now I prefer to wait and see what the audit uncovers."

Julia got up and began to pace the office, idly glancing

at the commendations on the wall. "Any reports back from the lab?"

Charlie sighed in dismay. "Yeah, but there's nothing. Nothing that means anything, anyway."

"No fingerprints?"

He shook his head.

"No foreign hair or skin scrapings or…?"

He kept shaking his head. "Nothing."

"How about Parker's alibi for the night Amber died?" she said, turning. "Anything more on that?"

Finally a spark lit in Charlie's dark eyes. "I had a talk with Wally over at the garage. Parker hasn't been in with any flat tires in about two years. And I noticed he isn't riding on his spare."

"Hmm." Maybe Charlie's theory wasn't so flimsy, after all.

"But how would a respectable-looking bank official like Jeff Parker get hold of a date-rape drug?" she asked.

"Looking respectable never stopped anybody from buying drugs. He could've picked it up any number of places in Boston. He reports to the home office once a month."

Julia sat on the corner of Charlie's desk. "Anything new with Bruce?"

Charlie nodded, sitting back with fingers laced across his thick waist. "He's started causing a stink over the house. I'm just about done with it as far as the investigation goes, but I won't release it to him yet. Hank and Viv Loring have petitioned the court for the right to claim certain personal effects of Amber's. As long as they're waiting to hear on that, I'm keeping the tape up."

Julia found herself tight with anger again. "Boy, didn't that turn out well for Bruce, getting ownership of the house."

"And the bar and everything else he and Amber owned."

Julia muttered a few choice words.

"I know, sweetheart. I feel the same. But there's no way I can prove anything yet." Charlie looked racked with frustration. "The evidence just isn't there."

"Well, you keep looking. I'm sure something'll turn up." Julia picked up her purse from the floor.

"I will," Charlie said halfheartedly. "In the meantime, if you want to give an update on your show, just say the investigation is continuing, people have been very cooperative, and I'm grateful for all the help they've given me."

Pressing her lips and nodding, Julia got to her feet and came around the desk. "Take care of yourself," she said, giving him a hug.

He chuckled. "I am, dammit, I am—except for one scotch when I get home. I can't turn into an angel overnight."

She smiled. "You've always been an angel, and don't you ever doubt it."

TIME WAS PASSING too quickly for Ben. Monday flowed into Tuesday, and Tuesday into Wednesday, and now Wednesday was nearly a memory, too.

He was in such a daze that he felt he was sleepwalking through work. The newspaper had become unimportant. So had the homicide investigation, except in how it might affect Julia. His life had come to revolve around her—meeting her for lunch, going to her place after work, spending the night with her. He was like a man possessed. Julia, Julia, Julia. Nothing but Julia on his mind.

When Scott Bowen called him Wednesday afternoon, he could barely remember why and had to be reminded of *his* call on Saturday requesting information about date-rape drugs.

"I've collected reports on all the recent cases throughout New England, even down into the middle Atlantic states," Scott said. "I've only looked through about half of 'em, but I already found something interesting."

Sitting at his desk in the newspaper office, gazing at one of the photographs he'd taken of Julia on Sunday, Ben suddenly tensed. "Go on," he urged.

"Three weeks ago a guy named Kenny Lopes was arrested in Hyannis and charged with rape. The woman involved went to a clinic as soon as she could and got a positive confirmation that she'd been drugged. The case hasn't gone to court yet, but it's a pretty sure bet Lopes is gonna get nailed. Anyway, what I find especially interesting is the person Lopes called to bail him out. Does the name Chris Normandin ring any bells?"

Ben got to his feet and began to pace. "The name Normandin does, yes. Bruce Davoll, Amber's husband, is seeing a woman named Nicole Normandin."

"Right. Chris is her younger brother."

Ben remembered Julia asking Nicole about a brother, but he could've sworn the name was Jack. Or was it Jake?

"So, this Lopes had Chris Normandin bail him out?"

"Yeah. Referred to him as his boss."

"Boss? What sort of business is Chris Normandin in?"

"That's what I'd like to know. He claims he's a fisherman, and he does own a boat."

Ben tried to concentrate. "Am I missing something here?"

Scott sighed. "No. I just thought it was odd, Chris turning up as this guy Lopes's buddy and then his sister turning up as Bruce Davoll's girlfriend, and that drug being involved in both arenas. By the way, Chris has a record, including a couple of narcotics violations.''

"Dealing?"

"No, just possession. But who knows, maybe he's graduated. It wouldn't be the first time a guy with a fishing boat decided to supplement his income that way.''

Ben understood what Scott meant. He, too, had heard the rumors of illegal drug traffic off the coast, reports of boats far out on the night sea approaching each other, their lights mysteriously blinking out as, presumably, an exchange took place. Most of the rumors were just that, however—rumors.

"Does he ever come around Harmony?"

"Uh-huh. I did harbor duty for a while—that's how I know. I got to recognize certain people, certain boats."

"Does he come here to fish?"

"Heck, no. Most of the time he's over at Davy's Locker sunning himself on the deck. That's one of the reasons I find this whole thing so interesting. I don't know a heck of a lot of fishermen who can waste time like that in the summer."

Ben tried to be objective. "Maybe he just likes visiting with his sister. She works there, y'know."

"Yeah, I know, but it does make you wonder where he gets his money."

It sounded to Ben as if Scott was on to something. In fact, it felt distinctly like a break in the case. But as yet there were too many pieces of the picture missing.

"I'll keep on it," Scott said. "Maybe take a ride down to Provincetown. That's where Normandin docks his boat."

"Keep me posted, will you, Scott?"

"Sure will."

"Talk to you soon."

As soon as Ben closed up the office, he paid a visit to Harmony's police chief and told him about Scott's call.

Suspicious of Ben's motives, Charlie received the information with caution.

"Why are you telling me this?" he asked.

Ben shrugged nonchalantly. "You're heading this investigation. You're the man to tell."

Charlie was undoubtedly aware Ben could've kept the information to himself and let Scott run with it. Then, after the case was solved, he could've written a bang-up article, questioning why Charlie hadn't looked through the records himself, records that even a rookie knew enough to investigate.

Charlie sat at his desk staring at Ben, dissecting him. Slowly he began to nod as if he saw right through him. "You really care about her, don't you?"

"What?"

"Julia. You care about her."

Ben sighed, feeling transparent and helpless. "Yeah, Charlie, I really do."

"She cares about you, too."

Ben leaned forward on his knees, looking at the floor. "But not enough to stick around."

Charlie eyed him narrowly. "Have you asked her?"

Ben laughed sardonically. "No. I already know what her answer would be."

"Well, you have to understand, since she was a kid, being on the radio is all she ever wanted. I tried to talk her into staying here, too. But I finally realized I had no right to hold her back."

"I don't want to hold her back." Ben sounded sulky even to himself.

"But you don't want her to leave, either."

"No."

"What are you going to do?"

Ben sat back with an exhausted sigh. "I don't know. Talk. Try to hammer something out. She's not really happy in Los Angeles. She says she is, but I wouldn't be surprised if she moved within the year. Why not here? And if she's worried about money, hell, I could support her. I could pay Preston Finch for airtime, too, if she wanted to continue doing a show over WHAR."

Charlie smiled sympathetically. "Somehow I don't believe it'd do any good. You could be a Vanderbilt and it wouldn't matter to her. She's determined not to depend on anybody but herself."

"Tell me about it." Ben sat with his forehead propped on his fingertips, thinking. "I don't get it," he said. "I mean, I understand women's issues as well as the next guy. I back their causes one hundred percent. But, hell, is the idea of a man supporting a woman really all that bad?"

"It is when you come from a home like Julia's. People talk about the effects of divorce on kids too casually these days. They don't realize how devastating those effects can be."

"Maybe that's my problem," Ben said wryly. "I come from a disgustingly happy family." He was surprised to hear Charlie laugh. "We didn't have a lot of money. My father drove a train for the city. My mother stayed home and raised us kids. There were four of us—me, my sister and two brothers. And I never remember her questioning the setup. She never thought of herself as a second-class citizen, either. She always said raising us kids and taking care of the house was the most important job there was."

"You're a lucky man," Charlie said. "There must've been a lot of love and trust in your family."

"There sure was. I never remember any of us, least of all my mother, doubting that my father would always be there for us. And he was. He'd never dream of cutting out."

Charlie studied Ben with new appreciation. "Is that where your mind is in regards to Julia? On marriage already?"

Ben steepled his hands at his mouth and blew out a long breath. "That's an unfair question. We've known each other less that two weeks. I *think* that's where we're headed, but we need more time to find out for sure. That's what's bothering me."

Charlie leaned forward, resting his beefy forearms on the desk. "I don't know what to tell you, son. God knows, I wish she'd come home. I'd love to see her settled here, married, with a couple of kids. Heck, that's about the only way I'm ever going to have any grandchildren. But I also want her to do what's best for her."

"I know."

"If it's any consolation, I'm pulling for you."

"Thanks." Ben got to his feet. "I'm glad we had this talk," he said with an uncertain grin.

Charlie gave a self-deprecating chuckle and rose, too. "We sound like a couple of old hens at the beauty parlor."

Ben turned and reached for the door, then paused, remembering the reason he'd come here in the first place. "You might want to give Scott Bowen a call. He's doing a lot of legwork just out of his own curiosity and initiative. You two pool your efforts, you might move a lot faster on this case."

Charlie tightened with resistance, then relaxed. "I'll consider it."

Ben extended his hand and the chief took it firmly in his.

THAT EVENING OVER DINNER Ben told Julia about his call from Scott, and while they ate, they discussed the possible implications of Chris Normandin's knowing someone

who'd obtained a date-rape drug. They agreed it might be
just an unlucky coincidence. Or it could mean Chris Normandin knew how to get hold of those drugs himself. Given
his history, that seemed a likely possibility. But did it connect him in any way to Amber's murder? That was the
question.

Julia's interest in the subject continued right up to the
time she went on the air. Ben, however, had other thoughts
on his mind—specifically the issue of Julia's leaving on
Sunday. They had to talk about it, and somehow he had to
convince her to stay—or at least arrange to come back.

But in spite of the depth of his concern—or maybe because of it—the evening passed without him broaching the
subject. He didn't want to set off an argument that would
spoil what little time they still had together.

Irresolution made for a fitful night's sleep, however. At
six in the morning he was lying wide awake, staring at the
shadowy ceiling and kicking himself for being such a coward. If he didn't take a chance, how would he ever find out
what she thought?

Ben turned on his side, wondering if he should wake her
or wait until breakfast, and found her awake already.

"Ben?"

He felt so much emotion when he looked at her he
thought he might die of the overload. "G'morning, love."
He brushed a kiss across her sleep-warm cheek.

"Is something wrong?" she asked drowsily. "You've
had a restless night."

"Sorry. I hope my thrashing didn't disturb your sleep."

"No. But something's obviously bothering you." She
yawned, sat up, folded her pillow and leaned back, clasping
her hands over her waist. "So what is it?"

Ben sat up, too, fear skidding through him. He took a
deep breath and let it out slowly. "I don't know how to

start. I've been lying here all night trying to find the right approach.''

"Ben, just say it. Whatever it is, it can't be as bad as what I'm beginning to imagine.''

He laid his hand over hers and nodded apologetically. "It's about Sunday and your leaving.''

"Oh.'' The sound was small and hesitant. "What about it?''

Ben stared at the dark hills formed by his feet rather than look at her. "I was wondering if maybe…considering how close we've become… Aw, hell, Julia, I don't want you to go.''

Her fingers curled over his forearm and gave it a squeeze. "I'm going to miss you, too.''

"Miss? No, you don't understand. When I say I don't want you to go, what I mean is, I want you to stay. I'm *asking* you to stay. Seriously asking.''

Her stillness put a knot in his stomach. He finally turned to look at her. The sun had begun to throw a pale peach glow into the sky, enough to faintly light her face, enough for him to see her expression. It wasn't good.

CHAPTER THIRTEEN

JULIA EASED HER LEGS off the bed and sat up, her back to Ben. "I thought we had an understanding," she said. "I thought it was perfectly clear that on Sunday I'd be getting on a plane and leaving, and whatever we'd shared would have to be put behind us."

Ben sat up, propped his elbows on his raised knees and plowed his fingers into his hair. "We did have that understanding, but that was before. Things have changed."

She looked over her shoulder, the dawn light sculpting the soft curves of her cheek and jaw. "Don't."

"Don't what?" His patience was becoming strained.

"Talk that way. Before you know it you'll be saying things you don't mean or can't live up to."

"That's precisely why we need more time. We need to find out for sure what we mean to each other."

"I don't have more time."

"Isn't there any way you can make more?"

"Aside from quitting my job, no!" Even in the shadowy light he could see the color in her cheeks deepening. She rose from the bed, her silk nightgown shimmering with the tension that emanated from her. "I happen to have a life beyond these shores. I have a job, I have colleagues, all sorts of opportunities opening up. I have an apartment and belongings in that apartment—furniture, books, dishes, rugs. I have friends I go out with, and my aerobics class three times a week, and my subscriptions to five magazines.

Have you ever even *tried* to understand who I am away
from Harmony?"

Ben let his hands drop between his knees and leaned his
head back against the wall. "Okay, you've got a point. All
I know of you is what I've seen here on Harmony. Maybe
I haven't wanted to think about you existing anywhere else.
Still, you have to concede me a point, too. *We* exist, you
and I. We have a life, and it's every bit as real as the one
you lead out in L.A."

Julia plucked her robe off the chair and punched her arms
into it. "What exactly are you asking me to do? Come here
and live with you? Not that I can or will. I'm just curious."
She tied the belt extra tight.

"If you wanted to move in with me, yes, I'd love it. But
you wouldn't have to. Just as long as we could see each
other and continue to explore what we've started."

Standing at the foot of the bed, she folded her arms under
her breasts. "And how long do you foresee this arrangement lasting? Not that I'm taking it seriously."

Ben felt nailed in place. This was the hard part, asking
her to do something that came with no guarantees. "Hell,
I don't know. However long it takes for us to decide if we
want to make it permanent."

"Permanent."

"Yes. Or not."

She began to pace, then abruptly stopped. "We've been
over this before. Didn't you hear anything I said? There's
no work for me here."

"Julia, I could support you. I make decent money with
the newspaper. And if you missed radio, there's always
WHAR."

"WHAR!"

"Yes. I could pay Preston Finch for airtime if you
wanted to continue doing your show."

Her mouth fell open as if she couldn't believe what she was hearing.

"Aw, hell, I'd be willing to buy the whole damn station if you decided to stay here. Think of the autonomy you'd have—no one to answer to. Think of the creative freedom. And the potential for growth!"

"Give me a break." She moved to the bureau and picked up her hairbrush. Ben could see there was no sense in telling her he was serious. WHAR was a joke to her. He was beginning to think that maybe he was a joke, as well.

"Sorry. It just seemed to me you were having a good time at the station."

"Sure, it's been fun, but that's neither here nor there. Bottom line is, it's not a paying proposition. I'd have to find work somewhere else. And as for you subsidizing me, that'd be worse than my taking a job as a chambermaid in one of the hotels. I'd be no better off than a...a kept woman."

Ben would've laughed if he wasn't so hurt. He wondered if that was how his mother felt when his father came home and placed his paycheck on her desk. Not bloody likely.

He took a couple of calming breaths as he watched her pulling the brush through her hair. "Look, I'm just trying to work something out here, see if we can stay together for a while. It doesn't have to be the way I just said. That was only one suggestion. I'm open to anything, so help me out, Julia. Talk to me."

She looked at him in the mirror as she fastened her hair at her nape with a large tortoiseshell barrette. "I can't come up with anything." She sounded as if to do so would be ridiculous.

"What about the idea of trying to get a job in the Northeast? There must be dozens of stations an hour away from here by plane."

"What good would that do?"

Exasperation got the better of him. "At least we could see each other once in a while."

She turned, folding her arms tight again, challenge in her eyes. "Why are you dumping all this on me? What's wrong with *you?* Why don't *you* pull up stakes and follow *me?*"

Ben squirmed. "You know how I feel about living here and owning the paper. This place is home to me now. I've sunk roots here."

Her anger rose visibly. "So you expect me to mold myself around your life, your job, your wants? That isn't fair!"

She was right, Ben realized. He was asking her to make one hell of a sacrifice, and he resented her for forcing him to realize it. The trouble was, he thought their relationship was worth it. Apparently she didn't.

"Okay, forget it. You want to go back to California, go back to California." He got off the bed and yanked on his jeans. "You want to think of me as just some chump you had a good time with while you were here, fine, you do that."

Her folded arms became unbraided and fell to her sides slowly. "You know that isn't true."

"Isn't it?" He pulled on his shirt and, as he buttoned it, pried his feet into his shoes.

"Of course not!"

"Could've fooled me."

"Ben, I wish I could make you understand." Her hands lifted beseechingly. Tears filled her eyes, though her voice, that magical voice, remained steady.

"Oh, I understand all right." He opened his gym bag and whipped a shirt into it. "From your point of view all we have is a physical relationship." He pulled a pair of socks off the floor and tossed those into the bag, too. "Fine. I can go with that. Hell, I should be glad it's just that. Most guys in my situation would be turning cartwheels.'' Into the bag went a T-shirt and a half-read novel. "A week of great sex with a beautiful woman, then adios amigo, no strings attached? Hell, that's a single guy's dream.'' He closed the bag with a force that almost broke the zipper.

When he looked up, her face was stricken. "That's not fair,'' she said again.

Ben's shoulders slumped with an abrupt exhalation. He rubbed his hand over the back of his tense neck. "Sorry. I didn't mean to start an argument.'' He went on rubbing his neck and thinking, but every avenue his thoughts took was a dead end. And *she* wasn't helping. She just stood there, silent, unwilling to even consider a future together.

"Maybe it's best we just say goodbye now,'' he said, swallowing over a lump in his throat as hard as a golf ball.

"Is that what you want?''

"You know what I want.'' He dared a look straight at her, challenging her one more time.

She tried to hold the look but couldn't. Her eyes lowered and a tear trickled down her pale cheek.

He gripped the handle of his gym bag. "I can see myself out.''

"Don't you want any breakfast?''

"No.'' He walked past her toward the bedroom door.

"This is crazy. It's all happening so fast,'' she said, still wearing that dazed look. Ben wished he could be more sympathetic, but he was feeling too hurt.

He turned and said, "It would've happened, anyway, right? And I don't think I want to invest any more of myself in something that's going nowhere. I feel cheap enough already.''

Her breath hitched, a small choking sound. He wanted to take her in his arms and say he didn't mean it. But he did. And so he made himself place one foot in front of the other until he was on the stairs. One foot in front of the other until he was at the door. Until he was outside, then in his vehicle and finally driving away.

CATHRYN CALLED JULIA at noon, looking for a favor, and Julia was in the perfect frame of mind to be distracted. She'd tried to keep her thoughts off her confrontation with Ben, but she'd failed miserably. She'd spent the entire morning alternating between spells of inconsolable crying and bouts of rip-roaring anger.

By the time Cathryn called, Julia had convinced herself that ending the relationship was for the best. It was already Thursday, anyway. She'd be busy the next couple of days, first preparing for the class get-together and then with the get-together itself. Before she could blink, she'd be flying out.

Besides, she'd gone into the relationship knowing it would leave her hurting. It would be hypocritical of her to complain about the consequences now.

Cathryn needed her to drive down to the harbor and meet Mike Fearing's boat when it came in. Mike was donating a mess of lobsters for the festivities, and Cathryn had told him she'd pick them up today. But she couldn't. She'd forgotten that Bethany had a doctor's appointment that afternoon.

After assuring Cathryn the errand was no trouble, Julia splashed cold water on her face, put on some makeup and went down to the harbor. It was nice seeing Mike again. After transferring the lobsters to her car, they crossed the street to the diner and spent nearly two hours talking over coffee and pie.

Leaving the diner, Julia felt a lot better than she had entering it. She went straight to Cathryn's to drop off the lobsters and stayed until it was time to go home and prepare her show. Cathryn had lists taped all over her kitchen—menus, things to pick up, chores to do, all in preparation for the weekend bash. Julia did the vacuuming, then offered to go to the market, but Cathryn insisted she had everything under control.

When she got home, the message light on the answering machine was blinking. She shrugged out of her jacket, her heart leaping with hope that the caller was Ben. Almost simultaneously she shrank from the thought. Why was she hoping that? What would she say to him? Nothing had changed since this morning, had it?

But the voice was a woman's. "Julia, this is Vivien Loring." Julia flinched with guilt. She hadn't gotten around to visiting the Lorings yet, and she'd promised she would.

"I'm sorry I haven't called you sooner," the message continued, "but the way things've turned regarding Amber's death, I think you understand. I'd still like us to get together, though, tomorrow if possible. Could you give me a call back?"

Julia rang the Lorings' house. No need to look up the number. It was indelibly filed in her memory.

"Mrs. Loring? Hi. It's Julia."

"Oh, I'm so glad to hear from you." The woman got right to her purpose. "The police are finally going to release Amber's house tomorrow, and Bruce will be taking it over. But I've been given permission to go through the place first and clean out Amber's personal belongings, and I was wondering if you'd join me."

Julia held her hand to the top of her head, wondering what to say. The very last thing she wanted to do was spend time in the house where her friend had died.

"Will you please come by?" Mrs. Loring implored. "I know there are photographs and other memorabilia that would mean more to you than anyone else."

Julia took a breath, firmed up her spine and answered, "Sure. What time?"

"I'll be there from two to five. Any time in there will be fine."

"Okay. See you then."

IT WAS GOING TO BE a long night.

Ben planted his elbows on the table and stared at the meal congealing on his plate. The sight of it turned his stomach, yet he knew he should eat. He'd skipped lunch and hadn't had anything but coffee all afternoon.

The music Julia was playing tonight wasn't helping matters any, either. Blues. Torch songs. Pieces designed to tear him up and knock him down a thousand ways to tomorrow. If he had any brains at all, he'd turn off the radio. But he couldn't. Couldn't sever this connection with her. He wanted to savor at least this much as long as he could. In fact...

He hurried to his stereo set and slipped in a blank tape. "Fool," he muttered, but that didn't stop him from pressing the Record button.

"That was old blue eyes, Frank Sinatra, and 'Guess I'll Hang My Tears Out to Dry.' And I'm Julia Lewis with you until ten on this rainy Thursday evening..."

Ben stared at the narrow bars of light on the receiver, jumping and dropping as her voice rose and fell, and imagined her sitting at her microphone. Without even half trying, he could see the lustre of her dark hair, feel the warmth of her cheek, smell the fragrance of her skin. Julia Lewis was burned into his sense memory, and he didn't know how he was going to get on without her.

Maybe he should give in. She was right. Why put all the responsibility of their relationship on her? Maybe he should surrender the newspaper, sell the building, leave Harmony, leave the Northeast where his entire family lived...

Ben felt as if his insides were being put through a shredder.

He couldn't do it. He'd never had any desire whatsoever to live on the West Coast, and he certainly didn't want to live Julia's nomadic life. Damn! Why *should* he?

Maybe he'd be better off thinking in terms of a long-distance relationship. Sure. He'd heard of couples who lived that way. But where would he and Julia get the money for all that flying back and forth? The setup would eat up their savings in no time. And where would they find the time? But the biggest concern was what sort of relationship would it be, apart most of the time? Were any of those long-distance couples really happy? Maybe they were, but not with each other, that was for damn sure.

"And now here's a number from Barbra Streisand called 'Some Good Things Never Last.' This is Julia Lewis at 91.2 FM, and ain't that the truth."

Ben pushed away from the radio and walked over to the drinks cabinet. Julia was right. There was no solution to this problem. They each had a separate life and neither was willing to give it up. She was absolutely right.

He poured two fingers of bourbon, took a step away from the cabinet, paused, turned and grabbed the entire bottle. It was going to be a long night, indeed.

WHEN JULIA PULLED UP in front of Amber's house the next afternoon, Mrs. Loring's automobile was already in the driveway, parked alongside a police cruiser. She turned off the engine and gave the long Cape-style ranch her reluctant attention. Amber's touch was everywhere. In the impatiens still blooming in the window boxes. In the jaunty scarecrow wind sock hanging by the door. In the one forlorn garden glove lying by the mailbox.

Don't think, Julia, she advised herself. *Just keep moving.*

Mrs. Loring let her in. They embraced and tried to chat, but the strain was clear in both their faces.

An officer was present, as well, one of Charlie's backups. As Mrs. Loring went on to explain, he was there to record the items she wished to claim, to avoid problems with Bruce later. She'd already boxed most of Amber's clothing for charity and set aside some Lladro porcelains to take back to her own house. She said they'd been birthday gifts to Amber from her and Mr. Loring.

"She had a lovely home," Julia said.

"You've never been here?"

Julia shook her head as her eyes roamed and her heart ached. It would've been so pleasant to have Amber show her around, proudly pointing out this and that, then to curl up on opposite ends of that couch and gab away an afternoon.

"I already have some things put aside for you." Moving briskly to a box on the coffee table, Mrs. Loring seemed determined to get through this awful chore without becoming maudlin. Julia decided the woman deserved at least that much from her, too.

"Oh, my gosh." Julia bit her lip as she picked up a stack of letters she'd written to Amber. They went all the way back to a postcard she'd sent from Disney World when she was eleven.

The box also contained dozens of photographs of the two of them, sometimes with other friends. "Are you sure you don't want these?" she asked Mrs. Loring.

"I have enough—unless you don't want them."

"Of course I do! These are wonderful. Oh, my!" She

burst out laughing. "Remember this? The summer we gave each other home permanents?"

Mrs. Loring rolled her eyes. "And nearly fried the hair off your heads? Yes, I remember."

There were several other items in the cardboard carton, including the crystal glasses Julia had given Amber and Bruce as a wedding gift. "Are you sure Bruce isn't going to want these?"

"I doubt it, but you can ask him now if you want. His car just pulled up." Mrs. Loring stood a few feet back from the window, arms crossed tight. "Oh, bother! He has that Normandin girl with him, too."

Julia wrapped the crystal goblet she'd been looking at, nested it back in the box and went to stand by Mrs. Loring. Bruce got out of his black Corvette first, his movements hard and vigorous as he slammed the door. He didn't wait for Nicole but started straight for the house. He walked in without knocking.

"Vivien." He nodded to his mother-in-law. "Julia."

Nicole opened the door that he had let close and entered timidly. She didn't meet anyone's eyes.

Julia felt awkward. She wondered if she should take her box and leave.

"We're not exactly done here, Bruce," Mrs. Loring said in a tone that wouldn't tolerate much opposition. "In fact, I think I'm going to be here well into the evening."

Bruce flexed one of his oversize shoulders and stared at her a moment. "No skin off my nose. Just show me what you've done so far."

Mrs. Loring showed him the clothing she'd boxed and the porcelains she intended to reclaim. He rummaged through the boxes, occasionally holding up a dress or sweater, but eventually he dropped it all and said she could do what she wanted with it. In the kitchen, however, he refused to give up the few small appliances Mrs. Loring had thought to take.

Julia felt obliged to tell him about the crystal in her box—and then was sorry she did.

"That was a present to the two of us," he told her. As she removed the glasses from the box, Julia suspected her mouth was as tight as Mrs. Loring's. Meanwhile Nicole stood off by herself, her eyes on the picture window.

"Before Julia goes, there are a few more things I'm sure Amber would've wanted her to have." Mrs. Loring led the way down a short hall, past the bathroom and the den to the master bedroom. Julia had to reach extra deep into her well of courage before entering, and even then she felt slightly nauseated as she glanced at the bed. It had been stripped of all linens, the mattress covered with a simple white sheet.

Bruce followed them into the room. Nicole trailed behind like a shadow, waiting in the doorway, her eyes cautiously roaming. Julia wondered what was going through her mind. Was Bruce planning to move in here? Would they be using this room? Sleeping in that bed? No wonder the poor girl looked so pale.

Mrs. Loring opened the closet door where a few items still hung. She unhooked something heavy and sealed in a quilted garment bag.

"What's this?" Julia asked.

"Amber's mink coat. Remember? It used to be her grandmother's. We had it restyled for her when she was a senior."

Julia remembered. At seventeen she'd thought it the most luxurious garment ever.

"She didn't get much use out of it. A few special functions in secretarial school. A dance or two here. I'd like you to have it, Julia."

"Me?" Julia flicked a look at Bruce. He didn't seem pleased, but he'd be hard-pressed to argue *he* deserved to keep it.

"Yes. Here, please. Wear it in good health."

Julia murmured a surprised thank-you, then stood by while Mrs. Loring quickly dispatched the rest of the clothes in the closet.

They moved to the bureau next. Bruce opened all the drawers. "Where're the coins?" he asked. "There used to be a coin collection in this drawer."

"I have no idea," Mrs. Loring said, affronted by his tone.

"A maroon leather book? Looked like a photo album?"

"Oh. I think I saw something like that in the den."

Bruce looked at Nicole and jerked his head. She slipped out of the room. When she came back a minute later, she murmured, "It's there."

By then they'd opened the jewelry box on top of the bureau.

"Where're the diamond earrings I gave her last Christmas?"

Mrs. Loring rolled her eyes. "Right there, Bruce!"

He didn't thank her for pointing them out.

Mrs. Loring continued to sort through the jewelry, picking out pieces that had been in the family and handed down to Amber. She insisted Julie take a pair of garnet earrings.

"Where's the gold chain I gave her on our first anniversary?" Bruce squawked again.

Mrs. Loring's eyes turned to chips of ice. "You mean the one with the heart-shaped pendant you had engraved 'To the only girl I'll ever love'?"

Although her tone was heavily sarcastic, Bruce didn't strike back. For one rare moment, in fact, he actually seemed to look sorrowful. "Yeah." His Adam's apple bobbed as he swallowed. "That one."

Julia glanced at Nicole in the mirror, curious and concerned about her reaction. Nicole's eyes veered to hers, as well. She looked stricken. Julia was surprised by how sorry she felt for the young woman, for in that brief exchange she'd caught a glimpse of understanding into the true nature of Bruce and Nicole's relationship.

A moment later Bruce had recovered his obnoxiousness. "I paid over three hundred bucks for that chain. It was solid gold." His thick fingers made a jumble of the necklaces and bracelets in the velvet-lined box. "She better not have sold it."

Mrs. Loring huffed. "She didn't. In fact, she was wearing it—" She left off abruptly and turned her head.

Julia wished she was anywhere on earth but where she was. Nicole looked as if she felt the same.

After a moment Mrs. Loring continued, "She was wearing it when she dropped by our house that evening." She placed just the slightest emphasis on the word *that*. "I remember because I commented on it. I said I didn't understand why she still wore it, and she said she didn't care who'd given it to her—she just liked the piece. So you see, Bruce, I'm sure it'll turn up eventually, if not in the house, maybe the police have it."

She turned from the bureau and scanned the room once more. "Well, I see no reason to keep Julia here any longer. I'll just go and see her out to her car, then I'll be back."

Julia breathed a sigh of relief. She hated being caught in other people's emotional crossfire, and the crossfire here was as bad as it got.

When she arrived back home, she carried her legacy up to her bedroom. She still couldn't believe Mrs. Loring had given her the mink coat. Julia wasn't all that fond of furs, but because it came from Amber, she'd take it and treasure it and, yes, even wear it on occasion.

There wasn't much left to the afternoon. Julia spent what little time there was vacuuming and straightening the house. She might not get another chance before she left, tomorrow being totally taken up with the reunion.

She went on the air that evening with conflicted feelings. She was looking forward to the get-together tomorrow and seeing her old friends. But as happy as she was about that, she was equally sad that her stay on Harmony was nearly over—and she still hadn't answered the question that had brought her here: Why did Amber die?

Of course, the question was no longer, why suicide? Now it was, who killed her? But at its heart it was still the same. As Julia stared out the window watching the night sky deepen from indigo to black, she regretted not being more help in solving the case. She'd so wanted to see it resolved before she left. That was a debt she felt she owed to her friend. But resolution would have to happen without her— if it ever happened at all.

There was another reason she felt bad about the unsolved case, and that was Charlie. She'd wanted to see him through it to a successful end. She'd wanted him to prove to Harmony, and to himself, that he could tackle it, that he was just as sharp and as dedicated as always. Now she didn't know what was going to happen to him. She feared it wouldn't be good.

Julia lifted the needle off a record and leaned into the mike. "That was Rosemary Clooney and her big hit from the fifties, 'Come on-a My House,' and that one goes out to Cathryn McGrath out on West Shore Road. Now from the same era, here's Peggy Lee with 'Till There Was You.'"

Julia sat back, thinking, *And this one's for you, Ben.* Her misery deepened immeasurably. She shook her head. She couldn't think of Ben, not if she intended to get through this show with any sort of composure.

Even without thinking about him, it was going to be a difficult night. She'd enjoyed her stint here. When she was sitting in her windowless high-tech cubicle next week playing her prechosen, preorganized noise, she was going to miss this drafty window-walled shed and the extraordinary music that lifted from it. She was going to miss speaking with her callers, laughing, arguing and sending songs out to them. She was even going to miss this quirky old equipment. Everything about the experience of broadcasting here had been personal and unique.

And autonomous, just as Ben had said. That was the real joy of it, playing and saying anything she wanted. For too long a time she let herself spin daydreams around Ben's proposal that she stay and work here. He'd made it sound so tempting and easy.

Tempting, it was. But easy, no. She couldn't give up her livelihood, couldn't surrender control of her life and put herself in a position of such utter dependence.

She wished she were different. She wished she could take the leap of faith that Cathryn had taken with Dylan. She wished she could trust that Ben would always be there for her, now and fifty years from now. She wished she could trust that the island would support her temporal welfare, as well. But she couldn't. Her insecurity was as basic as her genetic makeup.

Julia had nearly finished her three hours when she became aware of a faint crunching noise outside on the driveway. She turned down the sound of the receiver and listened harder. Nothing. All she heard was the sighing of the wind.

She turned her attention back to her program. She had

one more record to play in a set of big-band numbers, then she'd dedicate the last ten minutes to thanking her audience and reading a poem she'd found entitled "This is Not Goodbye." At last she'd finish up with the song "I'll Be Seeing You" from one of the tapes in Ben's collection.

Ben's collection! Good heavens, she'd forgotten. She'd have to return it to him somehow before she left.

She was wondering how she was going to do that when the sound came again, the distinct crunch of seashells, this time from right under the kitchenette window. It sounded like a human footstep. But that was impossible. She hadn't heard a car, hadn't seen any lights coming up the driveway.

Julia suddenly realized all the shades in the studio were up. She was sitting here in an illuminated fishbowl, seen but unseeing. Stiff with tension, she rose and reached for the shade on the east-side window.

"You're acting silly," she whispered to herself. The night was windy and full of strange sounds: dry leaves swirling over the patio, an occasional acorn skittering across the roof. Nevertheless, she continued to pull down the shades until all of them were drawn. Then she returned to her seat, cued up the Tommy Dorsey number, did a station ID and started the record.

No sooner had she turned off her mike than there came a faint muffled thud. From inside the house? Had something fallen over in the den? Or was it out on the breezeway?

Was someone there?

Impossible. She took a calming breath. All the outer doors were locked, as well as all the windows. She was definitely letting her imagination run away with her.

Still, her heart was pounding as, slowly, she turned and looked at the door of the studio, closed but unlocked. She hadn't even thought to lock it since it was inside the breezeway.

She waited through an interminable silence, listening, listening, watching the door. Maybe she should lock it, anyway, even though it was unnecessary, just for peace of mind.

The light within the studio was dim, the door cast in shadow. Still, it seemed to her she saw the brass knob turn. Her blood thundered as the moment froze, becoming infused with all the menace of those times when she was a child lying in bed, eyes on her closet door, sure she heard a monster breathing on the other side.

I'm seeing things. It's nothing. But even as she thought this, the knob turned again and the door began to inch open. She tried to breathe. Couldn't. Tried to move. Couldn't do that, either. And all the while the door continued to open, inexorably as a nightmare, revealing the darkness on the other side.

With a suddenness that made Julia jump, the door swung in and slammed against the wall. And there stood Nicole Normandin, malice in her eyes and a gun in her hand.

CHAPTER FOURTEEN

JULIA'S MIND EXPLODED. "Nicole?"

Nicole stepped into the studio, dressed in a black leather jacket and dark jeans. With one hand she pulled off a black scarf, releasing her blond hair about her shoulders. With the other she waved the gun toward Julia's chair. "Sit down."

Julia wasn't even aware she'd gotten to her feet. "Nicole, what are you doing?" She glanced at the gun and decided she didn't need an answer to that. "How did you get into the house?"

"What do you mean, how did I get in? You've got a back kitchen door with a lock a five-year-old could slip. Now sit down and put on some more music. Don't pull anything funny, either."

This couldn't be happening to her, Julia thought. Her legs wobbled as she lowered herself to her seat. Oh, God, Nicole was the killer? And she was *here?* Julia tried to piece together the whys and wherefores, but she couldn't think. Nicole had come to stand behind her and was pressing cold steel against the base of her skull.

The Tommy Dorsey record had been over for some time, the needle hissing through untold seconds of dead air. Julia lifted it, turned on the mike and in a shaky voice apologized for letting her attention stray. Then she reached blindly for one of the cassettes scattered across the table and plugged it into the tape player. "The time is eleven minutes to ten," she announced, remembering that the moment had arrived for her to wind down, thank her audience and say goodbye. Instead, here she was, cuing up a fast Neil Diamond number, one she didn't even like.

For a brief hopeful moment she thought about leaving the microphone on and letting all of Harmony hear whatever Nicole had come to say—or do—but suddenly a hand snaked around her and flipped the switch.

"I said don't pull anything funny."

Julia carefully turned her chair. The gun was pointed straight at her forehead. "It was you all this time? You killed Amber?"

"That's right. But you already knew that, didn't you."

Julia frowned. Nicole thought she knew?

"When did you figure *that* out?" she bluffed.

"This afternoon of course. At the house."

Julia tried to think back to the afternoon, but details blurred. Nothing of significance came to mind.

It didn't matter, anyway, *how* Nicole had come to believe she knew. The important thing was the implications of her believing it

It took every bit of Julia's stamina to say, "Are you here to do something about it?"

Nicole chewed on the corner of her lip, her expression serious, tense, unhappy. She nodded.

Terror enveloped Julia as she stared at the gun.

"Not yet." Nicole continued to gnaw on her lip. It was raw and cracked. "After you finish up here."

Julia glanced over her shoulder at the clock. It read nine-fifty-three. Seven minutes left to her show. Seven minutes remaining of her connection to the outside world. There had to be a way to let people know she needed help. But what? Nicole had already caught on to the switch on the microphone.

The only idea that came to mind was pretty lame. Still, it was worth a try.

Slowly she swiveled back to Nicole. "I've got to get some more music." She pointed at the shelves.

"What's wrong with all that?" The gun waved a broad careless S over the tapes and records on the table.

"I've already played those. You don't want me to repeat, do you? People might wonder what's going on."

"Uh, no. But I'm right with you."

"I know." Julia walked to the record shelves, her legs barely supporting her, and scanned the titles.

"What's keeping you? Come on, hurry up."

Julia finally located the particular album she was looking for. It was a compilation of themes from movies, all of the film noir genre. She walked back to the console and placed it on the turntable.

"That was 'Mama Don't Know,' one of my all-time favorite Neil Diamond numbers, and now we'll slow things down a bit with the beautiful theme from the 1975 flick *Laura.*" Julia glanced at Nicole from the corner of her eye, fearing a reaction, but there was none. Apparently Nicole wasn't a film buff. "This is Julia Lewis for WHAR FM. Stay with me awhile."

Could anyone hear the tightness in her voice? she wondered. Was anyone wondering how she could've misdated by three decades such a famous film? Was anyone thinking of *Laura* in terms of a murder mystery?

Was anyone listening at all?

She faced Nicole. "That's a pretty long piece. It'll give us a chance to talk." Her manner was outwardly relaxed, as if they were just a couple of girlfriends sitting down to chat.

"Talk?" Nicole scowled. "About what?"

"Well, how you did it, for starters. How you killed Am-

ber.'' She glanced at the gun, held in two hands now. Were
Nicole's arms getting tired? ''I have to say I admire your
ingenuity. You left no fingerprints, no tracks at all, and it
looked just like a suicide. The only mistake you made was
using that drug.''

Nicole seemed to take offense. ''It wasn't a mistake. If
there hadn't been an autopsy, I would've gotten away with
it, scot-free. I'm still gonna get away with it.''

Julia wondered if Charlie's reputation for negligence had
led Nicole to believe there wouldn't be an autopsy or if she
just hadn't known suicides needed to be investigated. Julia
decided she'd rather not find out.

The tense atmosphere shattered abruptly with the ringing
of the telephone. Nicole jumped, her eyes wild and brilliant,
her fingers whitening around the revolver.

''Whoever that is, get rid of them fast. And don't say
anything dumb.''

Julia picked up the phone. It was a caller correcting her
on the date of *Laura*. She thanked the woman for setting
her straight, then paused, searching for something to say
that would sound an alarm.

The caller didn't give her the chance, however. She said
goodbye and the next moment Julia was listening to the
dial tone. She replaced the receiver in its cradle and let out
a long disheartened sigh.

''Let's make sure we're not interrupted again.'' Nicole
reached for the phone and placed the receiver on the table.
Anyone calling in now would just get a busy signal. Julia
slumped. There went the phone as an avenue of help.

On the other hand...

She almost smiled. As usual, she'd set the phone line to
record all of the evening's calls. It was, in fact, recording
now, the open receiver picking up sounds generated within
the studio. Maybe she wouldn't be around to testify to Ni-

cole's guilt, but Charlie was still going to have an airtight case!

With that in mind, Julia sat back and resumed the conversation.

"The question that's got me most baffled, Nicole, is where you got roofies. Would you mind telling me?"

Nicole shrugged evasively. "A dealer."

"Here? On the mainland? Where?"

Nicole's lips parted, then snapped shut again. "Hey, I'm not here to answer your questions."

"Okay." Julia held up her hands. "Sorry for prying." She hooked her elbows on the arms of the chair and linked her hands over her waist, hoping she looked relaxed. For some reason it seemed important to calm Nicole and get her talking. If Julia could reach her on a one-to-one conversational level, maybe she'd be able to reason with her.

Beating back a wave of anxiety, she forced herself to smile. "Have a seat, Nicole."

"Why? Am I making you nervous?"

"No, you just look as if you'd like to take a load off."

"Just shut up and do your show."

Julia glanced at the timer. "Still a minute to go on this number."

Nicole sighed, pulled up a chair and sat, perching tensely on the edge of it, her eyes never straying from Julia.

"Was it your brother?"

Nicole's pale eyebrows lifted. "What?"

"The person you got the roofies from? Was it Chris?"

Nicole looked at Julia for a long stunned moment, then she whispered a quiet but heartfelt "Shit!"

"I guess that answers my question."

"Look, I don't know how you found out about Chris, but he isn't a bad kid. Sure he deals, but not big time. It's just a sideline, just a little extra money to get by on."

"Hey, I understand, believe me. These days you've got to do what you can."

"That's right. He had no idea I was gonna use those pills, either. I caught him trying to sell them down on the beach and took them from him. I didn't want him getting mixed up with that kind of stuff. As far as he knows, I flushed them down the toilet."

"Okay, don't worry about Chris. If he's not directly involved in this—"

"He's not."

"—then he won't get in any trouble."

Nicole's agitation abated somewhat. Her frown lines eased.

Just then, the theme from *Laura* ended. Julia didn't move.

"Aren't you going to put something else on?"

"Nah. Let's just let the LP play on and continue talking. I do that sometimes, don't worry," she said as the theme from *Body Heat* began. The only other time she'd let an album play on, Charlie had thought fit to come check on her. Would he think anything was unusual tonight—*if* he was even listening?

"You got here through the hiking paths, didn't you?"

Nicole tilted her head, eyes narrowed and full of questions.

"You have a twig of something caught on your jeans."

Nicole glanced at her leg. "Oh."

"That was how you got to Amber's, too, wasn't it?"

A brief smile flicked across Nicole's lips. "My house to hers, by road, is three miles. Through the woods, only half a mile."

"Clever. But didn't she find that odd, you showing up at her door without a car at…what time was it? Eleven?"

"It was only ten-thirty. And, no, she didn't think it was

odd. A little annoying maybe, especially as it was me, but not odd. I told her my car had broken down just up the road and I needed to use her phone.''

Julia tried not to envision the scene, but it flashed across her mind, anyway.

''While I was there I asked if she had something I could drink, because I was thirsty from walking. So she opened a soda and shared it with me.''

''And you slipped the drug into her glass?''

Nicole nodded.

Julia had to struggle to keep her feelings hidden. Inside she was weeping. How like Amber to be extending hospitality to someone with murder on her mind.

''It didn't take long after that.''

Nicole looked aside, her voice becoming hollow, almost mechanical. ''I helped her to bed. She was so out of it she could barely walk...''

Only the fact that Amber had not known fright or pain comforted Julia and enabled her to ask, ''And then you took the gun from her nightstand and shot her?''

Nicole stared fixedly, her eyes empty. ''Yes.''

''And you put it in her hand?''

''Yes.''

The theme from *Body Heat* faded out. Shaking off her numbness, Julia turned and checked the time. Three minutes to ten. Three minutes till the end of her show. The next selection from the album started—the theme from *The Third Man*.

''I imagine it must be difficult to think clearly in a situation like that,'' Julia continued, ''yet you did. You washed the glasses you'd been drinking from, I presume?''

''Oh, yes. Washed them and put them away. Wiped everything I'd touched.'' A frown creased Nicole's brow suddenly and darkened her entire face. "But then I made my mistake."

"Which was?"

"I went back into the bedroom and took the necklace."

The necklace? Julia wondered. And then it hit her. Nicole was referring to the gold pendant Bruce had asked about today.

"As soon as you looked at me," Nicole said, "I knew you remembered seeing it at my place. Your expression said it all."

Julia lowered her eyes to hide her reaction. Now that Nicole had explained it, she understood what had happened. But Nicole had made another mistake. Julia had *not* seen the pendant at her house. She'd seen a lot of jewelry on the kitchen table, and apparently the pendant had been among the lot, but Julia hadn't singled out any one item.

"Why did you take it, Nicole?"

"I don't know. It was stupid."

Julia gazed at the gun in Nicole's hand. It had drooped to her knees.

"Was it because of the inscription?"

Nicole must have noticed where Julia's interest was directed. She jerked the revolver back into place.

"The inscription?"

"Mmm. 'To the only girl I'll ever love.'"

Nicole's pained expression told Julia she'd struck a nerve. Gently she asked, "*Was* Amber the only girl Bruce loved?"

Nicole's chest rose and fell more rapidly. "He was always wanting to go over there. He said it was just to work out the divorce..."

"But you think he wanted to be with her, that he never got over her?"

Nicole's breathing became even more agitated, her eyes more pained.

"Is that why you killed her, Nicole?" For a moment Julia found herself actually sympathizing with Nicole. Love, ah, love—how completely it could consume a person.

But what Nicole felt for Bruce wasn't a healthy love. It was a warped obsession. So was whatever Bruce felt for Amber, if indeed Nicole's perceptions were right.

"I thought maybe if she wasn't around anymore, he'd finally notice me, see how I've always been there, in love with him."

"He notices you."

"Sure, when it's convenient."

"For sex?"

Nicole's nod was reluctant.

"For...releasing frustration?"

Nicole tilted her head quizzically. "Do you mean, does he hit me?"

"Yes."

She smiled wryly. "No. He's pushed once or twice but never hit. He knows better. My brother Chris knows some pretty scary people."

Julia leaned on the arm of the chair, thinking, her hand over her mouth, her eyes on Nicole, her awareness, as always, on the revolver. "Does that mean Bruce knows that your brother deals?"

"Bruce knows everything that goes on around the Locker."

Julia's head was pounding. "Does he know you killed Amber?"

The gun in Nicole's grip was trembling now. "I *told* him I didn't but, I don't know, he isn't dumb. I'm sure it's occurred to him that the alibi we made up about being together all night protects me, too.''

Julia's thoughts teemed with confusion and questions. Somehow what she was hearing didn't sound like Bruce. If he had even a hint of suspicion, he'd be tearing mad at Nicole. Mad enough to hit. Mad enough to tell the police. He wouldn't care who her brother knew, unless...

A thought zinged through her. Unless his revealing Nicole's guilt would reveal something about himself.

"What've you got on him, Nicole? What's Bruce into?"

Suddenly Nicole's blue eyes became more sharply focused. Her face hardened as if she realized and regretted how long they'd been talking. "It's ten o'clock," she said with chilling objectivity, waving the pistol toward the board.

Desperate to stall, Julia said, "Don't worry, I'll finish my show. But after that I really think we should reconsider why you came here."

"There's nothing to reconsider. You're the only person who can place me at Amber's that night, and I'm sorry, but that gives you a little too much power."

"Because of that necklace? Throw the damn thing away, Nicole. Take a ferry ride and drop it into the water. Then there won't be any evidence left."

"But you'll still know. And you'll tell."

"No, I won't. I promise I won't."

For a moment Nicole looked as if she wanted to consider the idea, but then she shook her head. "Forget it. Now hurry up and finish your program."

With a sinking heart Julia turned to the microphone. "That's it for another night, folks. As always it's been a pleasure." She paused. All she had to do was say it, the one little word, *Help*. But the gun muzzle was pressing into her neck again and so she just whispered, "Good night, Harmony."

Nicole switched off the mike. "All right, let's go."

"Where?"

"For a walk."

Julia was reluctantly pushing herself out of the chair when there came the sound of an automobile turning in at the bottom of the driveway. Nicole went stiff. She swore as the sound came closer.

It was Ben's Bronco, Julia was sure of it. She closed her eyes, sagging in relief. Wasn't it just like Ben to figure out something was wrong? But as quickly as her relief had risen, it gave way to alarm as she thought of the danger Ben was walking into.

"Hurry up, hurry up." Nicole hauled Julia toward the door. But the vehicle was approaching too fast. If they tried to leave the house now, they were sure to be caught in its headlights.

Gripping Julia's arm with one hand and pressing the gun to her back with the other, she said, "Get rid of him. I don't care how you do it, but get rid of him."

A sweat broke out on Julia's forehead as she waited. She heard the car door open, then shut, heard familiar footsteps scuffing on the path, followed by a firm knock at the door. At each step of the way, she felt the push-pull of her relief and her fear.

"Julia?" Ben called, knocking again.

Nicole whispered, "Okay, go out there and talk to him, but don't forget I've got this gun pointed straight at you, and I won't hesitate to use it—on both of you." She reached for the wall switch by the door and turned off the light in the studio, cloaking herself in darkness.

Julia stepped out to the breezeway and, trying to school her expression, turned her gaze on Ben. Her heart nearly burst with love. If she died right now, she realized, her deepest regret would be that she'd never told him how much he meant to her.

She unlocked the outer door but opened it only a few inches. "Yes?" she said stiffly.

"Hi, I know you weren't expecting me." He looked deep into her eyes, his own uncertain. Was she in trouble or wasn't she? they seemed to ask. "I tried to phone you, but your line was busy."

"I had a lot of calls tonight."

His eyes fixed on the slightly open studio door behind her. "Mind if I come in?"

"Ben, now isn't a good time. I'm..." She swallowed. She so wanted him to stay, but more than that she wanted him to be safe. "I'm awfully tired. Please go. I'll call you tomorrow, all right?"

She tried to close the door, but he startled her by pushing it open and stepping inside.

"It can't wait. I've been doing a lot of thinking about us..."

Julia feigned exasperation. "Not now, Ben."

"Yes, now." Despite her small cry of alarm, he pushed right on past her, flipped on the lights in the studio—and found himself face-to-face with Nicole's revolver.

Of the three of them, Julia thought Nicole looked the most unnerved. She was standing in the middle of the room like a parody of some gunman she'd seen on TV, feet braced, knees bent, gun held straight out at chest level. But in spite of her aggressive stance, her hands were trembling and she kept muttering, "Oh shit, oh shit." Evidently the situation had become more complicated than she'd planned, and she didn't know what she was going to do about it.

Ben emerged from his shock within seconds. He swung his right arm around, pushing Julia behind him.

"Get out of here," he ordered. "The keys are in the ignition."

"Don't move!" Nicole shouted at the same time, her slim body shimmering with tension. "I'll shoot you both."

Julia believed she was skittish enough to do just that. She remained where she was, half in, half out of the room.

"Calm down, Nicole," Ben said. "Take a deep breath. There's nobody here you want to shoot."

"Don't count on it."

"You want to go to jail for three homicides? I don't think so. So do yourself a favor and quit while you're ahead." Ben took a step farther into the room.

Nicole took a step back, the gun still aimed at chest level. "Stay where you are, I said. I can't think with you moving like that."

Ben smiled sympathetically. "Look at you. You're shaking. You're pale as the moon." He took another step.

"Ben, don't," Julia pleaded.

"It's all right, Julia. Nicole's a smart woman. She's not going to—"

But she did. She fired off a shot that zinged past Ben's left ear and splintered the door frame beside Julia.

"Julia!" He spun around.

"I'm okay."

He spun back to Nicole, his eyes blazing. "Give me the gun, Nicole."

She laughed nervously. "Nothing to lose now. Whether I go to jail for two years or fifty-two, it's all the same to me. Nobody'll be waiting when I get out. This way, maybe I've got a chance." Her face lifted. "Sure. I can call my brother. Before anybody even realizes you two're missing, he can come get me, take me someplace safe." Her expression became almost childlike in its desperate hope.

"Your brother's going to be a little busy for a while, Nicole. He was arrested this afternoon."

Nicole emitted a small strangled sound. "What?"

Julia was just as surprised.

"That's right. So you might as well do what you can to help yourself."

Nicole's disappointment seemed like a physical force moving through her. Her eyelids drooped, her shoulders slumped, her arms lowered so that the gun pointed toward Ben's feet. Faster than lightning, he seized the moment and lunged forward.

"Run, Julia!" he hollered, crashing with Nicole against the record shelves.

Why was he unable to understand that she *couldn't* leave him?

"Go!" he ordered again just before he and Nicole toppled to the floor and the gun discharged. Julia heard him grunt, yet he kept grappling.

"Ben!" She rushed forward, not knowing what to do, only knowing she had to do something. But then the gun went off again. This time Ben flinched and twisted onto his back, panting in pain. Bloodstains were spreading over his clothing, one on his jeans leg, the other on his shirtfront.

Fury seized her. She moved on animal instinct alone. In two swift strides she crossed the room, picked up the heavy microphone and had it poised, ready to come down on Nicole—only to find Nicole looking up at her from the floor, gun firmly in hand again.

"Drop it," Nicole ordered, her voice shaking, her eyes wild now that she'd actually shot Ben.

But Julia refused to listen. Ben was lying there consumed by pain, unable to help himself, bleeding profusely. If she didn't do something about Nicole, he'd die. The issue was that simple.

Riding on love and adrenaline, Julia brought the heavy instrument down, catching Nicole across the wrist. Nicole gasped. Her hand opened and the gun clattered to the floor. Julia dove for it but got shoved away. Springing back, she dove again. This time Nicole kicked her in the ribs. Pain colored the world red.

I can't pass out, she thought, feeling the room spin. *I can't let Ben die.*

With a strength she didn't know she possessed, she rolled to her knees, pushing Nicole aside, and searched for the gun. By the time she spotted it, however, it was too late. Nicole's hand was just closing over it.

"Hold it right there," a deep familiar voice ordered. Julia glanced at Ben, but already knew it couldn't be him; he'd slipped into unconsciousness. It was Charlie Slocum, standing in the doorway, service revolver drawn. "It's over, Nicole," he said. "It's all over."

CHAPTER FIFTEEN

JULIA RODE in the Harmony rescue-squad helicopter right by Ben's side as he was airlifted to a Providence hospital that night. She was oblivious to the racket of the chopper's engine, oblivious to the spectacle of city lights below. She was only aware of Ben, with a wound to his chest and another to his right leg, and three tense medics trying to keep him alive. She held his hand, and although he remained unconscious, she spoke to him continually, telling him it wasn't his time to die. He couldn't die; she loved him.

As soon as they touched down on the roof of the hospital, he was whisked into surgery and she was left to pace the waiting room for the next three hours. Fortunately one of Charlie's men had come along, too, so she wasn't completely alone.

During that interminable wait, she sent up prayer after prayer for Ben's well-being. She also cried a little and thought a lot, and rued the truism that we don't appreciate what we've got till it's gone.

Charlie showed up around one in the morning. He'd been delayed on Harmony because he'd needed to process Nicole's arrest. He kissed her forehead and gave her a hug, and then he let her hang on for a little while longer. Finally she stepped away, wiping two index fingers under her eyes.

"I'm scared, Charlie."

"I know." He smiled grimly. "But he's going to be all right. He's too ornery to die. You'll see."

She wished Charlie's assurances had lasted a little longer and not been quite so pat.

He turned to the other policeman. "Hey, Bill. Why don't you go down to the cafeteria and get yourself some coffee?"

The man smiled gratefully and rose. Charlie took the seat he'd vacated. Julia sat beside him. A long meditative moment passed before she spoke.

"I'm such a fool, Charlie."

He looked at her, one gray eyebrow curled. "In what way?"

"Every way. All the moving I do, all the different jobs."

"Hasn't each new job been a little better than the last?"

She nodded halfheartedly. "But I could've made the same progress staying put in any one of the cities where I've lived."

The eyebrow curled higher. "This is an awfully strange time to be talking about your work, sweetheart."

"That's because it's not about my work. It's about people. I keep moving away from them, too."

"Ah. And would you care to venture a reason?"

"Sure. I'm a rotten person."

His shoulders shook as he chuckled. "Besides that."

She lowered her eyes. "I don't know. For as long as I can remember I've been a loner. I've needed distance. I feel safer if people don't get too close."

"I think you're wrong there, sweetheart. You've let a lot of people get close. You're looking at one right now."

"Only to a point, and then, wham, up goes the drawbridge."

"Yeah, you *do* do that. But I understand. I know you

love the people in your life. You just have trouble believing they love you back."

Julia turned astonished eyes on him. "How do you know that?"

"I'm a lot smarter than I look."

She smiled. "Yes, you are."

"So, does any of this have anything to do with Ben?"

Julia nodded as she dug in her bag for a fresh tissue. "Where Ben's concerned, I've been the biggest fool of all. He put his life on the line for me tonight, Charlie. I wish you could've seen him. He went after Nicole as if he had no fear for himself. The only thing on his mind seemed to be getting me out of there."

"That's called love, sweetheart."

"I know. And you don't want to hear how many ways I pushed it away." She blew her nose. "I am *so* stupid!"

Charlie curled a hand over her shoulder and gave it a squeeze. "It'll be all right. You'll see."

Julia pulled in a bolstering breath. "Maybe," she said, but she doubted it. What sort of person was she that a man had to go to such lengths before she accepted that he loved her? If he chose to have nothing to do with her ever again, she wouldn't blame him one bit.

A young surgeon dressed in green scrubs came through the swinging double doors marked No Admittance.

"Julia Lewis?"

She shot to her feet.

"I'm Dr. Flynn, one of the surgeons who worked on your friend."

"How is he, Doctor?"

"He's out of surgery and resting comfortably."

That didn't exactly answer her question.

"How bad was he hurt?" Charlie inquired.

"It could've been worse. The bullet that entered his chest

just nicked his left lung. A few millimeters to the right and it would've entered his heart."

"And the leg wound?"

"It's caused him to lose a lot of blood, but that's the worst of it. Basically it's just a flesh wound."

Julia still hadn't taken a decent breath. "So he's going to be all right?"

"Yes." The doctor smiled reassuringly. "He'll be fine."

She swayed a little as relief washed through her. "May I see him?"

"He's still under the effects of anesthesia, but sure, you can take a peek."

Julia walked into the recovery area, reminding herself that Ben would look terrible. She'd seen other people after surgery before and knew he'd be gray and hooked up to lots of frightening equipment. But when she looked at Ben, her heart splintered. He was not "other people." He was Ben, the center of her universe.

She kissed his pale forehead, smoothed his hair, kissed him again and yet again, telling him, soul to soul, that she loved him. And when she'd taken her heart's fill of him, she let Charlie and the young surgeon convince her to go home and get some sleep, even attend her reunion with her friends the next day. Ben was in no danger, the doctor assured her. Neither would he be alone. His family had been contacted and were already on their way.

IT WASN'T UNTIL the Harmony chopper was in the air that Julia and Charlie finally got around to talking about Nicole and the earlier events of the evening.

"I'm just remembering something Ben said." Julia raised her voice against the clamor of the rotors. "He told Nicole her brother Chris had been arrested today. Do you know anything about that?"

"I sure do. His buddy, the one who was arrested on rape charges, turned him in as part of a plea bargain. Province-town police took Chris into custody today, along with five kilos of marijuana and a small stash of roofies found in his apartment."

"Do they realize he provided the drug that was used in a homicide?"

Charlie grinned rather smugly. "Of course. I've been in constant communication with the police both in Province-town and Hyannis for the last three days. Been working with that young summer cop, Scott Bowen, too. He's been invaluable."

"Charlie, I must say you've surprised me. You've been so diligent and on top of things."

His red-rimmed eyes fixed on her lovingly. "I had one very good reason."

What really surprised Julia, though, was Charlie's next revelation: Bruce Davoll was dealing, too. When the police searched Chris Normandin's apartment, they'd found a notebook that recorded transactions between him and Bruce.

"So that was why he didn't turn Nicole in!" Julia exclaimed. "He knew she'd turn him in in retaliation."

"Yep, they were holding each other hostage, so to speak."

"Has he been arrested?"

"Yep. We took him in tonight."

Riding along in the pale blue glow emanating from the helicopter's instrument panel, Julia's thoughts eventually turned to Jeff Parker, Amber's lover.

"I guess he had nothing to do with her death, then, huh?"

Charlie shook his head. "The only thing Parker was guilty of was having an affair—and being a first-rate sleeze.

When I ordered the audit of his bank, he finally realized how serious I was about linking him to Amber's death. He got scared and came to me with a confession. Apparently Amber wasn't the first person he'd had an affair with. She wasn't the last, either. He'd already taken up with someone new. That's where he was the night Amber was killed, with his new girlfriend.''

''Ah. So that's why he made up that story about a flat tire.''

''Yep. I should feel bad for him. With all the questioning he's undergone and all the rumors, his wife finally figured things out, and from what I hear life is pretty tense over at the Parker residence right now. But I can't; he had it coming. He's a married man, for cryin' out loud. Plus, he preyed on your friend when she was at her most vulnerable.''

They sailed through the night sky without speaking for a while, watching the dark ocean slide beneath them.

''I have one other question, Charlie, and I promise this'll be the last. How did you know I needed help? What made you come out to my place precisely when you did?''

Charlie shifted to look at her. ''Are you kidding? Do you know how many calls we got from people concerned about you?''

''Really?''

''Yep. They said you sounded odd and were playing odd stuff, especially as it was your last broadcast. And then leaving the transmitter on...''

''I left the transmitter on?'' Julia dropped her hands on top of her head. ''Oh, my Lord, I left the transmitter on!''

Harmony was a black smudge on the dark sea just ahead. Here and there a few lonely lights shone. One of them was red. Julia leaned forward in her seat and smiled. For the first time in her life, she truly felt she was coming home.

THE ATMOSPHERE at Cathryn's house the next day was different from anything anyone attending the reunion had anticipated. Julia arrived last. By the time she'd caught a few hours' sleep and pulled herself together, everyone had heard about her ordeal. As soon as she pulled into the driveway, they spilled out of the house, concerned and curious, and began asking questions, and the questions didn't stop until she'd narrated the entire story. It helped that Jake Normandin had opted to stay away. Julia felt sorry for him, though. He wasn't to blame for what his siblings had done.

With their curiosity satisfied, everyone at the gathering finally settled into reunion mode. While enjoying Cathryn's buffet lunch, they reminisced, pulled out photographs and asked one another about their current lives.

Julia was especially happy to see Lauren DeStefano. Lauren was a successful businesswoman now, which didn't surprise Julia one bit. Lauren had always been a scrapper. What did surprise her was that, except for Cathryn's wedding, Lauren hadn't set foot on Harmony in eleven years.

"When I left this sorry butt of an island," she explained in her inimitably breezy way, "I promised myself I'd never come back. And I haven't. Only for you, Jules. I couldn't let you go back to L.A. without seeing you."

Julia spent some time with Seth Connor and his wife, who'd flown in from New Haven. Seth had become a high-school English teacher. She talked at length with Mike Fearing and the O'Banyon twins, Tyler and Wyatt, whom she'd seen at the funeral, but just briefly. She also became reacquainted with Barry Devine, who'd recently left the air force and was hoping to become a commercial airline pilot.

She was pouring herself a third cup of coffee and marveling at what diverse paths their lives had taken when Jake decided to show up, after all. The room fell silent. He walked up to her directly and in his typically open fashion, apologized for his sister's actions. Then he apologized to the group in general.

After a moment of awkwardness Julia gave him a big hug. "I'm glad you decided to show up. Now everyone's here."

"Except for Amber." His eyes lowered with guilt again.

"Speaking of which," Lauren said with timely grace, "aren't we supposed to go to the cemetery sometime today?"

"Now's as good a time as any," Cathryn suggested.

IT WAS A SIMPLE TRIBUTE. When they got to the cemetery, Cathryn placed a large wreath of fall mums on the soft dirt of Amber's grave and then stepped back with the others.

"I didn't prepare anything formal. I thought we'd just pray quietly, say what we wanted from our own hearts."

Heads bowed. Eyes lowered. Hands folded one over the other.

Gazing at the newly carved headstone, Julia recalled standing here two weeks ago, racked with grief and questions. Now, she realized, she stood with a measure of peace, as if a debt had been paid, a responsibility met. She knew why Amber had died, and so did the world, and she, Julia, had played a major role in bringing that about.

But of course that wouldn't bring Amber back. That wouldn't stop the pain of missing her. All Julia could do now was move on and remember never to take loved ones for granted again.

As the circle began to break up and people stepped away from the grave, she lifted the sleeve of her blazer and glanced at her watch. She'd enjoyed the day and it was far from over yet, but her mind had been on Ben throughout.

Cathryn noticed her gesture, discreet though it was. "You're thinking about Ben, aren't you?"

Julia nodded.

"And you want to go see him."

Julia didn't answer. How could she? Cathryn had planned this party around her being here. But something in her expression must've betrayed her, anyway.

Cathryn lifted her shoulders in a helpless shrug. "Well, I guess there's nothing left to do but go see the man."

"No, it's all right. I'm fine. Besides, I'm supposed to be leaving tomorrow. I have to pack."

Cathryn's apple cheeks dimpled. "You're not going anywhere tomorrow and you know it."

Julia pressed the heel of one shoe into the grass. "Well, I have thought of sticking around a few more days, just till I'm sure he's really well."

By then Lauren had wandered over. "What's going on?"

"Julia's being polite. She's afraid she's going to hurt our feelings if she cuts out to go see her knight in shining armor."

"Oh, honey—" Lauren dropped a casual arm across Julia's shoulders "—listen to the woman. When it comes to matters of the heart, she knows what she's talking about."

"But he's not *my* knight. After the trouble I've caused him, he's not my anything. He probably hates me and doesn't ever want to see me again."

Mike Fearing joined the three women. "You talking about Ben Grant? The guy's crazy about her."

Julia's cheeks flamed.

Wyatt O'Banyon ambled over, too. "That right? So what are you worried about? Go see the guy."

And Lauren added, "Actually I was beginning to get sick of you, anyway, Jules."

"Me, too," Mike threw in. "I was secretly hoping you'd leave the party voluntarily. But since you won't, how about we escort you out?"

"Yeah. All the way out to the airport," Tyler chimed in.

"That's a great idea. The airport," Barry cheered. By now Julia's embarrassment had vanished and she was barely able to hold in her laughter.

After a quick stop by her house to throw a few things into an overnight bag, the three-car caravan took Julia to the Harmony airport, where her friends chipped in to buy her ticket to Providence and then stood on the edge of the runway waving her off. When the plane lifted into the afternoon sky, she was still smiling and counting her many, many blessings.

JULIA'S COURAGE deserted her outside Ben's hospital room. She could hear several voices within and knew they must belong to his family.

She gazed at the bouquet of roses she'd bought down in the gift shop and suddenly felt she had no right to go in there. How would he introduce her? As the woman who'd thrown him over for a life that was gutlessly safe and selfishly solitary? As the woman who'd rejected his offer of home, financial support and love? Or how about the woman who'd almost got him killed? That was sure to win her friends.

But then she thought, Ben wouldn't introduce her at all. He wouldn't even want her in his room. Why had she come here? Had she actually thought he might want to consider resuming their relationship?

She turned and gazed at the elevators far down the long corridor. There it was, the easy way out, the familiar escape.

"No!" she whispered. "Not this time."

Squaring her shoulders, she headed into Ben's room.

He was sitting up in a chair, dressed in a dark gray robe and slippers, when she spotted him. He was laughing and he looked wonderful. Healthy! His color was back and his eyes were bright. She'd never known such a surge of relief and love in her life.

He looked up as if drawn magnetically to her presence, and his laughter froze. His sobering expression made the others in the room turn and look at her, too. They fell silent. Insecurity weakened her knees for a moment, but then she fixed her gaze on Ben and made herself walk.

When she was an arm's length away, he finally broke the stare. "Hey, guys," he said to the others, "this is Julia. Would you mind leaving us alone for a while?"

His family's reaction seemed to indicate they already knew all about her. Without any further explanation, they left the room. Someone even closed the door.

Julia and Ben stared at each other a long tense moment, then both spoke at once. "I'm sorry..."

They fell silent again, frowning.

"What are you sorry about?" Ben asked. "I'm the one who screwed up."

Julia's eyebrows lifted. "You?"

"Yes. I acted irresponsibly last night. I could've gotten both of us killed."

Julia emitted an incredulous gasp of laughter. "Irresponsible! You were the bravest person I've ever known! I'm the one who messed up, and I want you to know I'm sorry for all the trouble I caused you, and if you never want to speak to me again, I understand, but I also hope you realize I intend to try and change your mind."

"Good, because you're going to have every opportunity possible to change my mind. I've decided it's time I went to work on the West Coast, got a different perspective on things, juiced up my creative life."

Julia scowled. "What are you talking about?"

Ben smiled. "I was wrong to place all the responsibility

of our relationship on your shoulders. I had no right to ask you to give up your life and come here. I can work almost anywhere. You can't. So—''

"But you own the *Record*. It's something you've always wanted. You love Harmony."

"Yes, but I love you more."

Julia opened her mouth to protest further, but then lost her train of thought. "What did you say?"

Slowly he struggled to his feet, putting all his weight on his left foot. He propped a crutch under one arm, took a careful breath and straightened. "I said I love you, and if you can't live here, I'll move."

Julia stared into fathomless blue eyes, speechless. Was there no end to this man's ability to give? She wanted to tell him she loved him, too, but tears suddenly thwarted her.

"Aw, hell, Julia," Ben said in anguish. "I know you're afraid to make a commitment, but you've got to give me a chance. You've got to give *us* a chance. And this is the only plan I can come up with."

Julia swallowed a sob. Ben thought she was unhappy with his proposal? He thought she didn't want him following her? "You idiot." She laughed and cried simultaneously as she wrapped one arm around his neck and moved into his confused embrace. "Of course I'll give us a chance. But you don't have to move anywhere. I'd like to give Harmony a chance, too."

Ben tilted his head, eyes narrowed and questioning. "Do you mean that?"

"Yes. That is, if you don't mind having me around."

"Now who's the idiot?" Ben held her to him gingerly. "I just want you to know that if the arrangement doesn't work," he said, his gaze steady and deep, "we're out of there."

She smiled, her lips trembling. "Okay."

He dipped his head and sealed their bargain with a kiss.

"By the way, how are you feeling today?" she asked.

"Numb." He grinned. "Oh, you mean this?" He looked down at his chest. "Sore as hell! So's my leg. But they say I'll live."

His comment was innocent enough, but it stole her smile. "Oh, God!" She hugged him to her again, trying not to hurt him. "I thought I'd lost you last night. Let's never do anything like that again."

"That's a promise."

They didn't let go of each other until a nurse eventually tapped on the door and walked in, complaining that his other visitors wanted to know what was going on.

Ben looked at Julia. "Are you ready to meet the family?"

She took a deep breath. "Bring 'em on."

EPILOGUE

JULIA CAREFULLY maneuvered her arms into the delicately beaded sleeves of her wedding gown, then held the confection of satin and tulle in place while Cathryn, her matron of honor, zipped up the back. Beyond the partially opened windows of Charlie Slocum's spare bedroom, the late-April sun was coaxing daffodils and crocuses from the cool spring earth and filling the afternoon with their perfume. The song of robins entwined with the caw of gulls. In the distance, wild shad blossoms turned the hills and hollows of Harmony into a fantasy of white.

When the last satin button had been fastened, Julia turned around for her friend's inspection. "Oh!" Cathryn covered her mouth with the fingertips of two hands and struggled to hold back her tears. "You look like a dream."

Julia smiled shyly, turning back to the mirror, barely able to believe her reflection. Her cheeks had never been so aglow, her eyes so filled with happiness. But it wasn't a giddy girlish happiness. It was one based on the surety that she and Ben were right for each other, that their life together would be productive, fulfilling and blessed with peace.

She'd been living on Harmony for six months now. Although she'd been certain of her commitment to Ben when she'd made the move, he'd wanted to give her plenty of time to think about it. He didn't want her ever to say she'd been rushed. The wait had seemed interminable at times, but at least it had given them the opportunity to plan a large wedding.

"Okay, now for the crowning touch." Cathryn was lifting Julia's veil off the bed when Lauren rushed into the room, her spring green bridesmaid's gown the perfect complement to her copper red hair and her flushed, faintly freckled cheeks.

"Where've you been?" Cathryn exclaimed.

"I'd say I was caught in traffic, but something tells me I'd never get away with it." She shrugged and grinned. "I got sidetracked checking out some property. Hey, you look snazzy, Jules. You're gonna knock Benjie off his pins."

Cathryn and Julia glanced at each other, then stared at Lauren. "You were looking at property?" Cathryn cried in disbelief.

"Yeah. Real-estate values are really rising here, aren't they?" Lauren leaned toward the mirror to reposition the small spray of silk flowers in her short hair. "I'm beginning to see why you and Ben were so excited about buying the Finch place. You got the bargain of a lifetime."

"It needs a total rehab," Julia said, bending so Cathryn could pin her veil securely, "but, yeah, we did okay." Her coy smile punctuated her understatement.

Preston Finch had returned from his motoring tour of the states in November and decided that his wife's condominium cottage was far more suitable for their new life-style than his rambling old house and its five acres. So he'd offered it for sale, and Julia and Ben had snapped it up.

Julia was especially pleased because they'd arranged to transfer ownership of WHAR to her, as well—although she and Ben often got ribbed about their now being a communications monopoly on the island.

She'd expanded her evening show to four hours, with Preston occasionally filling in to give her a break. And she'd begun selling advertising time to local merchants, thus making the station a paying proposition. At present she had so many plans for WHAR she sometimes thought she needed another lifetime to implement them all.

A light tap sounded at the bedroom door. Charlie poked his head into the room, his salt-and-pepper hair meticulously combed. "It's time we started for church, Funny Face. Are you ready?"

"Just about. You can come in. Let's see your tux."

Charlie stepped into the room, full of its feminine fragrances and rustling gowns. Julia brushed a piece of lint off his lapel. "You look very handsome. I'll have to keep my eye on you at the reception."

"Oh, go on." He waved a hand, his ruddy cheeks darkening.

Julia's life wasn't the only one that had changed these past six months. Charlie would be walking her down the aisle today as *retired* Police Chief Slocum. He'd stepped down soon after Amber's case was resolved. To Julia's deep satisfaction, it had been with full pomp and honors.

These days he spent his time fishing, volunteering with a youth group at the church, participating in singles activities and occasionally filling in as a backup on the force, which was now headed by a capable young man from New Hampshire.

Cathryn handed Julia her bouquet, then gathered up the train of her gown. "Got my flowers, Lauren?"

"Right here. Are you ready, Jules?"

Julia took a deep breath and let it out on a smile. "You bet. Let's go get me married."

Firming up his trembly chin, Charlie opened the door and she stepped through.

THAT NIGHT Ben carried Julia in his arms from his Bronco to the front steps of the old house on Peggoty Hill, her veil trailing over the crushed seashells of the driveway, her gown making her a difficult bundle to hang on to. Panting and laughing, he made his way up the steps and across the porch.

"You can at least put me down while you unlock the door," she said, nuzzling into his warm neck. His collar was undone, the gray cravat that was part of his tuxedo lost somewhere back at the reception.

"No, I can do this. Watch." Propping her on one unsteady knee, he got the key in the lock, turned it, and the door swung in, nearly spilling them onto the foyer floor. He caught her to him as he regained his balance. "See?" He beamed proudly.

"Benjamin, you're drunk."

"I believe you're right, Mrs. Grant." He swung her into the living room, with its stripped walls, and skated her across the gritty floor, around a sawhorse table and a paint-splattered ladder, all the while singing, "'I will always love you-oo-oo...'"

He finally set her on her feet in a puddle of moonlight, letting her slide down his body slowly. By the time her white satin pumps touched the floor, the laughter had faded from their eyes, leaving them serious and adoring.

"Oh, God, Julia. I love you so much." The reverence in his tone weakened her. "Sometimes I think I'm just dreaming and I'm going to wake up and—"

"Shh." She placed her fingers over his lips. "I love you too, and I'm not going anywhere, ever, unless you're with me."

He dipped his head, kissed each of her eyelids, her cheeks, her jaw, the soft underside of her chin, before finally settling on her mouth. It was a kiss full of tenderness and promise.

Julia rested her head on his chest, steadying her breathing, listening to his heartbeat. "We had a nice wedding, didn't we?"

"Nice?" Ben pulled back a little to look down at her. "Darlin', it was legendary." They both smiled, remembering.

The church had been full to overflowing. Even people who hadn't been invited showed up, eager to watch Julia and Ben, two of the island's most popular personalities, tie the knot. And of course all of Ben's family and friends from Boston were there. Julia had met most of the Grants while Ben was in the hospital and by Thanksgiving already felt like one of them.

The ceremony itself was a romantic's dream. There was a forest of lighted candles, flowers everywhere, a five-voice choir to accompany the organ and personal vows exchanged to deepen the meaning of the traditional ones.

As soon as the ceremony was over, though, the solemnity ended and the celebration began. The words "You may kiss the bride" had barely left the minister's lips when Ben did just that, resoundingly, and the congregation cheered. Then they'd exited the church to the triumphant strains of "The Wedding March" and a shower of rose petals and rice.

After a quick session of picture-taking on the lawn, the gathering moved to the Surf Hotel. Its panoramic view of the ocean served as a backdrop to the head table. They'd dined on a sumptuous buffet; they'd drunk toast after toast of champagne; they'd cut their five-tier cake, and danced and danced and danced. Julia's feet were throbbing from it.

"Your family certainly knows how to have a good time," she said dryly.

"Your friends aren't exactly wallflowers, either."

"Aren't they great?" Julia smiled proudly, pleased that

everyone had made it back for her wedding. "I still can't get over the stunt Lauren pulled, though. That had to be the topper of the day."

They laughed, their eyes still somewhat glazed with disbelief as they recalled the incident. Just as they had been about to leave the reception, a muffled thump went off on the lower lawn, followed by a long arcing whistle. They'd turned, startled, just as the night sky exploded in a dazzling display of shooting stars. It was a surprise fireworks presentation, a wedding gift from Lauren.

"She claims she's not the romantic sort and tries to be so tough and business-minded," Julia said, "but that was just about the most romantic gesture I've ever seen or heard of."

Ben locked his hands behind Julia's back. "What's her story, anyway? Has she always been that way?"

"No. But I'd rather not get into that tonight. It's long and involved and, quite frankly, pretty sad. It involves Cameron Hathaway."

"Cam?" Ben's eyebrows lifted. "From the marina?"

"Cam from the wealthiest family on the island," she added with unintentional derision. "You notice he wasn't at the wedding."

"Hmm. He said he had a prior commitment. So what happened between him and Lauren?"

"Some other time." Julia glanced toward the kitchen. "Are you hungry?" she asked, thinking of the food left over from the rehearsal dinner Ben's parents had hosted.

Ben's eyes glittered with mock lasciviousness. "Very."

Julia ran her hands up his pleated shirt and rested them lightly on the sides of his neck, while fitting her body closer. Suddenly the lasciviousness in his eyes wasn't so mock anymore.

"Oh, lady, what you do to me." His head lowered and he angled his mouth over hers. They kissed deeply.

"Shall we take this party someplace more comfortable?" she suggested. He didn't answer, just lifted her into his arms and climbed the stairs to the room facing the ocean where they'd set up makeshift quarters while working on the house. He kissed her the entire way.

Later that night, Julia awoke from a dreamless sleep. In the thin gray moonlight seeping into the room from the edges of the window shades, she could see Ben lying beside her, asleep. His jaw was slack, his dark hair tousled. His broad muscled back rose and fell in a peaceful rhythm.

As quietly as possible she slipped out from under his arm and tiptoed to the window. She lifted the shade slowly, with an occasional glance over her shoulder.

The moon was full and fat, drenching the sky with its light. Julia's lips parted in wonder as she gazed at it. There was also a huge ring encircling it like a halo—why, she wasn't sure. There was undoubtedly a scientific explanation, something involving moisture and atmospheric conditions, but at the moment she wasn't interested in science. She just thought it was the prettiest sight there was.

Unexpectedly her thoughts turned to Amber. She wished her friend could've been at her wedding today. She would've been maid of honor. Staring up at the moon, Julia could easily picture her sitting at the head table, lending her beauty to the occasion. She could hear Amber's contagious laughter, feel the joy of dancing with her while they clapped their hands overhead and sang, "Celebrate good times..." just as they had at her wedding seven years earlier.

But if she hadn't died, Julia thought, frowning, I wouldn't have come home and met Ben. The irony was too sad to think about and certainly too profound to fathom, and so Julia let it go, knowing only that somehow Amber had managed to attend the wedding, anyway.

Inadvertently she fingered the new wedding band on her left hand, its shape symbolizing the unending nature of her and Ben's love for each other. Was it an ideal? Of course. But she would do everything in her power to make it come true, and she knew Ben was just as committed. They were in this for the long haul. Already they'd laid a strong foundation.

She turned and watched him slumbering in the moonlight, loving him more than she'd ever thought it possible to love another person. Life was full of circles. Some came undone. Some took us out and brought us back to where we'd started. And some went on forever and ever.

Julia gave the moon one last look, smiled under its benediction, and then returned to bed.

HARLEQUIN SUPERROMANCE®

MEN OF GLORY

They're ranchers, cowboys, men of the West!

O LITTLE TOWN OF GLORY

by Judith Bowen

**Visit the town of Glory in December 1998!
A good place to go for Christmas...**

Calgary lawyer Honor Templeman makes a shocking dis-
covery after her husband's death. Parker Templeman had
another wife—and two children—in the small town of
Glory. Two children left to the care of their uncle, Joe
Gallant, who has no intention of giving them up—to
Honor *or* her powerful father-in-law.

Available wherever Harlequin books are sold.

HARLEQUIN®

Makes any time special ™

Looking For More Romance?

Visit Romance.net

Check in daily for these and other exciting features:

Hot off the press

View all current titles, and purchase them on-line.

What do the stars have in store for you?

Horoscope

Hot deals

Exclusive offers available only at Romance.net

Plus, don't miss our interactive quizzes, contests and bonus gifts.

PWEB

MEN *at* WORK

All work and no play?
Not these men!

October 1998
SOUND OF SUMMER by Annette Broadrick

Secret agent Adam Conroy's seductive gaze
could hypnotize a woman's heart. But it was
Selena Stanford's body that needed saving—
when she stumbled into the middle of an
espionage ring and forced Adam out of
hiding....

November 1998
GLASS HOUSES by Anne Stuart

Billionaire Michael Dubrovnik never lost a
negotiation—until Laura de Kelsey Winston
changed the boardroom rules. He might
acquire her business...but a kiss would cost
him his heart....

December 1998
FIT TO BE TIED by Joan Johnston

Matthew Benson had a way with words
and women—but he refused to be tied
down. Could Jennifer Smith get him to
retract his scathing review of her art by
trying another tactic: tying him *up?*

Available at your favorite retail outlet!

MEN AT WORK™

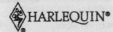 

Look us up on-line at: http://www.romance.net   PMAW3

What do you want for Christmas?

A DADDY FOR CHRISTMAS

'Tis the season for wishes and dreams that come true. This November, follow three handsome but lonely Scrooges as they learn to believe in the magic of the season when they meet the *right* family, in *A Daddy for Christmas*.

MERRY CHRISTMAS, BABY
by Pamela Browning

THE NUTCRACKER PRINCE
by Rebecca Winters

THE BABY AND THE BODYGUARD
by Jule McBride

Available November 1998
wherever Harlequin and Silhouette books are sold.

 HARLEQUIN®
Makes any time special ™

 *Silhouette*®

HARLEQUIN SUPERROMANCE®

Love THAT MAN!

He's the guy every woman dreams of.
A hero in every sense of the word—strong, brave,
kind and of course, drop-dead gorgeous.
You'll never forget the men you meet—or the
women they love—in Harlequin Superromance®'s
newest series, **LOVE THAT MAN!**

BECAUSE IT'S CHRISTMAS
by Kathryn Shay, December 1998

LOVE, LIES & ALIBIS
by Linda Markowiak, January 1999

Be sure to look for upcoming **LOVE THAT MAN!** titles
wherever Harlequin Superromance® books are sold.

HARLEQUIN®
Makes any time special ™

HARLEQUIN SUPERROMANCE®

COMING NEXT MONTH

#814 O LITTLE TOWN OF GLORY • Judith Bowen
Men of Glory
Honor Templeman is a Calgary lawyer, who makes the
shocking discovery that her husband, Parker, had another
wife, another family...in a small ranching town called Glory.
Now that he's dead, she wants to meet Parker's children—but
their uncle and guardian, Joe Gallant, is fiercely protective of
them. Inevitably, when Honor fills in because Joe's desperate
for a nanny, she grows to love these kids. *And* their uncle....
He's a man for all seasons, from the heat of a prairie summer
to the joys of a Glory Christmas.

#815 BECAUSE IT'S CHRISTMAS • Kathryn Shay
Love That Man
To most people in the small town of Bayview Heights,
Seth Taylor's a hero. But Seth can't forgive himself for a
mistake in his past. And neither can Lacey Cartwright—the
woman he loves. If Lacey takes his side, she'll lose what's
left of her family. It's a risk she can't take—and a choice Seth
can't allow her to make.

#816 LET IT SNOW • Sherry Lewis
Marti Johansson has brought her troubled teenage son to
spend a quiet Christmas on his grandfather's Colorado ranch.
Unfortunately, the holiday is anything but peaceful. Her father
is feuding with his neighbor, Rick Dennehy. Her son wants
her to forgive his father, who has his own reasons for wanting
Marti back. And then there's Rick....

#817 THE HEART OF CHRISTMAS • Tara Taylor Quinn
Abby Hayden is at loose ends until Nick McIntyre persuades
her to spend the Christmas season helping out in a home for
pregnant teenagers. This place is where Abby learns about
trust and happiness and letting go.... And this Christmas is
when she falls in love with her very own Saint Nick! By the
author of *Father: Unknown*.